I0685187

RACKED

ASH FITZSIMMONS

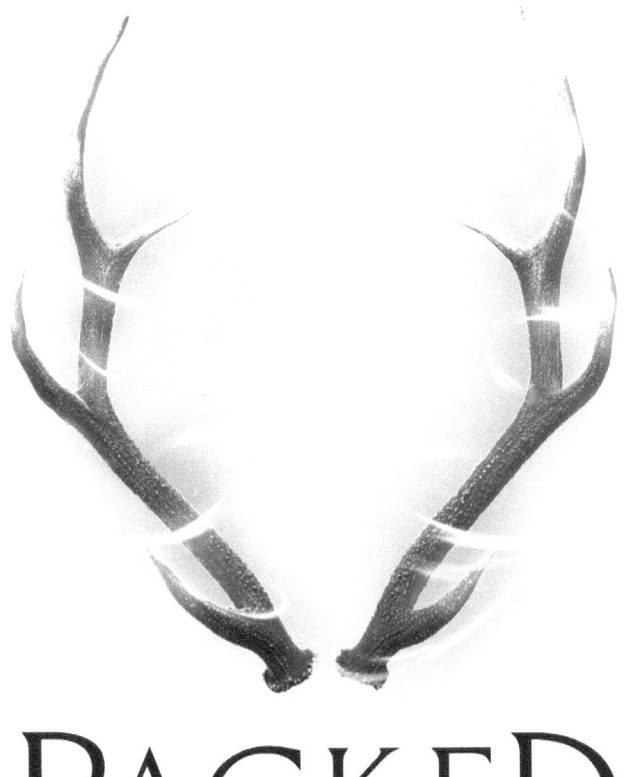

RACKED

The WILD HUNT, BOOK ONE

This is a work of fiction. Names, characters, places, and incidents are products of the author's imagination or are used fictitiously and are not to be construed as real. Any resemblance to actual events, locales, organizations, or persons, living or dead, is entirely coincidental.

RACKED. Copyright © 2023 by Ash Fitzsimmons.

All rights reserved. No part of this book may be used or reproduced in any manner whatsoever without written permission except in the case of brief quotations embodied in critical articles and reviews.

Print Edition ISBN: 978-1-949861-53-2

Cover design by MiblArt.

www.ashfitzsimmons.com

CHAPTER 1

Things could always be worse. Mantra of my life.

I mean, sure, it was Monday morning, which seldom thrilled me. But I'd learned the rhythm of our week, and the day was looking up now that the breakfast rush was behind us, that frenzied two-hour period in which Maya took each order as she plated the one before it, leaving me to work the espresso machine until my hands ached and my apron was stained with splashes of hot milk. *That* was a miserable time, especially on Mondays, when the DPP agents who'd had all weekend to relax stumbled into the café for their necessary chemical stimulation. But the rush was past, and while Maya hid out in the kitchen, putting the finishing touches on the lunch specials, I had a chance to properly clean the equipment, rearrange the display cases, and breathe. The café was so much more pleasant when it was quiet.

Relatively speaking.

Oh, Mangia Due was a friendly space, and Maya had put her touches on the café to make it her own: tables and comfy chairs to accommodate a variety of groups, a small wooden stage in one corner for weekend karaoke sessions, a television on the wall for background noise, and an assortment of minimalist light fixtures, sleek but annoyingly low-hanging. Unless it was late on one of our weekend bar evenings, the café tended to smell like coffee and baked goods. Our customers were seldom rude, and most tipped well. I might have enjoyed working behind the counter, had I wanted to be there in the first place.

I wasn't a restauranteur like Maya—I was a private investigator. Okay, a *very* green PI, but I had a license and business cards, the whole shebang. As far as I knew, my website was still out there, inviting suspicious spouses and worried parents to contact me for a confidential consultation. But if I'd had any potential customers since Halloween, I didn't know. I hadn't even checked my email in nearly eight months, as my jailers grew twitchy whenever I got too close to a machine with access to the real world.

But things could have been worse.

I could have still been locked in the windowless holding cell in the Division of Plants and Potions where I'd awakened last November. Sure, I'd basically been abducted by aliens, but they weren't the human-eating sort, by and large, and they'd finagled a cover story to allow me to reassure my parents that I wasn't dead in a shallow grave. My family believed I'd been thrust into witness protection for my own safety, and they understood that I couldn't contact them so as to keep them safe. Nonsense, all of it, but I couldn't very well tell them the truth: I'd wound up stuck in a magically created world, unsure whether I'd ever see home again, because I'd gone to Maya's Halloween party.

I'd considered skipping the festivities that year, but Mom had encouraged me to go. "You're only young once," she'd cajoled when I'd told her I was thinking of spending the night passing out candy in my comfy pants. "Go be with your friends, Annie! Have a good time!"

My mom would have had kittens if she'd known how much liquor was always on offer at Maya's parties—never mind the pot and the occasional harder drugs—but she'd meant well. I'd been working my ass off that October, spending most of the month looking for a runaway who didn't want to be found, then wrapping things up by trailing an old horndog professor and his coed girlfriend around Richmond at the behest of the dirtbag's wife. I'd needed a night to let my hair down. Plus, with my birthday on November 3, Halloween had always been a sort of pregame for me—and considering the desserts that came out of Maya's restaurant, I knew I'd be in for a sugary, boozy, carb-heavy evening of fun.

So I'd thrown together my best sexy cowgirl outfit, resolved not to sulk about the fact that the woman in the mirror was on the cusp of twenty-nine, and taken an Uber to Maya's townhouse in Carytown. I'd laughed and chatted with our mutual friends, opened a beer and eaten way too much cheese, and tried to forget about the things I'd seen my client's husband and his sidepiece get up to at an hourly motel. (The two had used pseudonyms to check in—Dick Nixon and D. Throat—and after watching the girl's admittedly impressive oral skills through a zoom lens, I had no doubt about why she'd gone with that moniker.) And then, like almost everyone else there that night, I'd partaken of the joints being passed around the party. Nothing odd about that—Maya had a dependable dealer who offered great product at a low price, and a little pot was just the thing to take the edge off.

I don't know when I passed out. The next thing I remember is needing to pee like a racehorse and stumbling toward the bathroom, only to see Rose Thorn lurking outside. Between my grogginess and unexpected vertigo, I almost didn't recognize her, but the red hair had narrowed the field of possibilities. Rose was a fixture in Maya's social circle, a painter a few years younger than me, and I'd been disappointed when Maya had explained that Rose was blowing off the party to spend the evening with a guy—just a friend, Rose had insisted, not a boyfriend, but no one had believed her on that front. When I'd found her that morning, I hadn't known what was going on. I'd had no idea that most of the guests were still unconscious, that a guy with whom I'd shared Jell-O shots hours before was dead on the bathroom floor, or that we'd all been drugged.

And then Rose had mentioned my antlers. Prosthetics,

she'd assumed, until she'd given them a good inspection in the kitchen and realized they'd taken root.

Things could be worse.

Unbeknownst to any of us at the time, Maya's dealer was a rogue sorcerer—I hadn't realized that was a career option—who'd liked to experiment with potions and viewed us as oversized guinea pigs. He'd tainted the pot he sold Maya and several other people with his latest creation, then sat back to see what happened. Most just passed out for a few hours and woke unharmed. Maya sprouted wings overnight—two pairs of delicate, iridescent wings like those of a scaled-up dragonfly—while I'd awakened with a rack like a trophy buck. And three of our friends—plus at least another two victims who'd also bought from the bastard—never woke at all.

Like I kept telling myself, things could be worse. I could be dead.

The folks who were studying the potion had dubbed it "Roulette," as whether you had a nice nap or wound up a freak of nature or a corpse seemed like a matter of chance. Months later, they had yet to identify a factor to predict how the potion would behave with a particular subject, but given the odds, they didn't exactly have a line of test subjects to work with. Instead, they'd staged the corpses and sent our unaffected friends home with a mind wipe to make them forget about having been whisked off to Neverland. Maya and I weren't so lucky.

But again, things could be worse.

Sometime after waking up in a sealed room, dressed in institutional scrubs I didn't remember putting on and under observation by a decidedly inhuman staff of babysitters, I'd learned what had happened and where we were. Magic was real. My friend Rose wasn't quite human, and her guy friend, Yven, was a blond, blue-eyed, full-blown *elf*—not to mention an agent of a government I was never meant to know existed. Back in the sixteenth century, faced with a growing population of humans and running out of safe places to hide, the world's magical races had banded together and split. They'd created their own little pocket world in which they could go about their lives without fear of torches and pitchforks, and while some of them occasionally made trips back across the border, humans *never* found their way in. "The Pactlands," they'd dubbed it.

And because Yven had taken one look at the after-effects of Maya's party and called it in, we'd become guests of the Pactlands agency that dealt with unknown potions.

I couldn't blame the guy. Finding a corpse on the floor would be enough to make almost anyone call for backup, never mind the fact that Maya and I had mutated in our sleep. The folks in the Pactlands had a vested interest in not informing the rest of humanity about the reality of magic, and for all they knew, we'd been hit by something both magical and communicable. As it turned out, we weren't contagious, and the sorcerer was soon off the street (and dead—no great loss there, as far as I was concerned). But until DPP could figure out a way to undo the effects of Roulette on Maya and me, they couldn't let us go home.

Things could have been *so* much worse.

Had I been taken into custody by anyone from outside the Pactlands, I'd probably either be in a cell in a black site or in pieces on a dissection table. Our jailers felt terrible about the situation—Pactlands agencies didn't make a habit of kidnapping humans, and we were the victims in this mess—so they tried to make us comfortable while we waited for a cure. DPP paid for a well-appointed two-bedroom apartment for Maya and me a few blocks from their headquarters in downtown Beukal, convenient for when the research team asked us to come in for yet another round of bloodwork, measurements, and magical examination. They gave us agency credit cards to buy food and other necessities, and they even loaned us vehicles. Maya had been handed the keys to a well-used sedan, while

I'd been given an old van, which had a ceiling high enough to accommodate my antlers. Neither one needed gasoline, and DPP allowed us to drive outside the capital and go sightseeing, but Maya and I seldom went far. She could hide her wings with a long coat, but I had no such luck. When even centaurs and trolls look at you like you're a sideshow attraction…well, you become a homebody.

It had been Maya's idea to open the café. Unable to return to Mangia, her restaurant in Carytown, she'd offered our services to the DPP director in compensation. DPP's only on-premises dining option had been some sad vending machines, and with a willing chef on hand—plus one displaced PI with minimal culinary skills—the director had quickly agreed. Mangia Due turned a profit and kept the agents happy, and DPP deemed it a fine and useful thing to fund.

But making lattes and working a panini press in a magical pocket world hadn't been part of my ten-year plan. I missed my parents like crazy, and I wanted nothing more than to go home and put this weird adventure behind me. I wanted to see my friends in Carytown and trade memes with my high school crew and watch angsty, overwrought teenage dramas that hadn't been dubbed in Pactish. I was sick of the stares and whispers when I walked down the pristine streets, weary of the prodding and testing in the lab, and fed up with the daily burns from the espresso machine.

Sometimes, I joked with Maya that DPP should make us the face of whatever D.A.R.E.-like initiative they used in schools: *Don't do drugs, kids, or you'll end up looking like Tinkerbell and Bambi here.*

Maya didn't have it so bad. When she wasn't hiding her wings, she'd figured out how to use them—not *gracefully*, but well enough to let her grab items on high shelves without a stepladder. She was never going to trade in her car in favor of flying around town. But my antlers were useless ornamentation. Given the general lack of deer to fight off in the capital, I could do nothing with them but try to keep my hair from tangling around them and the prongs from snagging the hanging lights in the café. I couldn't ride in a normal car anymore, I had to carefully gauge doorways to determine whether I needed to stoop or turn sideways to fit through, and I'd slid my bed into the middle of the room and removed the headboard to give my antlers a place to go at night. Pullover shirts no longer had a place in my wardrobe.

Though Maya blamed herself for our situation, I never put that on her. She hadn't known that she'd been sold tainted weed—she'd just wanted to be a good hostess. She cooked for us both, picked up after herself around the apartment, and only smoked outside, and as roommates went, I couldn't complain.

Things could have been worse…but *man*, things could have been so much better, too.

Grateful for breathing room in the lull between the breakfast and lunch crowds, I oversaw the front of the house while Maya prepped and baked in the kitchen. The woman had an impressive memory for recipes and had adapted several of her standards to the food on offer at the nearest grocery store. She'd even bought a few cookbooks and tried her hand at gnomish meat pies, an elven gazpacho-like soup, and a few troll dishes with names unpronounceable to the human tongue. Her daily specials drew in loyal agents every afternoon and usually earned her accolades. As for me, I did my bit by avoiding the kitchen. I kept a laminated cheat sheet of coffee staples beneath the counter, to which Maya and I had added once people started coming in and asking for off-menu options. Exotic flavorings, floral teas, a high-octane coffee bean that came from a Pactlands greenhouse and could keep you up for two days—if people wanted it, we tried to provide. Eight months in, I could be trusted with the drinks, the microwave, and the panini press, leaving Maya to work her magic in the form of pies and cheesecakes.

The place was dead that Monday, which suited me nicely. As I cleaned the espresso machine and wiped down the counters, I glanced through the wide windows at the morning beyond the glass. Pactlands weather was seldom horrible—a hurricane outside might result in gentle showers within—and even in late July, the temperature hovered in the high seventies. Anyone whose job didn't keep them tethered to a desk was surely enjoying the summer day, and I'd have been tempted to join them if not for my work behind the counter…well, and the stares. Our regulars barely batted an eye at Maya and me, but out in public, away from DPP, I couldn't escape the whispered comments and wide eyes. Some days, I'd smile and nod, but I often just hunched my shoulders and tried to ignore the gawkers. It's hard to lose yourself in a pleasant day outdoors when the greatest attraction is you.

With the counter smelling faintly of ammonia and the bakery case tidied, I pulled up my neglected stool and took out the paperback I'd stowed under the counter for just such an occasion. Mystery novels were my guilty pleasure, and while no one needed my help, I returned to my whodunit. Like most of the secondhand books I'd found in Beukal, mine was old and dogeared, the cover creased and fraying at the edges. While there was a market for human media, it was considerably niche, and I took what I could get. My favorite bookseller, an overly enthusiastic sorcerer who wore her hair in a pink-streaked bob and accepted payment in coffee, had even begun putting merchandise aside for me when she found English titles among the trade-ins. That she couldn't read a word of English was only a minor stumbling block, and if she excitedly offered me the occasional find in French or German, I never pointed out the mistake. I tried Pactish titles, too—thanks to a potion, Maya and I could speak the most common of the local languages—but there was something comforting about books from home.

I'd just turned the page to start a fresh chapter when the bell over the external door jingled. We had two doors into the café, one connected to the DPP lobby and the other to the street, and most of our midmorning traffic came from outside the building. Slipping my bookmark into place, I sighed to myself and plastered on a smile as I looked up. "Hi, welcome to Mangia...uh..."

The customer was standing on the threshold, holding the door open and staring at me. Nothing unusual about that. But his appearance surprised me almost as much as mine apparently did him. He was relatively cute, about six feet tall and moderately built, more like a swimmer than a football player. His light brown hair hung loose and fell just below his shoulders, which wasn't uncommon around Beukal. Clean-shaven, I noted, with a hint of the stubble to come. His eyes, though, were different, large and closer to a honeyed amber than to true brown, and his ears seemed ever so slightly pointed—not like an elf's, and nowhere nearly as extreme as a nymph's, but unusual all the same.

What really drew my attention, however, were his antlers, which were every bit as obnoxiously large as mine. That, plus his attire. I'd seen a variety of fashions in my time in the Pactlands, but in DPP, almost everyone wore either a formal robe or the sort of tactical clothing appropriate for fieldwork. This guy sported a rough-spun off-white shirt, held together with a crisscrossed thong up the front in lieu of buttons, and what appeared to be loose leggings...in leather, if I wasn't mistaken.

Leather leggings in *July*?

I cleared my throat. "Sorry, uh...frog. Welcome to Mangia Due. What can I get you?"

He stared a moment longer, then collected himself and stepped inside. "Uh...um...hello," he managed.

Baritone. I didn't hate it, though I couldn't place his accent.

I smiled again. "Hi. Any questions about the menu?

Want a minute to look it over?"

"I...um..." He frowned at the chalkboard behind me, upon which Maya had carefully written out the beverage menu. "I...don't know..."

"Ever had espresso?"

He shook his head.

"Tell you what, why don't I make you a latte? That's an easy first step."

As I rummaged in the fridge for milk, I noticed him creeping closer to the counter and felt the weight of his stare on my back. "Lactose allergy?" I asked. "I've got soy, if you'd prefer."

"No, thank you," he murmured.

When I turned around, he was perhaps a yard away from me. "I'll have it up in a jiffy. Let me get the coffee going..."

I'd just attached the portafilter to the grouphead when he blurted, "You have a very impressive rack."

I froze. In Pactish, the term wasn't slang for boobs— he really was talking about my antlers—but still, my muscles tightened as my face began to flush. "Thanks," I muttered.

"They're beautiful," he continued as if I weren't trying to shrink into myself in front of him. "Lovely symmetry."

Saying nothing and hoping he'd take the hint, I pulled a shot and kept my eyes on the machine.

"Are you from this city?" he asked.

"No."

"Then where?"

"Outside." Grabbing the milk pitcher, I cranked up the steam and swirled.

"*Where*, outside?" he pressed. "I admit, I've not seen the full breadth of the Pactlands—"

"Virginia," I said, raising my voice above the noise. "I'm from Virginia." The milk wasn't quite as hot as I'd have liked, but I quickly assembled his drink and slid it across the bar. "There you go. Sweeteners are on the side table."

His brows knit. "Where is Virginia?"

"Like I said, outside. Outside the Pactlands," I continued when his confusion didn't let up. "Not from around here, don't want to talk about it."

"*Oh* I didn't realize there were women with racks as beautiful as yours beyond the borders—"

"There aren't," I snapped. "I'm cursed, okay? Happy? Anything else you need to know?"

But I didn't give him a chance to answer. Red-faced and ready to either punch the wall or burst into tears, I marched off to the kitchen.

As the swinging door flapped closed, Maya glanced up from the cookies she was decorating and dropped her piping bag. "Annie? What's wrong?"

"Could you please ring him up?" I asked, cocking my head toward the front of the building. "I need a second."

"Sure." She squeezed my shoulder as she passed me, and I slunk into the walk-in refrigerator.

I hid in there for a good five minutes, long enough to calm down, start shivering, and berate myself for losing my temper in front of a customer, and emerged to find Maya back in the kitchen. "Sorry," I told her. "Is he still out there?"

"I switched his drink into a takeout cup," she replied. "Are you all right? Need a break?"

"I'm fine. Better go clean up my mess," I said, and forced a smile as I left.

Things could have been worse, I told myself. He could have been standing there, staring at me. But the café was empty once again, and with a sigh, I wiped down the steam wand and dumped the grounds.

CHAPTER 2

I hadn't given the stranger much thought after the Monday lunch rush. Once we closed down for the day, Maya and I had gone upstairs for our appointment with the research team working on Roulette for more bloodwork and the monthly interview. Any changes—physical, emotional, or magical? How were we feeling? Any signs of illness?

We told them what they wanted to know, but as usual, they had few answers for us. Their data suggested that Maya and I were stable, still very much affected by Roulette but unlikely to wake up with gills or worse. But as for an antidote to the potion, they remained baffled. Considering that some of the top potions experts in the Pactlands were working on the problem, this didn't give me much hope, but I forced myself to smile and insist that everything was just fine on my end.

I'd given up on expecting overnight miracles, but out of habit, I checked my DPP-issued phone first thing Tuesday when my alarm buzzed, just in case there'd been a breakthrough while I was sleeping. No such message appeared, however, and so I sighed, rolled out of bed, and shuffled to the shower. Mine came equipped with a detachable showerhead, a real perk when one was trying to rinse shampoo from around antlers. Drying my hair was another matter entirely, as half the time I spent trying to style it was devoted to untangling it when it blew around my rack and snarled.

As I toweled off, I briefly considered my reflection: wet clumps of dark brown hair turned black with moisture, green eyes that might be pretty once the morning puffiness subsided, a zit trying to erupt on the side of my chin. I'd lost a little weight since coming to the Pactlands—even though I was working at a café, Maya's meals were healthier than the snack foods I'd lived on for much of the previous year—which gave my collarbones a bit of definition but hardly left me looking like a waif. I flexed my right arm, appraised the muscles, and resolved to spend more time at the DPP office gym. Lord knew I needed a diversion, and I could do worse than arm day.

Screw the hairdryer, I decided, and turned away from the mirror as I pulled the damp mess back in a ponytail. I still hadn't acclimated to my freakish new look, and if I avoided reflective surfaces, I could almost pretend that I wasn't trying to cosplay as a deer.

Maya and I made it to the café around three-thirty, and while she baked and prepped, I got the drip coffee brewing and checked our supplies, as getting caught without enough takeout cups on hand during the middle of the rush was a pain in everyone's ass. To my relief, the morning went off without a hitch—well, one tiny burn on my wrist from a splash of hot milk, but that was barely worth noting. The usual crowd of agents knew better than to order off-menu, the microwave and toaster cooperated, and no randos came in to gawk at the baristas. By nine, the place was calm and clean once more. Maya returned to the kitchen, and I took out my book to pick up with the car chase I'd begun the day before.

When the doorbell jingled at ten, it jerked me out of the story. My head shot up in time to see Rose push her way into the café, her arms laden with Kroger bags.

"Hey, Annie!" she called, grinning. "Got the loot. Where do y'all want it?"

"You didn't have to—"

"But I did. *Oof.*" She slung the bags onto an empty table and rubbed her bare forearms, which were striped with red indentations from the handles. "Found some

BOGOs that were too good to pass up, you know?"

When it was just the three of us, Rose always spoke in English, which I appreciated more than I let on. She was as conversant in Pactish as I was—and she spoke Low Elvish, too—but Rose sounded like *home* when she reverted to our first language, and for a moment, I could pretend I was a world away from Beukal.

Unlike Maya and me, Rose had special dispensation to come and go at will. Though she was basically elven royalty, she'd grown up in Richmond like we had, and she still had a house and a studio there. But over the last month, Rose had begun making arrangements to wrap up her life in the city. Whether she would sell her childhood home remained an open question, but she'd notified her landlord that she wouldn't be renewing her lease on the studio, and she wasn't accepting new commissions. She told us she'd explained the situation to our Carytown clique by claiming she was moving overseas for an intensive graduate program. In reality, she'd landed a job with DPP, she was spending hours each week with a tutor to work on remedial magic, and she and Yven had a wedding to plan. A *distant* wedding, Rose insisted—Yven understood that she had too many flaming chainsaws in the air to add a wedding to the mix—but the fact remained that the two of them were engaged now and deep in the googly-eyed phase.

Though she was, genetically speaking, overwhelmingly elven, Rose could go home on a whim because she didn't look the part. She seemed perfectly human, a gray-eyed redhead of average height who could drawl with the best of us. Only once she wiggled her fingers and items flew across the room to her did the illusion fail. More than that, Rose was a farseer, able to focus on distant people and see what they were up to, which made her *highly* useful to DPP.

Still, the agency hadn't always been sure of what to do with her. Until seven weeks ago, she'd been unacknowledged by any of the elven halls and therefore legally human. While she'd been tutored on the sly and cracked a few cases for DPP, once it slipped that she and Yven had fallen for each other, the director had kicked her out in an effort to keep Yven from running off with her. A Pactlander who decided they couldn't live without a human—or in Rose's case, someone who was legally human—had no option but a potion known as the death draught, which neutralized any power they had and killed them in less than thirty years. Rose and the director had since reconciled, particularly as the great-grandfather who'd finally acknowledged Rose had ripped the director a new one, and Rose and Yven had gone public with their relationship. Rose Thorn had become Rose ti'Dana, and she did as she pleased.

I was glad to have her back. Rose had been a lifeline for Maya and me during our first two months in the Pactlands, but after the New Year, she'd stopped coming around Pars Mera, one of DPP's Interdiction agents and Yven's buddy, had finally told us about her banishment in late January. I'd protested that the decision to cut her off wasn't fair, and Pars had concurred, but we'd had no say in the matter. Now that Rose was getting her life in order, she frequently dropped by the café, and more often than not, she came bearing gifts.

I knew Rose felt awful about the Roulette situation. Of our friend group, she'd been the only one not stuck in quarantine, and she'd raised a stink until our accommodations improved—caffeine, a place to smoke, a DPP tech on hand who spoke English. But she was also the reason we'd ended up in the Pactlands in the first place. Emily, Maya's sous chef, had been the first to awaken after the party and had called Rose in a panic when she found a body, and as Yven had been spending the weekend with Rose, he'd tagged along to investigate. I wasn't upset with her—the Richmond PD certainly wouldn't have known what to do with me and my new antlers—but I didn't think I was imagining that Rose carried a bit of something akin to survivor's guilt.

Now that her portal credentials were secure, Rose made it a point to check with us at least once a week and get a shopping list. While DPP was great about financing the café, some of Maya's preferred ingredients were available only outside the Pactlands, and Rose didn't mind swinging by the grocery store or specialty shops on her way out of town.

"All right," she said, and cracked her knuckles before she began unpacking that day's haul. "I think this bag is nothing but coffee…"

"Ooh," I replied, noticing the familiar labels. "You're *good*."

"I got everything in whole beans except this one, which they only had ground." Handing me a sealed package, she waggled her eyebrows as I smiled. "You said you'd been craving it."

"I didn't mean for you to *buy* me flavored coffee," I protested, but gratefully accepted my pound of French vanilla. Adding syrup to the regular brew just wasn't the same.

Rose continued to unpack as I moved the boxes and bags into piles on the counter. Loose-leaf tea in several varieties. A big cannister of Maya's preferred curry blend. Whole peppercorns. Flaky sea salt. Several pounds of lemons and limes. Bags of perfectly ripe red cherries. Three types of cooking spray, one designed for baking, and a half-gallon of olive oil. The muffin tin liners Maya liked. From the cold bag came enough boxes of Philly to get the average baker through the holidays and Maya through at least a week.

And then Rose revealed the bonus items she'd picked up for me: two boxes of Cinnamon Toast Crunch, a family pack of Velveeta Shells & Cheese, a cannister of instant stuffing, and three bags of Reese's Cups. She finished it off with big bottles of shampoo and conditioner—nothing too fancy, I was an Herbal Essences girl—and a twelve-pack of Mountain Dew.

"This is too much," I said as I ripped into the candy.

"Nah." She stole a cup from the bag and quickly unwrapped it. "Maya said you'd like this. I really don't mind, Annie."

"It's not cheap—"

"Pa-eme reimburses me. Go wild," she replied, shrugging. "Let me know when y'all want a tenderloin."

"*Right*, like the director's going to pay for a tenderloin."

"He won't put up a fuss. Trust me."

"If you say so." I stacked my personal stash under the counter as Rose folded her shopping bags. "Something to drink?"

She perked. "Iced coffee?"

"Coming up."

I made two, deciding not to interrupt Maya. She could be as social as they came, but bothering her during her pre-rush prep time was unwise unless you had a good reason.

Popping a pair of cookies on a plate, I joined Rose at the cleared-off table with our drinks, and she rolled her eyes with pleasure as she took a sip. "*Nice*. I needed that."

"Long drive?"

"Eh, it's really not so bad, but I've been craving one of these. I was in the studio all day yesterday."

"Could have come by on Saturday," I replied.

"Not last weekend." She smiled and leaned closer over the table. "Yven took me home to meet his folks."

My eyebrows rose. "And?"

"Still alive, aren't I? And the engagement's still on. Actually," she said, relaxing back into her chair, "they were lovely. Tana and Runat put me up for the weekend at the family manse."

"Ooh, the *manse*. Would this be bigger or smaller than the mansion you're currently living in?" I teased. I hadn't actually set eyes on Lord ti'Dana's house, but from all accounts, it was palatial.

Rose snorted. "Not quite as large, but very nice. You've seen the mural I painted inside Mangia?"

"Sure..."

"Make the trees shorter and take out the vineyard, and that's basically it."

Not too shabby, indeed. The painting in Maya's Carytown restaurant featured a two-story home with an orange tile roof and several outbuildings scattered across rolling countryside. Little but grass grew well in the Pactlands unless the area was anchored to the outside world, and from what Rose had told me, the apple orchard from which Yven's parents made their cider grew on fertile rented land elsewhere.

"Some of Yven's siblings came by, too, but don't ask me to name them all—that's a work in progress," said Rose, laughing. "Gileg still lives with their parents because he's just thirteen, and Yven's immediate elder sister, Melari, hung around most of Saturday. She's an artist, too, so I think we're off to a good start."

"And the rest?" I asked.

She made a face. "So Yven's the fourteenth of fifteen, right, and some of his siblings are, like, five hundred years old. Melari's eighty-six this year, and the next youngest is...wait"—she screwed up her face in thought—"Bascir, right. He hangs around because he's in on the family business. But he's about a hundred twenty and has two kids, so it's not like he and Yven have oodles in common."

"Imagine buying Christmas gifts for all of them."

"Thankfully, that's not on the agenda. Anyway, things got a little awkward on occasion," she continued. "Sometimes, I wasn't sure whether the siblings had come to gawk at the ti'Dana or the human in their midst."

"I hear you," I muttered.

Rose flashed a sympathetic smile. "You doing okay?"

"Eh." I sipped my coffee and shrugged. "Getting by. Same old same old. The folks in the research division remain optimistic, but..."

"But they have no answers yet," she finished. "Shit."

We contemplated the unfairness of the universe while we ate Maya's cookies.

"Any decision as to your house?" I asked, changing the subject. "You going to sell?"

Rose sighed. "I *should*, but I can't yet. All of my parents' stuff is still there, and...I mean, I know it's stupid," she said, picking up speed, "and they're not going to come back and yell at me from beyond the grave if I donate their furniture, but..."

"It's okay," I told her. "You're allowed."

"It's a waste of money to keep it up."

"Maybe, but is that actually a legitimate concern?"

"Not really," she admitted. "I've got enough in savings over there to handle the place for a while, and I can exchange currency here."

"I was talking about the family fortune."

"Okay, true, but I don't want to keep going to Pop with my hand out for home upkeep. He's already letting me stay with him now."

I smirked. "That's on him."

"To be fair, Yven's apartment would be tiny for the both of us, all my art supplies, and his orchid collection. We'll get a bigger place together soon enough." Grinning, she added, "Pop has offered us our own apartment at his house, but I'm not sure if Yven's ready to take that step. He still gets tongue-tied around Pop."

I could only imagine what sort of setup Rose had at the ti'Dana mansion, but something told me it was at least as large as Maya's and my apartment. Diriem ti'Dana might have surrendered his throne to sign the Pact—bringing his people into the new pocket world and thereby saving them from extinction—but he hadn't left himself destitute.

"I want to have you and Maya out for a weekend once things settle down," said Rose. "To Pop's place, I mean. A change of scenery wouldn't hurt, right?"

"Thanks. Sounds like fun." I adjusted my straw around

the ice cubes and sipped. "How are your lessons going?"

In response, Rose groaned and planted her face on the table.

"That bad, huh?"

"History, politics, magical theory...those are all fine," she replied. "It's the physical stuff that's the problem. I've got one tutor for the delicate side of casting, and she's great, but Pateme has me working with Emarae and his Interdiction group again, and..." She stood and lifted part of her shirt, revealing a discolored patch up and down the left side of her ribcage. "He's a good teacher, but *man*, he hits hard."

"Shit," I muttered. "Did he crack a rib?"

"Three. I got sloppy in practice, and then I spent an hour with the healers. At least swimming wasn't on the weekend itinerary," she said as she sat again.

"You ever think about where we were this time last year?"

Rose smiled wistfully. "Yven's lessons never hurt as much as Emarae's..."

"Before that, then. Do you ever wish you hadn't found out about this place?"

She hesitated. "Sometimes, a little. When my lessons are overwhelming or Pop takes me out in *society* and I can't enjoy myself because I'm so paranoid about committing an unspeakable faux pas..." With a brief huff, she returned to her coffee, then said, "Things were simpler in Carytown, and no one ever shot at me there. I miss that. But on balance, I wouldn't go back in time and run away."

Rose didn't ask me what I would have done, had I been given a do-over for last Halloween, and she quickly directed the conversation onto a different topic. "You and Maya are still coming to Yven's for dinner Sunday, right?"

I nodded. "Assuming one of y'all gives us the address..."

"Gah. Sorry." She fumbled in her purse for a pen and a piece of scrap paper, then scribbled out directions. "It's not far from DPP, and there's visitor parking beside the building." Lowering her voice, she added, "He's excited to cook but slightly intimidated to cook for *Maya*, if you know what I mean, so——"

"I'll tell her to be gentle."

She smiled and finished her drink, then stood and gathered her things. "We're glad you're coming. Tell Maya that I'm planning to make another run to Richmond on Friday if she needs anything—and you, too," she added. "Seriously, I deliver."

I thanked her and hugged her goodbye, and Rose opened the door to the sidewalk. Before she could step out into the pleasant morning, however, she frowned and pulled something from the ground. "Sorry, I think this was stuck in the doorjamb. Must have missed it on my way in."

"What's that?" I asked, dumping our dishes into the washtub.

"Looks like a letter." She passed a folded piece of paper over the counter—not sealed with wax, the preferred method in the Pactlands, but rather with a crossed piece of twine like a tiny package. "Is your mailbox not working?"

"Orders have been coming in since five this morning," I said, pointing to the translucent tub on the counter by the kitchen. The Division of Parcels and Letters didn't bother with daily delivery, but rather sent mail through the system as soon as it was received and sorted. As I watched, another order form appeared in midair above the tub and fluttered down to join the few below it. "I'd better check on that," I told Rose. "Thanks again."

She saw herself out, and I added the carryout lunch forms to the queue in the kitchen as I lugged the groceries back to the storage room. Maya slid a quiche into the oven and gushed over the spices Rose had found, then chided me to tell her that Rose had stopped by the next time so that she could at least thank her properly. I promised, and once I'd cleaned up from our delivery and left Maya to pack the takeout, I turned my attention to the letter left by the door.

It had no stamps, and it was addressed only to "Annie"—or, more precisely, one of the several Pactish approximations of my name's spelling. Curious, I snipped the twine with a pair of kitchen shears, then unfolded the note to see who'd left the strange correspondence. The writing within continued in the Pactish script, a neat, blocky hand that slanted slightly to the right:

To Annie,

> *Please permit me to apologize for my behavior yesterday. I had no intention of causing you distress.*

I almost dropped the letter as I realized the weird guy with the antlers like mine must have left it, but curiosity kept me reading.

> *It's no excuse, but I was shocked to see you. I've never seen a female of my kind—they almost certainly don't exist, I fear—and to simply chance upon you knocked me off my feet. But I understand that my initial assessment was mistaken. Your friend explained your predicament in very firm terms.*
>
> *I'm terribly sorry for grieving you and embarrassed for having done so. I'm a newcomer to the capital, and I was unaware of your situation. Again, that's no excuse, and I sincerely apologize.*

> *Wylan*

He'd *apologized.*

No one did that. People stared at me, then tried to pretend they hadn't been when I caught them in the act, but they never apologized for making me feel like an exotic zoo exhibit.

I had no idea what this Wylan was—I'd yet to see his like around Beukal—but given that explanation, he must have been excited and confused when he walked in. The truth had to be a downer...though I wondered how long a male-only species could get by, even in the Pactlands. The fact that he hadn't used our mailbox confirmed that he wasn't a local. DPL's standards for properly addressing an envelope were ridiculously lax, so maybe Wylan didn't have a mailbox of his own yet.

Feeling ever so slightly bad about storming off to hide in the kitchen, I tucked Wylan's letter between my cereal and pasta boxes beneath the counter for safekeeping. While there was no question that this was a matter to discuss with Maya, experience counseled me against bothering her while she was busy and close to sharp objects.

CHAPTER 3

I didn't know how Maya did it. She could labor in the kitchen for hours, meticulously organizing and timing half a dozen dishes, but when she stepped out to the counter, she was suddenly *on*. She laughed easily, recalled customers' names as if they were old friends, and even seemed to flirt on occasion. No one had ever taken her on a date during our time in the Pactlands—at the end of the day, she was still just a human with a bad potion reaction—but people gravitated toward Maya like moths to a porch light.

Maybe she was born with that confidence. I certainly didn't know—we'd been three years apart in school, and we hadn't crossed paths until we were adults, when I stumbled upon Mangia and fell under her spell. Sociable to a fault, Maya knew everyone worth knowing in Carytown. She was more selective about those she admitted to her inner circle, a beachcomber on the hunt for shells of a particular shape and hue, but once you were in with Maya, you were *in*. Interesting people, wild parties, her notorious tipsy party bus tours of Christmas decorations…Maya was a generous friend, effervescent when in her element. Even post-Roulette, she carried herself as though nothing were amiss—as though restauranters often came in a winged variety. Sometimes, she hid her wings beneath a long sweater or coat, but that being impractical in July, she let them hang freely behind her as she worked. When we went out, if people stared, she smiled and waved, even stopped on occasion to let curious kids have a better look. Hell, she'd gone to a few DPP house parties—on the whole, the Regulatory folks were fairly staid, though Interdiction knew how to have a good time. But I wasn't nearly as easygoing as Maya was in an unknown crowd, and after nursing a beer in the corner all night at one of those parties, I'd begged off from future events.

Honestly, I felt drained. As fun as Maya's parties could be, they were the sort of thing that required a degree of psyching-up for me to enjoy, and I was always useless the day after. I needed space and quiet, time alone with my thoughts, which was why the PI gig worked so well. You don't have to be social if you're surveilling. I'd lived alone in Richmond, and my favorite group events had been hitting the woods with my dad and his buddies, all of us silently freezing up in tree stands in the predawn while we waited for deer to wander by. Now...well, I wasn't particularly comfortable in kitchens to begin with, I faced a steady glut of customers six days a week, and while Maya made a lovely roommate, she was still a *roommate*.

At least I had my books...and on that front, I had Syvin.

DPP's chief deputy, Syvin Deop, was a petite faun with curly brown hair and a penchant for accenting her robes with floral scarves. And she was *petite*: a couple inches below five feet, by my estimation, if one didn't take into account her horns, which curled back from her bony forehead and wrapped around by her ears. She may have been short, by Syvin was perfectly proportioned to administer one hell of a headbutting, should she have cause—and judging by some of the stories I'd heard in my time around DPP, she'd done so to great effect in her younger days. Of course, no one in the Pactlands gave her a second look unless they recognized her from the agency. Beukal had a growing population of fauns, and physically, Syvin was an unremarkable example of the species. She was goatish below the waist, and like most fauns I'd seen, she eschewed anything resembling pants or shoes. Even her eyes had a caprine quality to them, golden-brown and set with rectangular pupils.

And she was, without question, my best customer.

Syvin took her coffee large and black, and she preferred drip to espresso. She never asked me for anything more complicated than a reheated pastry, which I could confidently manage, and she tipped. But more important—at least for me—was the fact that Syvin was a connoisseur of mystery novels. When she came in midmorning one day before Christmas and caught me rereading *The Maltese Falcon*, one of the few paperbacks I'd managed to scrounge from the secondhand shop, her face had lit up like she'd just met her new best friend. As it turned out, Syvin *adored* mysteries, the more hardboiled, the better. "I read one once involving a knitting circle of elderly women," she'd confided to me with disdain. "Everything of interest happened offstage, and there wasn't even a proper murder. Won't make that mistake again."

Upon realizing that she'd found a kindred spirit, Syvin became a regular at the café, and she frequently came bearing gifts. I had no idea how large her home library had to be, but she'd brought me dozens of books: classic English-language detective fiction, a few that had made the bestseller lists within my lifetime, and a selection of her favorites by Pactlands writers. When she had time to spare, she'd linger by the counter with her coffee and chat with me about my reading, asking me about my bookstore finds and answering my questions about the nuances of the stories set in a world I was still exploring. Thanks to Syvin, I quickly learned about the different agencies—particularly the Division of Laws, which oversaw both the police and the prosecutors—and I discovered that it took very little encouragement to get her started on her own war stories, of which she had *plenty*. As ignorant as I was of norms among the different Pact races, I couldn't begin to tell anyone's age, and it had taken me aback when Syvin had casually mentioned her four-hundred-year career at DPP.

On Wednesday morning, she dropped in around nine, carrying a canvas tote on her shoulder. "Morning, Annie," she said, her hooves clicking on the hardwood floor as she approached the pastry case. "Let's see, I've got a workout scheduled tonight, so...hmm." She frowned at the offerings as I poured her drink. "What do you recommend?"

"Carrot cake," I replied without hesitation. "Maya makes the cream cheese frosting from scratch."

Syvin sucked her teeth. "Tempting as the frosting sounds. I make it a point not to mix my sweets and vegetables. Second choice?"

I pointed to a thick, dense slice of chocolate cake. "Flourless torte. The raspberry ganache in the middle is to die for."

"Done." She smiled and pulled out her wallet as I plated her selection. "I'll need that to go today—nothing but meetings this morning," she explained with a sigh. "What do I owe you?"

"Six marks fifty."

With a nod, she placed a ten on the counter and said, "Keep the change. Also, I brought you more books. No new titles," she added apologetically, "but these are good ones. I tried to get my book club to read this," she continued, pulling a thick paperback from her tote, "but alas, the girls wanted no part of it."

The cover depicted a troll's legs lying in a pool of blood. "Little much?" I asked.

"They decided that the decapitation in the first chapter wasn't appropriate for wine and cheese," she replied, her lips tightening to a thin line. "Oh, a mystery's just fine when it's a talking horse doing the amateur detective work, but throw in DOL and a serial killer, and...well, what can you do?" Shrugging, she added two more books to my stack, then took her cake and coffee. "Let me know what you think, eh?"

"I'll pop it in my pile," I said, and smiled as Syvin slipped back into the lobby, armed for the long morning. But she'd piqued my curiosity, and as I'd finished my novel from earlier in the week, I decided to go ahead and give the rejected book club title a try. I hadn't read about a good decapitation in a while, and I was curious to see what had put Syvin's friends off their snacks.

Ten minutes later, as a rookie agent was running outside so as not to puke on the headless corpse, the jangle of an incoming customer pulled me out of the story. I quickly marked my place and slid the book beneath the counter, then looked up to find Wylan standing there, once more hesitating on the threshold.

"Hi," I called.

He smiled nervously. "May I come in?"

"Last time I checked, this wasn't a private club."

As he slipped inside, he took care to gently close the door, then took a few steps closer to the counter. "Did you, um, get my—"

"Your letter?" I finished. "Yeah, I did."

"Again, I'm very sorry—"

"You didn't know. I didn't mean to be quite so dramatic about the whole thing, but it's…"

"Sensitive?"

"Yeah."

He winced. "You're allowed. Really, I'd never heard of this, uh…"

"Roulette?" I offered.

"*Right*. Strange name. I've never had much to do with potions, and as I mentioned, I'm quite new to town, so please forgive my ignorance. I didn't intend to upset you."

He seemed so earnest that I couldn't be angry with him. "I think we got off to a bad start on Monday," I said, and extended my hand over the counter. "Annie Humphries."

"Wylan," he replied, clasping it.

"Just Wylan?" Pactlands naming conventions remained a weak spot in my admittedly patchy education. Elves were easy—all elven surnames started with *ti'*—but nymph surnames changed based on which of three genders the person claimed, trolls favored long descriptors, and as for everyone else, I couldn't yet tell species based on name alone.

"That's all," he confirmed as some of the tension left his shoulders. "Nice to meet you properly."

"Likewise." Releasing him, I cracked my knuckles and grinned. "What are you drinking today?"

He rubbed the back of his neck. "See, that's the problem. I've heard that people are supposed to like coffee, but I'm not entirely familiar with the stuff, and…"

"Didn't like your latte?"

"Perhaps it's an acquired taste. I mean no insult," he hastily added. "My landlord highly recommended this place when I said I wanted to try coffee—"

"You should sweeten it next time," I said. "But for today, how about I make you something else?"

"Such as?"

"Ever had matcha?" He shook his head, and I swept one hand toward the empty tables. "Take a seat. I'll have it up in a minute."

Rose had been kind enough to bring us a big cannister of matcha powder the week before, and I'd added it to the drink menu as a temporary special. Though I needed coffee to function, drinking the occasional cup of green tea made me feel moderately better about my abysmal dietary choices.

Wylan watched me as I pulled the pitcher of premade matcha from the refrigerator and added it to a glass three-quarters full of ice and milk until the concoction turned the color of lime sherbet. "Do you like mint?" I asked.

"Sure."

"Perfect." I stuck the iced latte under the pumps for

simple syrup and mint, then stirred and added a straw. "Give this a shot," I said as I brought it to his table. "What do you think?"

His eyes widened as the sweet liquid hit, and he grinned up at me like a kid. "This is great! What *is* it?"

"Ground-up green tea leaves, milk, mint, and a healthy dose of sugar. Enjoy."

"Wait," he said as I headed back to the counter, "what do I owe you?"

"On the house today," I replied. "Welcome to town, I guess. Where are you from, anyway?"

With his straw back in his mouth, Wylan gestured toward the world beyond the café windows until he came up for air. "Middle of nowhere. Pactlands, I mean, but nowhere exciting. I thought I'd give the city a try."

"I get it. Let me know if you need anything else," I said, and returned to my book without asking the one question I was dying to pose: *What are you?* One didn't need to be a Pactlands native to appreciate that the question was rude at best, so I kept my thoughts to myself and tried to focus on the story. Unfortunately, though the book was excellent, my mind kept wandering to Wylan. It wasn't just that he was new—in eight months, I'd yet to see another person with a rack like mine, and now there was one sitting a few yards away, reading a newspaper.

Quaint, I mused. Technologically, the Pactlands was on par with the world I'd left behind, though their tech was sometimes augmented by a hint of magic. Most of the people I'd seen reading in the café did so on a phone or tablet, and the only place I'd found an actual paper for sale was in the convenience store two blocks away, which kept a dilapidated dispenser by the front door.

As I surreptitiously observed Wylan over my book, I noticed that he wasn't just reading, but rather making notes on the paper with a red pen. My curiosity finally got the best of me, and I asked, "Reading anything interesting?"

He glanced up with a smile. "Job advertisements. I'm looking for work."

"What do you do?"

"Well, at the moment…nothing."

"No, sorry. What profession are you in?"

"*Ah*." His expression shifted toward embarrassment. "I've, uh…I've always worked for my father. Never had a job outside the family, so I'm eager to see what's available."

I knew I shouldn't pry, but I couldn't help myself. "How did your dad take the news that you were branching out?"

"Not well. He didn't try to stop me, but he's displeased. Thinks I'm wasting my time," Wylan replied, and rolled his eyes. "My family situation is somewhat fraught—"

Holding up my hands to stop him, I said, "None of my business. Sorry, I can be nosy."

"No need to apologize." His smile returned as he continued. "I've found a place to live a few streets over, and now I need to find work to pay the rent. Hence this," he said, tapping his pen against the newspaper. "I'm not sure of my qualifications at this point, so I'm circling anything that looks intriguing, and I'll follow up this afternoon." With that, he paused, considered the empty café, and quickly asked, "Is it all right if I stay? If you're closed—"

"Oh, no, you're fine," I assured him. "This is the slump before lunch. I'll let you get back to your ads."

For the next hour, while Maya worked her magic in the kitchen and I babysat the counter, Wylan studied the newspaper as if cramming for a test. I read my book, keeping an eye on our lone customer. Foot traffic was low—not unusual for a midweek morning—but around ten-fifteen, Maya emerged with a cooling quiche in her hands and game face on. "While I cut this, would you please bring out the sandwiches from the prep table?" she asked. "They're wrapped…"

Her voice trailed off as she noticed Wylan, and she shot me a questioning look. "He's fine," I murmured, and slipped past her to retrieve the bounty. Mangia Due's lunch menu leaned toward the grab-and-go end of the spectrum, perfect for the agent on the run, and most of the offerings were a variant on the "filling in carbohydrates" model. She kept a few premade salads on hand, along with single-serving tubs of fruit, potato salad, her perfect coleslaw, and a few other cold sides she'd played with in recent months, and of course, the coffee flowed.

For us, the lunch rush began around ten-thirty and didn't let up until after one. Those agents who worked the early shift didn't want to wait until noon, while on the back end, we often had stragglers wander down as late as three to pick over the sandwiches. Right on schedule, six of our usuals came down in a group, and Maya and I got to work, dancing around each other behind the counter in the choreography we could almost intuit. When customers approached, Maya took their orders, plating and giving change while I worked the espresso machine and churned out beverages. I also kept an eye on the to-go shelves, where the orders we'd received by mail that morning were packed and ready for pickup. The pace seldom slacked, and grabbing a two-minute break for a drink of water could be tricky, but we did our best to keep the line moving.

As I worked, I sneaked peeks at Wylan, who continued to study his paper and occasionally sip the watered-down dregs of his melting drink. He caused no trouble—he'd snagged a two-top out of the way, and a good chunk of our customers carried their meals back to their desks or out into the summer sunshine. But I was somewhat taken aback when I noticed the way other customers reacted to his presence: surprise, maybe a whisper passed between friends, and then avoidance. Even as the tables filled, folks gave him a *wide* berth.

It shouldn't have shocked me, I thought. Hell, I'd seen much of the same reaction directed at me as I walked through Beukal—some people actually crossed the street when they saw me coming. The fact that in a city full of magical beings, I was freakish enough to make parents pull their children close was demoralizing on a good day, but I'd come to expect it around strangers. That said, our regular customers knew me and acted normally, so their avoidance of Wylan struck me as odd. Making a note to enquire about it later, I focused on the more pressing task of not scalding myself.

By one, I was weary of pulling shots, but the press had slowed to a trickle. With our few remaining customers busily eating, I took a break, grabbed a ham sandwich from the dwindling supply, and brought it to Wylan. He glanced up and smiled when he saw me, then looked bemusedly at the sandwich as I put it on the table beside him. "What is—"

"You'll probably make a better impression on your job search if you don't faint from hunger," I said. As he fumbled for his wallet, I quickly murmured, "Save your money. I know what it's like to be starting out and short on cash, and you've got rent to pay."

"Thank you," he said, and tore into the wrapping.

He'd wolfed down half the sandwich by the time I'd pulled out the other chair, and I chuckled. "It's already dead—it's not going to run away from you."

"Rediscovered my appetite," he replied between bites. "And this is *really* good."

"I'll tell Maya you said so. Find any possible jobs?"

He turned the paper around to show me a dozen red-circled options. "I thought I'd start with these today. Any tips?"

"Not specifically," I admitted, grimacing. "Pactlands hiring isn't my specialty. Just follow the application directions, be polite, and show eagerness to do whatever you're applying for. Fingers crossed," I added, making the gesture.

Wylan cocked his head, perplexed.

"It means good luck," I explained. "Back home."

As I started to leave, he cleared his throat. "Annie? May I, uh…would you mind a somewhat personal question?"

Having been a twenty-something woman in a bar on too many occasions to count, I braced myself but shrugged. "What's on your mind?"

"I'm sorry to bring this up, but are you…that is…"

"Go on."

His face colored. "Are you *truly* human? Maya said you both were, but I, um…wanted to be sure," he mumbled in a rush.

I waited a beat, watching as Wylan's cheeks flamed scarlet, then quietly said, "Yeah, we are. The antlers are just the Roulette's doing, and that damn potion's the only reason I'm stuck here. Sorry if that's…disappointing?"

"Surprising," he amended, "and I apologize if this is a stupid question, but why are you *stuck*?"

My incredulous laughter slipped free before I could stop it. "Because if I walked around at home with these babies," I said, pointing to my rack, "and people realized they were actually attached to my head, I'd probably end up in a government lab somewhere. That, and if I started raving about how they're the result of a potion gone awry, I'd be labeled insane. When no one around you is able to use magic, you don't tend to believe in its existence," I explained.

He nodded. "Granted. But I've heard that there are items sold in places like Beukal that can change one's appearance. Could you not use something like that and go home?"

"Masking jewelry," I confirmed. "I've heard about it— agents who don't pass as human and can't mask themselves use it for fieldwork outside the Pactlands. But DPP and their buddies at DOL won't let Maya and me anywhere near it."

"Why not?"

I sighed. "Roulette is a novel potion, right? Well, the researchers are afraid of cross-reactions. Like, the spell on the jewelry will have a negative effect with whatever the potion has done to us. Is *doing* to us, I should say."

Wylan's brow furrowed as he listened. "Are you worsening?"

"Nope, but we're not getting any better." Sliding into my vacated chair again, I lowered my voice and leaned closer to him. "DPP tried to remove my antlers once. Brought a horn specialist in, and he took them down to nubs. He said he wanted to study my scans overnight and determine how deeply to cut the next day. Reasonable plan, so I went to bed…and when I woke up, they were back, like he'd never even touched them. Good thing they experimented with me instead of Maya," I added as Wylan's face worked. "Wing amputation is probably pretty painful."

"I'm so sorry…"

"Could always be worse," I replied, forcing lightness into my voice. "And there's another reason why I can't go home with masking jewelry: the potential of catastrophic mask failure. If I got caught out far away from a portal, with no way to get back, and my mask failed…" I made a face as I let that mental image sink in, then said, "So yeah, Maya and I are stuck here until DPP finds a cure."

Before Wylan could press me for more information, the bell jingled, and I got up to see to the new customers. He'd finished eating by the time I had them situated, and after he tossed his trash, he caught me at the counter. "Would it be all right if I returned tomorrow?"

"Sure," I said, smiling to myself as the worry melted from his expression. "Hey, good luck with the job hunt."

He raised his folded newspaper like a soldier with a sword, primed for battle, then strode off into the warm afternoon in search of gainful employment.

As the door closed behind him, Maya slipped out of

the kitchen and whispered in my ear, "He's not bad. Awkward, maybe, but not horrible."

I whipped my head around, almost snagging a low-hanging light on my stupid antlers, and she grinned. "He's new in town and lonely," I retorted.

"Yeah? Those things aren't mutually exclusive," she said, then dropped an exaggerated wink and returned to work with a teasing flutter of wings.

CHAPTER 4

Knowing next to nothing about the job market in Beukal, I couldn't guess how difficult a time Wylan would have in his quest, though I held out hope for him. But when he showed up midmorning Thursday with a fresh newspaper, he shook his head before I could even ask the question. "No luck," he said, joining me at the counter. "Perhaps I need to cross more fingers, eh?"

"None at all?" I replied, stowing my book back in its hiding place.

"Unfortunately, no. Either the positions had already been filled or I wasn't qualified. Or maybe the people in charge of hiring just didn't like me," he mused, squinting into the distance as he considered the possibility, then brightened. "But that's only one day of searching, and I'm ready to try again."

At least his spirits seemed high. "Sounds good. What'll you have today?"

"Could you make me that green drink from yesterday?"

"Sure. And have a seat," I said as he dug for his wallet—not in a pocket, I noticed, but rather in a pouch hanging from his waist like a loose-slung fanny pack. Wylan had worn different shirts during the course of the week, but his pants hadn't changed, and I wondered if he owned more than one pair of leather leggings. "This is on me."

"That doesn't seem fair…"

"My espresso machine, my rules, and Maya won't mind. Sit."

When I finished his iced latte, I found him at the table where he'd camped the previous day and slid into the chair opposite him. "Did you get any feedback yesterday?" I asked. "Any hints about what they were looking for?"

"No," said Wylan. "The ad is old, you're not quite what we had in mind, thanks for coming…" He took a sip and smiled at the hit of matcha and sugar. "If I may ask, how did you find your job here?"

Chuckling, I explained, "I got drafted. DPP is housing Maya and me until they find a cure, and she suggested opening this place as a way to chip in. *And* because that woman gets bored, I swear. But yeah, DPP renovated this space and fronts the money for supplies, and we've been turning a profit almost from the beginning. Even if folks get tired of coffee and sandwiches, you have to admit that the convenience factor is unmatched for the agents here." As he mulled that over, I said, "Sorry that's not much help. I don't know how I'd fare on the market—school around here goes to thirty-five, right, and I finished my associate degree and started working at twenty. Even for jobs that don't require magic, I'd probably be underqualified."

"Likewise, I fear," said Wylan, pushing his drink away before he could drain it. "I did a bit of research last night—my landlord loaned me his computer. I never went to school, which may be a problem."

"*Never?*"

"Nothing formal. Father and my brothers taught me what I needed to know. Out here, though…well, I suppose there are gaps in my education. But there must be *something* I can do," he continued. "I'm decently strong, and I know how to clean—surely one doesn't need thirty-five years of schooling to do *that.*"

I left him to his search. Wylan worked more quickly that day and was out the door with his fresh possibilities before the height of the lunch rush.

But when he returned Friday morning, he seemed dejected. "No luck again?" I asked, heading for the matcha pitcher.

"No." He huffed a sigh and ran one hand back between his antlers, pushing his hair into place. "More old ads, vacancies already filled...or maybe I really am unqualified for everything in this city."

"Has anyone said that?"

"Not specifically. No one's been rude, but I'll admit it's distressing to have no possibilities."

I started assembling his drink. "How many places have you tried?"

"Thirty-seven," he muttered, then noticed what I was doing. "Annie, wait, you don't have to—"

"I don't mind," I interrupted, and headed for the pump bottles. "Get settled with your paper, and I'll be right there."

I microwaved a cookie and brought it out with the latte. Maya marked the previous day's baked goods at half price, and one oatmeal cookie wasn't going to dent our bottom line. "We've all had lean times," I said as he started to protest. "Enjoy."

While Wylan scoured the want ads, I helped a few takeout customers with complicated drinks and warmed-over breakfast sandwiches, then returned to his table once the café was quiet again. "So," I said as he closed the marked-up newspaper, "just putting this out there, since I'm guessing you don't have much of a social calendar yet, but we reopen on Friday and Saturday nights around dinner and stay open late. Wine and beer instead of coffee, and Maya has a rotating tapas menu. Karaoke, too. My warbling is considered a war crime," I added with a little laugh, ' but a lot of folks around here seem to enjoy the mic. There's no cover charge, so if you want to stop in, we'll be here."

"Thank you," he replied, but cocked his head. "What's tapas?"

"Oh, uh…small plates. Like, instead of getting one big thing for dinner, you and your friends might order an assortment of small dishes to share. Personally," I said, lowering my voice, "I'm not sold on the idea. Going for tapas always seems to leave me with less food and a bigger bill, but Maya's the boss. Hang on, I'll get you tonight's menu."

I slipped back behind the counter and returned with her handwritten notes, which I needed to type and print during our brief break that afternoon. "Let's see…okay, yeah, the barbeque meatballs are my favorite, no contest. She serves them as a plate of five, but if you get a couple, you can make a decent meal from that base. The crostini…meh. Cute bites, but not filling. She's doing her chicken salad sampler in endive cups, and that's not bad. Mac and cheese balls are tasty but not the best value. Mini crab cakes—delish," I said with a groan. "The crudité and fruit platters are made to serve three to four. Oh, and the baked brie—she always has that on the menu. Ever had it?"

He shook his head. "What is—"

"Brie? It's a soft French cheese. Comes in rounds," I explained, spreading my hands to give him an idea of the size. "Wrap one of those bad boys in pastry, pop it in the oven until it gets melty, and serve with her homemade preserves and dried fruit…" I mimed a chef's kiss and grinned. "Might not cure what ails you, but it won't make matters worse, know what I mean?"

"I think I follow you," said Wylan. "But I take it most people don't come here alone to eat tapas, correct?"

"We wouldn't hold it against you."

"Appreciated. Once I have an actual job, perhaps I'll take you up on your undersized food."

"Think about it," I told him, and rose from the table. "And if you should stop by one night and ask nicely, I could probably sneak a few extra tidbits onto your plate. You know, since you're becoming a regular around here."

He patted his newspaper, then began collecting his things. "Here's hoping I won't be around to bother you all morning for much longer."

"You're not *bothering* me."

"You're kind to say so. But since my landlord will want payment eventually…"

"Go on, then," I replied, shooing him toward the door. "Good luck. I'll want a full report, now," I added with mock gravity.

Wylan bowed, tossed his empty cup in the trash, and headed out to try again.

I wasn't surprised when Wylan didn't return that night, though his absence on Saturday morning left me…well, there wasn't a good word to describe exactly how I felt, but *unsettled* was close enough. Disappointed, perhaps— he'd grown on me. Curious, as I hoped he'd found a job on Friday. Maybe a touch on the worried side, since he seemed to knew few people in Beukal. He was probably just sleeping in, I chided myself—he didn't need a mother or a babysitter.

Still, I wished I'd gotten his number in the past week, just in case.

Maya was no help. After the lunch rush, she nudged me in the shoulder and said, "Looks like your boyfriend's run off."

"Who, Wylan? He's not my boyfriend," I retorted, snorting as I wiped the sandwich crumbs off the counter.

"And yet you keep making him lattes."

"Because he's new in town and broke, and I kind of feel bad about how I reacted on Monday."

"Uh-huh." She slung her arm around my shoulders and laughed to herself. "He's sort of cute. I wouldn't be upset."

"Thank you for your approval," I said dryly, extricating myself. "But I would think it's obvious that we're not dating."

Maya let it go, but she kept shooting me sly looks during the night as I poured wine and filled pitchers, often with an eye toward the door.

Our one day off was Sunday, and unless absolutely necessary, I didn't get out of bed until ten. My social calendar being only slightly more booked than Wylan's, I seldom had no reason not to lounge in the apartment with my paperbacks and comfy pants until guilt made me take a walk around the block. That Sunday, however, I had actual plans—dinner at Yven's place at six—meaning I needed to shower at some point.

Rose had given me good directions, and right on time, I pulled up beside his building in my old van. Like most of the apartment buildings downtown, Yven's was immaculate, a ten-story stone structure surrounded by an iron fence and tidy landscaping. Few plants grew well on their own in the Pactlands, but grass was the big exception, and the lawn-like spaces where flowerbeds would have been back home looked nice enough to golf on. We'd asked what we could bring, but as Rose insisted all week that they had everything well in hand, Maya had snagged a nice bottle from the café's wine stash as a token.

She'd taken pains for the evening out, going with a lilac sundress she'd found in a secondhand clothing store and altered to free her wings. Unlike me, Maya could sew, and the dress looked like it had been made for her. Add to that a flowy printed silk scarf and wedges, and she looked ready for a night on the town. As for me…well, I was grateful that before one of Rose's trips back to Beukal the previous November, she'd sneaked into my place and raided my closet. DPP had been generous in trying to outfit us, but I'd arrived with little more than a stripperiffic Halloween costume to my name, most of our allowance necessarily went to basics, and I couldn't wait to get back into my own clothes. My fashion sense and Maya's ran in different directions, and so I'd opted for white jeans and a loose-fitting blouse with decently comfortable sandals for the occasion.

We buzzed in at the main entrance, then took the elevator up to the fifth floor. By the time we arrived, Rose was waving from down the hall, and she beamed as Maya extended our offering. "Y'all didn't need to do that," she protested. "Come on in, Yven just put out the appetizers. Get you something to drink?"

"Hello!" Yven called from the kitchen as we entered. "Make yourselves comfortable!"

That he'd greeted us in English was a welcome change of pace. Yven's accent was unplaceable, a quasi-American base with strong hints of northwestern Europe in the finish, but his potion-granted fluency seldom left me guessing.

I'd seen my share of single guys' apartments, which often tended toward minimal real furniture and décor inspired by beers. Yven's place left them in the dust: unscuffed eggshell walls, a pristine tan-colored couch beneath the den window, an actual coffee table and rug that couldn't possibly have come from Target, a modern metal bookshelf bearing neat stacks of reference manuals. He'd hung paintings, too, a mix of muted abstracts and familiar landscapes that had to have come from Rose's brush, all with nary a Pink Floyd poster in sight. But the feature of Yven's den that stopped me in my tracks was the orchids, dozens of flowering plants in a rainbow of colors that grew atop custom shelving and spilled over onto handy flat surfaces. A vine-covered trellis obscured an entire wall, and as I stepped closer to examine the long pods, I felt a cushion of warm, moist air clinging to the plant.

"Vanilla orchid," Rose explained. "He's got a temperature and humidity spell going to keep this baby happy. See the pods?"

"Yeah…"

"That's where the flavor comes from. Yven makes his own extract."

"No *shit*," Maya marveled, joining us for a closer look. "How does it taste?"

Rose shrugged. "Like vanilla?"

She rolled her eyes. "Closer to Tahitian? Madagascan? Ugandan?"

"Bottles are in the pantry," Yven offered. "See for yourself."

I was still admiring the flowers when I heard Maya screech, "Are you *kidding* me? You made this? Damn it, Yven, you've been holding out on me!"

He laughed over the sizzling grill plate. "Will trade for cheesecake."

"Done. Sold."

As Maya reluctantly returned the bottle to its shelf, Rose poured us glasses of a chilled blush wine, sweet and with peachy overtones. The three of us settled in with a boule of warm spinach, artichoke, and sundried tomato dip while Yven roasted vegetables over the stove, kitted out in a stained navy apron. "Your apartment is lovely," I told him as I dug into the cheesy goodness. "And not just because it looks like a deranged florist lives here."

He grinned. "Thanks. It's been a good place, but I'm looking for a larger alternative."

"Oh?"

"One bedroom, one bath, not nearly enough space for two people and a ton of flowers. I know there are some larger apartments in this building, but catching one of them available takes miraculous luck."

"Or," said Rose, swirling her wine, "there's always the backup option."

"Which is?" Maya prompted.

"Move in with Pop. Once we're married, that is. I mean, sure, the commute would take longer, but with ample space and no rent…"

"In the *ti'Dana* mansion," Yven mumbled, cutting her a look over his shoulder.

"And? I've seen your family home—you didn't exactly grow up in squalor, babe."

"Well, no," he admitted, "but my parents' house is nothing like *that.*"

"We don't have to decide anything tonight," Rose soothed. "Anyway, remember that Pop likes you."

"That's only mildly terrifying," he muttered over his blackening peppers.

Rose laughed to herself and scooped up a bite of dip. "So, y'all, what's new at Mangia? Any crazies this week?"

"No crazies," said Maya while my mouth was full, "but there's the *tiny* matter of Annie's new boyfriend." She shot me a sly glance as I frantically tried to swallow.

"Boyfriend?" Rose echoed. "You've met someone, Annie?"

Her tone seemed almost neutral, but I couldn't blame her for not squealing and bouncing off the walls. Antlers aside, I was human, which meant I was off-limits to Pactlanders as a girlfriend. Both of Rose's grandfathers had taken the death draught and been exiled, and had she not been acknowledged into Hall ti'Dana, Yven might have gone for the draught as well.

"He's not my boyfriend," I explained once I'd cleared my mouth of goopy cheese. "Just a guy who's been coming around this week. He's new in town and doesn't know anyone."

"Uh-huh." Rose pointedly looked at Maya as if waiting for the real scoop.

And Maya wasn't shy. "His name's Wylan," she reported. "Kind of cute. He's looking for a job, so he's been hanging out, scouring the want ads in the newspaper."

Rose's brow furrowed. "That seems…old-fashioned."

"What does?" Yven asked from the stove.

"You're on a job hunt," she called back over the

sizzling of the steaks he'd just thrown on. "Where are you going to look, in the paper or online?"

"Online," he replied without hesitation. "Gosh, I don't think I've subscribed to the paper in...fifteen years?"

I reminded myself that elven aging *drastically* slowed once they hit their twenties. Though Yven and Rose looked to be of an age, he was twenty-odd years her senior. Given their longevity, however, the elves I'd met didn't seem particularly bothered by age discrepancies in a couple.

"Guess Wylan didn't get the memo, then," said Maya.

"He told me he doesn't have a normal Pactlands education," I added. "Maybe he was homeschooled by a tech-averse family or something."

"We do have our share of those here," Yven offered. "Particularly among sorcerers, for some reason. *I* don't get it. Not to be crass, but what is he?"

I paused, dip halfway to my mouth. "Haven't asked. I thought it'd be rude."

Rose frowned. "You don't know? What's he look like?"

"About Yven's size," I estimated. "But broader. No offense," I added to our chef, "but it looks like he's got a serious gym membership."

Yven chuckled and flexed his lackluster bicep. "None taken. You *have* met Pars, yes?"

Considering his coffee addiction, it would have been difficult to miss Pars, even if the Interdiction agent weren't a seven-foot-tall sorcerer with a twisted nose, a linebacker's build, and frequently sparkly nail polish. Yven's buddy came off as a bruiser—and from some of the stories I'd heard, he could hold his own even without magic on his side—but he was a pushover for his little girls.

"Anyway, he's decently sized," I continued. "Brown hair, kind of long. *Pretty* eyes—they're almost amber, not even a true brown. Ears are short, but I think they're pointed—"

"And she's overlooking the key feature," Maya interrupted with a playful huff. "He's got antlers just like hers. Poor dude was so confused when I broke it to him that we're human—"

I twitched in my chair at the clatter from the kitchen as Yven dropped his tongs onto the tile floor. "Everything okay?" I asked. "Did you burn yourself?"

"*Antlers?*" he demanded, agitated. "You're sure? Not horns?"

"Uh, *yeah*. I've been seeing them in the mirror on the regular since November."

"And he's definitely not a faun," Maya added. "Why, what's wrong?"

I glanced at Rose, but she looked as confused as I felt.

"Hold that thought," said Yven, then grabbed a clean pair of tongs from a drawer and briefly stepped away from the meat. "You've been visited by a member of the *Hunt*," he said, folding his arms as he stared down at us. "Has anyone at DPP seen him? Does DOL know?"

The three of us traded bemused looks, and then Rose took the lead. "Sorry...what hunt?"

"*The* Hunt," he replied, as if emphasizing the article would explain everything. "The Wild Hunt."

That, at least, I'd heard of, but I only had a vague sense of the term from scraps of long-forgotten stories.

"You're going to have to give us more than that," said Maya.

Yven looked troubled, but he returned to the kitchen. "Let me see about the steaks before they burn, and then I'll tell you everything."

With the festive mood subdued, we picked at the cooling dip until Yven finished cooking and carried a massive platter of meat and vegetables to the table. "Sorry, I should have plated this..." he began.

But Maya cut him off. "Forget the presentation. What the hell is the Wild Hunt?"

He accepted a glass of wine from Rose and sank into

the empty chair. "That's actually a good question. We don't know everything about them. Ostensibly, they're somewhere in the Pactlands, but no one's ever been able to find their hiding place..." He sipped, considered his glass, then sighed and pushed it aside. "Better start at the beginning, eh?"

"Probably wise," Rose coaxed.

"Right. So, uh...most of us here fall into distinct species groups, yes? You've got your sorcerers, your elves, trolls, gnomes, fauns, centaurs, nymphs—"

"Sirens."

Yven shuddered at Rose's suggestion. "Them as well, and more besides. But there are...outliers. Unique pockets. Magic is a weird thing," he muttered.

I frowned. "Pockets?"

"Of things that maybe shouldn't exist. Like the Hunter. He leads the Wild Hunt," he explained, leaning into the table. "Been around for ages, but no one knows where he came from. The theory is that he was never born."

Maya's face scrunched in query. "What do you mean, he was never born? Everyone's *born*."

"Everyone who exists due to biological means," he countered. "The Hunter has no progenitors. We read a few hypotheses in school, but the most likely is that he was born from belief and fear. He's this personification of the primal hunt—the need for bloodshed to survive."

"That doesn't make sense," I started to protest, but Maya's eyes widened as comprehension dawned.

"Like the Philip experiment," she interjected.

It was Yven's turn to register confusion. "Sorry, what?"

"A parapsychology experiment. One of my friends at culinary school was *deeply* into the paranormal," she offered. "Anyway, this group got together and came up with a fictional ghost named Philip. They made a whole backstory for him, and then they tried to communicate with him through séances. And it *worked*," she insisted. "Philip, like, tapped the table and messed with the lights and answered questions. Shit started moving. But they'd *made him up*. He was this ghost, this entity...this delusion, what have you...made from their collective minds. Fascinating and freaky as hell, I think, but does that sound like your Hunter?" she asked Yven.

He grimaced. "Perhaps, though if he's akin to your Philip, he's exponentially more powerful."

I reached for my wine. "What does he do? Hunts, I take it."

"About once a year. Maybe more often—there's no set schedule. He calls up his followers, the Wild Hunt, and they chase prey outside the Pactlands. I've never seen them, but rumor says their horses' hooves don't touch the ground."

"Ghost riders in the sky," Rose murmured.

"Something like that. Back when the Pact was forged, the Hunter appeared, signed on, and then took his leave. Like I said, no one knows where he hides, and no one can find him. He never comes to the Forum, nor does he send a representative. And no one knows much about his band—they resemble him with the antlers and such, but beyond that, they're a mystery. We don't know if they're kin to the Hunter or just people he's picked up along the way."

"If he's a hunter, though," I said, "what's with the antlers? Deer are a prey species."

"Granted," said Yven, "but he's...well, it's like he embodies the hunter and the prey simultaneously, you know? I told you magic's weird. Oh, and this is the fun part: *if* you can locate him, he's virtually unstoppable. I've never heard of anyone giving him so much as a scratch. And now you're telling me that one of his minions has been lurking around the café? I've got DOL contacts—I could ask for someone to sit there undercover until he reappears," he offered. "The Hunt is dangerous."

Maya seemed unsure, but I jumped into the opening. "Wylan didn't come yesterday, and anyway, he's been...*harmless*. A little goofy and broke, but he doesn't strike me as a threat."

"Yet," Rose murmured.

"I'll handle it," I insisted. "If I can't, then you can bring in the big guns with my blessing. I mean, for heaven's sake, we're in a *government building*. If we needed backup, we could always call Interdiction and tell them someone's trying to steal the espresso machine. But let's not drop a SWAT team on the poor guy when he's just looking to pay his rent."

Though no one appeared to be fully convinced of my logic, they let it go, and we helped ourselves to the main course. Yven made an excellent steak—Maya was sure to compliment him, which left him flushed with pleasure—but as I ate and laughed and let Yven describe his favorite orchids, I couldn't help but wonder if what he'd said about Wylan was accurate.

Wylan liked iced matcha lattes and grinned at my terrible jokes. Sure, he had weird taste in clothing, but he wouldn't hurt me.

Right?

CHAPTER 5

I hadn't known quite what I'd do when I met Wylan again. Part of me hoped he'd found a job over the weekend and might return some Saturday to let me know he was still alive and in town, and I was disappointed for him when he arrived at the café midmorning Monday, newspaper in hand and sheepish smile on his face. "Hi, Annie. No luck yet," he announced, and reached for the bag at his waist. "But I'm paying my bill from last week, and—"

"Hold it," I interrupted, and pushed open the kitchen door. "Going on break," I called to Maya. "Back soon."

"What *break*?" she yelped. "I need to watch the oven—"

"Front of the house is dead. Carry on."

"Annie, wait—"

The swinging door cut short her complaint, and I marched around the counter. Wylan regarded me curiously as I pointed to the bathroom, but he dropped his paper on a table and didn't fight me when I ordered, "In."

The café's bathroom was a single-use facility, large enough for the toilet, the sink, and two people standing almost close enough for their antlers to entangle. "What's this about?" he asked as I locked the door.

I turned to him and folded my arms. "You need to be truthful with me, all right?" I said, keeping my voice low.

He frowned. "Very well…"

"What's the Wild Hunt?"

His shoulders slumped when the words left my lips, and he rubbed his elbow as the sound faded. With a soft sigh, he muttered, "I was hoping you wouldn't find out."

"About the Hunt?"

"That I belong to it. How did you guess?"

"I didn't. Never heard anything about it until last night," I explained. "But Maya mentioned you at a dinner party, and when she brought up the antlers, our host was concerned."

"But why? I've seen others in town with—"

"*Horns,*" I interjected. "Not antlers. I've been the only one around until now. Before you walked in, I thought this might be unique," I added, pointing to my rack. "Like Maya's wings, just a weird effect of the damn potion. But if what I heard last night is true, then maybe it's no surprise people avoid me on the street."

Wylan seemed to sink lower into himself. "I haven't spent much time away from home. Not in the Pactlands, I mean. And I thought...you know, if I didn't mention the Hunt...maybe I could pass for something else."

"Yeah, apparently, that's a big, fat, no." I quickly checked the sink counter for wet spots, then hoisted myself onto the ledge. "So what are you about? Seems like most folks have a lot of guesses and little else."

He leaned against the far wall and folded his arms in turn. "What did your friend tell you?"

"Well, let's start with basics. Who's the Hunter, and where did he come from? I heard he's a Pact signatory, and that's it."

Wylan nodded. "That's accurate. Father signed on—"

"*Father?*" I echoed, my eyebrows rising.

"Yeah. He signed on for the same reason everyone else here did: protection. Too many humans, wild spaces disappearing...he could hide, but coming here seemed simpler. So he invited himself and signed on, and we've been based here ever since."

"And by 'we,' you mean..."

"Father and the rest of the Hunt," he finished. "My brothers."

"Huh. Big family?"

He chuckled. "All things are relative, I suppose. You and your siblings, how many are you?"

I paused before answering. "Uh...well, I had an older brother. He died when he was eight and I was five..."

Wylan's face, which had shifted toward cautiously guarded, fell as I spoke. "Oh, I...I'm sorry, I didn't mean to—"

"It's been almost twenty-five years. I'm okay," I quickly told him. "I know Alan mostly through my parents' stories. He had a pretty aggressive form of cancer, and he didn't even live with us for the last few months of his life. But, uh...yeah, it was just us two. What about you?"

Though he seemed unsettled—perhaps embarrassed—Wylan answered my question. "There are forty-seven of us at the moment."

"I'm sorry, *what?*"

"Forty-seven," he repeated. "Two were lost before I came along, and I'm currently the youngest."

"Shit," I muttered. "Your poor mother."

"Don't worry, I don't have one."

It was my turn to remove my foot from my mouth. "Oh, gosh, I'm so sorry for your loss—"

"There's no loss," he reassured me. "I *never* had a mother. None of us did."

"Then...huh." I scowled as I processed that. "I mean, you had to come from somewhere..."

"Of course," said Wylan. "When Father wants another of us around, he wills us into existence."

He made that statement far too matter-of-factly for my taste. "I, uh...I don't mean to be insensitive, but...*how?*"

He shrugged. "All I can say is it's Father, and I've learned not to ask too many questions. But you understand now why I was so shocked to see you for the first time—I've never laid eyes on anyone like me who isn't male, and...well," he allowed, "I suppose my initial assessment was incorrect on that front, but..."

A family of forty-eight dudes. I couldn't imagine.

"So what was it like?" I asked. "Growing up with forty-six older brothers?"

"What do you mean?"

"You know, you're the baby, and even once you hit puberty, I'm guessing they still thought of you as a child..."

"Oh," he said, laughing softly, "I was never a child."

"Excuse me?"

"We...I'm not certain if you'd say we're 'born,' exactly," he mused, "but we come into existence as adults. As I am now," he offered. "I can't imagine that Father would have the patience for children." Wylan paused, considering my expression, then asked, "Did you enjoy being a child? I've always wondered what that might be like."

"It...it had its moments, I guess," I managed, trying to keep my jaw off the floor. Even by Pactlands standards, Wylan was *far* too blasé about the weirdness. "Let's, um, put a pin in that. What are you doing in Beukal?"

He flashed a strained smile. "I did mention my forty-six brothers, didn't I? Wanted to have a taste of life beyond the lodge."

"You quit the Hunt?"

His smile morphed into a pained grimace. "Difficult to say. I told Father I needed to explore, see the world, and he allowed me to leave. But when he calls again, when the Hunt rides...I don't think I'll have a choice. At least for a night or so." He hesitated, then murmured, "I don't know what you must be thinking, Annie, but I'm no monster. I mean you no harm. If you'd prefer that I stay away from this place—"

"You're fine," I interrupted. "And thanks for being honest with me." Cocking my head toward the door, I asked, "Matcha latte?"

"I've heard about something called a mocha..."

"Easy. Come on," I said, and unlocked the bathroom

door. "I'll get that brewing for you…"

My voice died as I noticed that we had a lone customer waiting by the counter. Syvin, sporting a red robe and a thick gold necklace, looked at us for mere milliseconds before one of her eyebrows headed for her horns.

"It's not what it looks like," I said, hurrying away from the bathroom. "Uh…plumbing issue. All better now."

"*Really*, Annie," she said dryly. "I brought you a book—"

"Aw, thanks!"

"—which we can discuss another time. Who are you?" she asked, wheeling on Wylan.

I hastily poured her coffee, hoping she'd grab it and run, but the chief deputy had slid into interrogation mode. As Wylan looked to me for cues, I took the lead. "This is Wylan," I told Syvin, keeping my voice calm. "He's new in town, and he's trying to find work. Also doesn't know much about coffee, so I'm attempting to set him straight."

She grunted and walked over to his table. With Wylan seated, she was able to look down at him, but only barely. "Scrawny for a Huntsman, aren't you?" she said.

He nodded. "Young, too."

"Your business here?"

"As Annie said," he replied, lifting his newspaper, "searching for a job."

"Why?"

"Curiosity. Also, if I don't find something, my landlord will kick me out. He's been clear about that."

Syvin turned around and fixed me with an incredulous stare, then huffed and returned to the counter. "Enjoy— this is one of my favorites," she said, pulling a thick paperback from her bag and plopping it in front of me. She handed me cash for her drink, then glanced back at Wylan. "I'll be keeping an eye on you, Huntsman," she said, and retrieved her cup. "Annie, if he puts one foot out of line, let me know. Be *careful*," she quietly added, and marched out.

As the doorbell jangled behind her, Wylan rubbed his face and sighed. "I'm sorry about that. Not trying to make trouble. I can go—"

"Stay there," I said, and quickly made a mocha. Bringing it to his table, I caught him reaching for his money pouch and tutted. "Pay me once you're employed. And happy hunting," I added, giving the paper a tap.

"I hate to admit it, but I've had easier prey," he replied, then took a test sip. "*Oh*, this isn't bad at all."

"You can try it with whipped cream next time, bub," I said, and headed for the counter to claim my paperback prize.

Monday's job search proved fruitless, as did Tuesday's. During the lull on Wednesday, I sat down with Wylan to read over the want ads and check for any possibilities he might have missed. "Fair warning," I said, pulling my chair closer, "but I've never had to look for work here, and the only reason I can read Pactish is because of a potion, so I make no guarantees."

He slid aside to allow me room. "I was wondering how you came to know the language."

"Someone at DPP gave me a tube and told me to drink, and I wasn't in a position to ask questions. Probably for the best—it's not like Pactish is taught in my neck of the woods. I didn't study anything more exotic than Spanish." Eyeing him, I said, "Let me guess, you never had to learn it."

"No—*ow*." He laughed and rubbed his arm where I'd punched it. "What was that for? You didn't study it, either!"

"Yeah, but the potion gave me a fever and made me puke my guts out all night. And why *do* you speak Pactish, anyway?" I pressed.

Wylan regarded me bemusedly. "Because everyone here does?"

"Well, yeah, but I thought it was, like, the officialized creole or something. It wasn't any group's language to begin with, right? I've heard snatches of Elvish and Trollish and stuff, and when Syvin swears, I have *no* idea what she's saying. So if the Hunt never comes around, then how'd you pick up Pactish?"

"I'm afraid you'd have to ask Father," he replied. "He speaks many of the old tongues, that I'm sure of, but this is the only language I've ever known."

I narrowed my eyes, and he shrugged.

"Freaking magic," I muttered, and pulled the paper closer. "All right, let's see. Show me which ones you've already tried."

Ten minutes later, I was shocked to see how many places he'd applied. Wylan had been proactive, and the ads he'd pursued ran the gamut: reception, janitorial, security, warehouse work, retail, even nannying. The man wasn't proud—he was desperate, and he was doing his best.

"I realize I don't have full qualifications," he said as he marked through another ad that had proven to be a bust, "but I'm not stupid, and I'm happy to learn. I just need to find someone willing to take a chance with me." Frowning at the newspaper, he dropped his red pen and sighed. "It must be the Hunt that's hamstringing me. I *know* I'm capable of stacking crates, but if people here are too afraid of the Hunt to consider me as a candidate—"

The doorbell cut our conversation short, and I got up to attend to the customer, a sorcerer from off the street who took one look at Wylan and me and made a hasty exit once she had her drink in hand. Returning to the table when we were alone again, I sat and asked Wylan, "Why *are* people so freaked out about the Hunt, anyway? I mean, half of DPP has at least *some* magical ability, and we're in a building with literal eight-foot trolls, and yet you're the guy everyone avoids. Okay, so you're a reclusive bunch, and your dad may be tough to kill, but where does this fear come from? Any ideas?"

"Unfortunately, yes." Folding his paper, he avoided my gaze and murmured, "We've never ridden after prey in the Pactlands. That was part of the deal: if Father wanted to sign the Pact and stay here, he had to agree not to hunt within the Pactlands or pursue humans outside it. It's not that the other signatories had any particular care for your kind—they were concerned that humans seeking to end the Hunt might track us back here."

"And now I feel all warm and fuzzy inside."

He didn't laugh. "Father agreed to the terms. But that…marked a change for him."

"Oh?"

"Prior to the Pact, he didn't discriminate," Wylan said softly, still looking at the neat newspaper. "The Hunt pursued whatever prey he chose, or so I've been told. And though we've upheld our end of the bargain, I suspect there are still some hard feelings. Hence the reason I was hoping not to be immediately identified."

"Shit," I muttered. "But you know, I think they had a similar situation with sirens…"

"The sirens were invited. We were not. Father simply walked in and reached for the ink," he explained. "There were few sirens still living in those days, and though they're dangerous, they can be defeated. It's almost impossible to kill Father."

"Why? What makes him so strong?"

Wylan shrugged. "I suppose it's all part of who Father is. *What* he is."

"I heard that most weapons can't touch him," I pried.

At that, he finally looked up at me. "It's not the weapon that's the problem—it's the *wielder*."

"Huh?"

"I've watched Father shrug off any number of things— swords, arrows, staff blows that would down a lesser man. Occasionally, he lets us take swings at him. I think it amuses him, to be honest. Nothing so much as bruises him. Granted, I've never seen magical weapons in play," he allowed, "but my older brothers assure me the result is the same. Strike him with whatever you like, and he'll treat it like a fly on his arm. That said," he continued, lowering his voice and leaning closer to me, "he does have one weakness."

Smirking, I teased, "Which you'll never tell me, right?"

To my surprise, he shook his head. "No harm in it. Father can only be killed by his prey. For instance, say he rode in pursuit of a bear but drew too close, and the bear swiped at him. The claws could do damage. He's been injured before when we ride, but it's rare, and these days, he often pursues prey with little chance of wounding him. Nothing worse than a moose in the last decade, if memory serves."

"Must be convenient," I said. "What about you, then?"

He grinned and spread his hands. "Not so lucky."

"Then I'll do my best not to accidentally shoot you," I deadpanned, and patted Wylan's shoulder as I stood. "But you're not the Hunter, and surely someone's bound to recognize that. Don't give up on the job search, okay? Something will come along."

"I hope you're right," he replied. "It would be ideal not to end up sleeping on the street."

By closing Saturday evening, when I'd gone a full twenty-four hours without encountering Wylan and kept glancing at the door to see if he'd brave the tapas menu after all, I admitted to myself that he'd become more than a random customer.

Ours was a weird sort of friendship, a common bond forged from being the two people in the capital most likely to make strangers gasp and scurry off. At least now I understood why folks gave Maya curious glances when her wings were out versus the bug-eyed stares they shot my way. None of our DPP contacts had bothered to explain that average citizens who didn't know me might mistake me for some sort of immortal, unstoppable killing machine in poor lighting—maybe they hadn't wanted to freak me out more than I already was by being stuck in the Pactlands with antlers that regrew no matter how desperately I tried to remove them. Frankly, with the secret out, I felt better knowing that the problem was the antlers and not the rest of me.

While I wasn't overly social by nature, having few friends around took its toll. Maya had been a fantastic partner through the madness, and Rose, now that she was allowed back in the Pactlands, was nothing but supportive. I could joke with Yven and Pars and a couple dozen other agents when they made their coffee runs, and at least I'd found a fellow mystery lover in Syvin. But I didn't exactly have a *crew* in Beukal like I'd known back in Richmond, a support network who would let me bitch about work and go out for drinks and mimosa brunches and even do the odd bit of sloppy dancing.

And then, all of a sudden, there was Wylan, a fellow freak with prospects even worse than mine and zero support.

He wasn't haunting the café for the free drinks—not a day went by that he didn't offer to pay his tab at least twice. And with the summer weather as nice as it had been, he didn't need to hide from the elements while he conducted his job search. If my instincts were good—not guaranteed, but decently likely—then he was stopping by for the companionship. I didn't panic and edge away when he walked into the room, which after a few weeks in Beukal must have come as a pleasant change of pace for him.

Plus, damn it, he was oddly cute. Poor wardrobing choices aside, Wylan had pretty eyes, a great smile, and muscles that suggested he might give *really* nice hugs. I mean, yeah, the antlers were less than ideal, and I knew better than to pursue a relationship with anyone in the Pactlands, but...

But.

He'd become my friend. My broke, unemployed, possibly dangerous but definitely awkward friend, and as Maya and I locked up that night, I hoped I'd see him again on Monday.

CHAPTER 6

Luck was with me, as Wylan slipped in around ten that morning. "Hey!" I called from the counter, pausing in my bean grinding to wave. "Just a minute, let me finish this batch."

He dropped his newspaper and pen at his usual table, then contemplated the drink menu as I finished my prep. "What are you doing?" he asked.

"Getting ahead of the lunch crowd. We had a bigger than usual breakfast rush, and my grounds were running low." Satisfied, I locked the top onto the airtight plastic box in which we stored our stash and rinsed my hands. "Any prospects over the weekend?"

"Nothing," he replied with a frustrated huff. "But it's a new week, isn't it? And perhaps I should try something new as well."

"Hmm." I sized him up, stroking my chin as I pretended to contemplate his leather leggings for the first time and deeply ponder our options, then suggested, "Chai. It'll pep you up, it's spiced, and you can add sugar to smooth it out however you like it."

He repeated the word and squinted at the menu board over my head.

"It's not on there," I said, cutting short his search. "Rose brought me a nice blend on her last trip home. Here, smell," I offered, opening the cannister.

Wylan leaned over the counter, and his eyes widened as he caught a whiff. "Interesting."

He loitered nearby as I brewed it up in latte form. "I

like it with one sugar," I said, sliding him an oversized teacup and a paper packet. "Brings out the flavor without turning it into candy."

He took my suggestion and smiled with pleasure after his taste test. "You're very good at this, you know?"

"You just haven't seen a proper barista yet," I said, and wiped down the steam wand. "Enjoy. I'm going to sort through these lunch orders for Maya," I added, pointing to our inbox as another form materialized and floated down to join the stack.

We worked in silence for a time, me with my to-go requests and Wylan with his want ads, interrupted every fifteen minutes or so by a customer who ran in for a drink or pastry and quickly departed. As I was arranging the lunch pickups on their shelves, Wylan cleaned up his table and sidled closer to me. "Um…Annie?"

"Yeah?" I muttered as I tried to figure out where one of the bags went. Alphabetizing had only become a problem for me once I attempted to do so with a completely different character set. Mentally running through the children's song Pars had taught me was my only saving grace.

"I was, uh, wondering…"

I slotted the bag into the correct spot and turned around fresh from my mundane triumph, to find Wylan's cheeks flushed. He was hunching slightly, as if he anticipated a blow, and I caught him nibbling on his lip before he cleared his throat. "What's wrong?" I asked.

"Uh…would you, um…be interested in coming over after work?" he finished in a rush. "My apartment's not great, but if you'd like a change of scenery, and I really do owe you dinner for all the drinks and snacks over the last two weeks—"

"Whoa, *whoa*," I interrupted, cutting him off as his words sped toward garbled indecipherability. "Hold on. You're asking me over for dinner?"

He nodded.

"Tonight?"

"If you have nothing better to do," he mumbled, his flush deepening.

"I suppose I could clear my *very* busy calendar," I replied, chuckling at his embarrassment. "But on one condition."

He perked. "Yes?"

"Let me bring takeout. I don't want you spending money you don't have right now. Deal?"

Though he sighed, Wylan relented. "Deal. But I *do* owe you—"

"And I appreciate that you want to clear your tab, but I mean it—don't worry. Look," I said, planting a hand on my hip, "I did two years at community college right after high school, and I was *broke*. I had a part-time job waitressing at this shitty restaurant at night, and I stupidly insisted on moving out of my parents' house, so most of what I earned went to pay my rent. There was a little all-night diner near my place, and after my fourth two a.m. dinner of toast and coffee in a row, the manager, this grandmotherly lady who'd run the diner longer than I'd been alive, took a seat in my booth and asked me about myself. Then she started adding things to my orders: eggs, bacon, pancakes, a freaking steak on my birthday. I tried to pay her, but she wouldn't hear of it. So this is me paying it forward, huh?"

"Thank you."

"Sure. What time tonight?"

Wylan grinned. "When will you be available?"

We had barely crossed into August, and the light still lingered past eight p.m., so I was in no rush to get to Wylan's before sundown. I left work late that afternoon, showered off the smell of coffee, and tried to choose an ensemble. Had this been a date—which it certainly was not—then I had a sundress stashed in the back of the closet. Since this was merely two friends sharing takeout, however, I opted for jeans and one of my ubiquitous button-down shirts. My closet back in Richmond had more interesting options, flowy shirts with V-necks and flirty off-the-shoulder tops, but the antlers grossly limited my sartorial choices.

The *fucking* antlers.

I silently seethed every time I stopped the dryer to untangle my hair from around them. If I had to have been cursed by the damn potion, then why couldn't I have ended up with something less cumbersome? Maybe cute cat ears or a weird hair color—hell, a prehensile tail would at least have been useful. But there was nothing I could do about it unless the brain trust at DPP found a way to reverse the potion's effects, and so I put on a little makeup, popped in the earrings I seldom wore around the café, and tried not to pretend that it looked like I'd merged my skull with that of my dad's favorite mounted buck.

Oddly enough, I didn't mind the antlers on Wylan. He could carry them off, and he seemed to move naturally around low-hanging obstacles. I hadn't seen him so much as bang them into a doorway. But then he'd been born— or come into existence, rather—with them, whereas I still regarded them as a particularly annoying headdress I couldn't remove.

Whatever, I told myself, giving my reflection a last check before I headed out the door. This was passable. Better than passable, really.

Maya concurred with a teasing wolf whistle when I hurried through the den. "Have fun, kids. I won't wait up."

"Oh, my God," I muttered. "It's not like that at all."

"Uh-huh. *Sure*, Annie. Make good choices, now," she called as I let the door slam behind me.

Wylan only lived a few blocks from the café, albeit in the opposite direction from Maya and me, but it wasn't a long enough trek for me to bother with the van. I strolled through the city around six-thirty, ignoring the motorists' stares and trying not to be offended when parents pulled their small children closer to them, and wound up in my favorite hole-in-the-wall establishment to pick up dinner. The owners, a couple of sorcerers who knew our place as well as we knew theirs, didn't bother handing me a menu when I ducked into the building. "Hello, young lady," the wife of the pair called, barely glancing over her shoulder as she tended the grill. "The usual?"

"Two, please," I replied, sliding onto a stool to wait. "And whatever appetizers you recommend."

She turned and smiled. "I recommend everything on the menu, my dear."

"*Right*. But if you had to choose…"

"Understood." She pushed a mass of sizzling vegetables around and added a splash of the secret sauce, which to me tasted strongly of teriyaki. "Where's Maya? Did she send you to forage alone?"

"No, she's hanging out solo tonight," I said. "I've got a friend who's new in town, and I said I'd bring dinner by."

Again, she turned from the grill, but she looked alarmed that time. "Don't tell me it's another Roulette victim—"

"No, *no*," I hastily reassured her. That shit was well and truly off the streets, as its maker had met his nasty end before bothering to share his recipe. "Someone I met at work."

"Mm." Mollified, she returned to her cooking. "A…male someone?"

I sighed to myself. "Yes, but really, we're just friends. I, uh…don't get many opportunities to dress up these days."

She nodded and dropped her line of inquiry, for which I was grateful. A few minutes later, she presented me with two takeout boxes of lightly spiced chicken strips, grilled vegetables, and a creamy dipping sauce that worked surprisingly well with the whole entrée, plus a few smaller boxes of appetizers. "Have fun tonight," she said as she packed everything into a bag with two bottles of water.

"Oh, and when you see Maya next, tell her we'd like to buy a cake for the weekend, wouldn't you?"

"You've got it," I said, then paid and hurried on my way.

The address Wylan had scribbled for me on a paper napkin turned out to be a five-story walk-up with a bit of age on it. While Beukal in general looked clean and shiny—the pristine streets would give Singapore's a run for their money—Wylan's building was a far cry from the DPP and DOL skyscrapers, or even from the more modest apartment building where Maya and I had landed. Yven's place, ordinary as it was for the downtown district, seemed like the pinnacle of bourgeois opulence beside the burnt-red brick edifice with its institutional windows and off-white For Rent sign in the front window.

I pressed the buzzer for Wylan's unit, 5B, and waited until the door clicked open. Turning sideways to maneuver my overburdened head through the narrow doorway, I noticed the row of ten mailboxes in the lobby wall, a few with softly glowing blue indicator lights. Wylan's box was dark—either he'd already retrieved his mail or, more likely, he'd received nothing. Taking note of the door at the end of the hall with MANAGER stenciled on the dark wood in yellow paint, I adjusted my food bag and started the long climb to Wylan's place.

He met me at the top of the landing, beaming in the dim yellow light of the hanging lanterns. "Annie! You made it," he said, sounding delighted but fidgeting with his shirt. "Here, allow me," he continued, taking the bag from my arms. "I apologize for the stairs—"

"Don't worry, I needed my cardio before we eat," I replied, and ducked into his apartment after him.

On first impression, the apartment was *definitely* not designed for antlers. Mine would have scraped the low ceiling had I stood on tiptoe, and Wylan, a good four inches taller than me, had to slouch. A few gouges in the plaster revealed the locations of his accidental straightening. The den was perhaps half the size of Yven's and barely furnished: a cheap pine end table, at least secondhand, a wooden crate for a chair, a nail in the wall near the door where his waist pouch hung. He didn't have a single knickknack, nor a rug, nor so much as a candle to make the place seem homier. I'd known guys back in college who had decorated with beer memorabilia, and their lousy apartments looked like designers' showpieces beside Wylan's.

The den gave way to what could be called a galley kitchen, were one feeling generous. From what I could see, the appliances were limited to a short refrigerator and a stove that was probably older than me. A single pot lay drying atop a cheap dishtowel on the counter.

The dining nook, demarcated by a slightly decorative hanging light, was missing a table and chairs.

Though I tried to keep my expression neutral, Wylan appeared to divine my impression of the place. "It's a work in progress," he said, glancing around the largely empty den. "Rent first, then furniture, yes? But here, come with me."

He opened a door, but instead of the coat closet that I'd imagined lay behind it, I found a steep wooden staircase heading up. "Where are we going?" I asked.

Grinning, he replied, "I thought you might like to see the view."

I carefully climbed behind him, almost bending over to squeeze my antlers through the cramped space, then emerged onto the building's flat roof. There was no protective railing, nor was there any furniture to suggest that rooftop access was a perk of top-floor tenancy, but the area over Wylan's apartment seemed freshly swept, and he'd anchored a sheet to the roof with four bricks. Beyond the edge of the roof lay Beukal, the blue of the summer afternoon giving way to the golds of the setting sun, the air cooling with the coming night, the office towers and government buildings glinting a few blocks away. Sure, it wasn't exactly a grand panorama—I'd been to the top of DPP, and twenty stories of elevation made for a great view—but Wylan's roof was charming all the same.

And besides, he'd set up a picnic area.

"Will this suffice?" he asked, barely masking the hopeful note in his voice.

"Perfect," I told him, and took a seat. "Let's unpack, and I'll show you what I got."

Wylan practically drooled as I opened the takeout containers, but he waited until I took a turn with the shared boxes. He grunted appreciatively as we ate, and though he scarfed his food at first, he soon realized that I was setting a more sedate pace and came up for air.

"Haven't had a big meal in a while, huh?" I quietly asked, wishing I'd slipped him more cookies at the café. From the way he'd been wolfing his food, I guessed he hadn't had a proper dinner in days.

"True," he admitted, reaching for the box of fried cheese bites. I'd been pleased to discover that the Pactlands had its own version of a dish in the mozzarella stick family. "And habit," he murmured. "Forty-eight men, one table, communal dishes…"

"Survival of the quickest?"

He nodded. "I learned early on that if I wanted to eat my fill, I needed to grab food before someone bigger claimed it. Father doesn't step in with mealtime squabbles. Believes they make us stronger," he said, rolling his eyes. "But since it's hard to fight back when you're weak from hunger…"

"Your table manners suffer," I finished.

"Sorry."

I patted his arm. "You're fine. Just don't stab me if I help myself to these, eh?" I teased, popping a vegetable fritter in my mouth.

"I wouldn't dare." He took another bite while I

chewed, then said, "You know, even though we're sitting on a roof and eating out of boxes, I think this is far more civilized than mealtimes at home."

"Hey, there's nothing wrong with boxes. My folks are proud believers in the occasional 'Chinese takeout and a movie' dinner in front of the TV," I said, trying to ignore the sudden pang of homesickness. "We'd spread out the cartons on the coffee table and grab paper plates, and I'd sit on the rug while they took the couch. *God*, I used to make myself sick on sweet and sour chicken," I said, and laughed to myself.

But Wylan grew pensive. As I returned to my grilled vegetables, he said, "Maya told me you haven't been home in months."

I nodded. "It'll be a year in November."

"Probably a stupid question, but do you miss it?"

Again, I nodded and focused on my dinner. "Yeah."

"I'm sorry, I shouldn't have—"

"No, it's okay," I interrupted. "I…" Dropping my fork, I collected my thoughts and sighed. "I haven't been able to talk to my parents in ages. When DPP let us out of quarantine, Maya and I each got one call from an untraceable line to our families. We told them we'd seen a pretty serious crime and had been put in a witness protection program to keep us safe…" Noting his bemusement, I explained, "Murderers generally don't like to leave witnesses to testify against them. Back home, there are programs in place to keep government witnesses alive until trial, or even after. But part of that protection can mean taking on a new identity. You're sent away with doctored papers, maybe to a safehouse, and try not to draw attention to yourself. Keeping in contact with the people in your old life makes it easier to find you, so…it wasn't a perfect lie to explain why Maya and I dropped off the face of the earth, but it was plausible enough. I'm sure my folks are worried sick about me, but there's nothing I can do." I paused to swallow the lump in my throat, willing myself not to cry and ruin the evening. "I just want to tell them I'm okay," I mumbled. "We were always close, and I don't want them to worry…"

"It's not your fault," said Wylan when my voice cracked. "You didn't knowingly take that potion, right?"

"No, but…" I struggled briefly, then managed, "Mom and Dad already lost Alan. I'm the only kid they have left, and now they think I'm hiding from some scumbag with a vendetta. And I *really* miss them," I said before I realized the words were slipping free. "I miss my apartment and my job and my friends, but my *family*…" Stopping myself, I cleared my throat and returned to my dinner. "Sorry, I—"

Wylan surprised me when he reached for my arm and gave it a firm squeeze. "Don't apologize. I'm the one who brought it up."

"Yeah, but I don't mean to be a downer. DPP's been great to us, and things could be so much worse…"

"But?" he prompted.

"But it sucks to be stuck here. Not *here*," I hastily amended, patting the makeshift picnic blanket. "Your roof is lovely. Stuck in the Pactlands more generally, I mean. And the longer we go without a cure, the more I worry that I'm never going to see home again."

He said nothing for a time, but his face worked as if he were considering a dozen variables. "What if I could sneak you back?" he finally asked. "DPP wouldn't need to know. We go, you reassure your parents, and we return before anyone misses you."

"I appreciate that blatantly illegal offer," I replied with a tight smile, then pointed to my antlers. "But you're forgetting about these."

"You think they'd take it that poorly?"

I whistled low. "Don't know many humans, do you?"

"Mm. Present company?"

"As a rule, we don't tend to do well with things we can't explain by non-magical means, since magic absolutely doesn't exist."

Wylan smirked at my straight face.

"Besides," I said, "even if I were to turn up with the world's largest hat on, they'd still have a million questions, and people in witness protection don't just pop by for a chat. Since I can't tell them the truth…" Hoping to lighten the mood, I tried to shift the topic. "How about you? Have you heard from your dad lately? Going to go home for a visit?"

The tension in his expression told me everything I needed to know before he opened his mouth. "No to both. My father and I…we don't always fit together well, if you understand me. And I'm in no hurry to go back there."

I picked at my meal for a minute while Wylan quietly grazed on the appetizers. As I returned to the cheese bites, he asked, "What do you miss the most? Besides your family, that is." I frowned, and he said, "Maya told me you were from a place called Richmond. I've never been, so…"

I mulled it over while I nibbled at the fried cheese. "It's a nice enough city, but you want the truth?"

"Absolutely."

"This is going to sound so vain, but what I miss the most is being able to walk around in public without the stares. It's not just because I'm not in love with my new look," I added. "Before all of this mess, I was a private investigator, but it's tough to keep a gig like that when you have such a distinctive appearance. I *can't* go unnoticed these days, so instead, I'm stuck working in the café."

"You're good at making drinks," Wylan offered.

"You only say that because you missed my trial-and-error period. I brewed a *lot* of bitter coffee—" Hearing myself, I recalled who was with me and tried to wrench my foot from my mouth. "Shit, I'm sorry, I shouldn't gripe about my job."

He chuckled and finished the half loaf of herbed bread. "You're allowed to complain, Annie. I made the choice to come here—you didn't." After wiping his mouth, he said, "You could be wrong about why people stare at you. It might have nothing to do with your, uh…resemblance to us."

My eyebrows rose.

"You're beautiful," he said simply. "Whether you have antlers is another matter. People around here might be surprised, but I'm confident they're not all blind."

I froze there on the roof, startled and trying to come up with a response.

He was serious—he'd said that as bluntly as if he'd been remarking upon the color of the sky. But he wasn't giving me the usual suggestive hints that might accompany such a declaration. He wasn't flashing bedroom eyes or a come-hither smile, but rather attacking the last of the fritters.

"Uh…thank you," I mumbled, and drained my water bottle as my face burned.

When I caught his gaze again, I noticed an unexpected brightness in his eyes. Though the evening was growing darker, the setting sun hit them at just the right angle, making the amber glow.

Eyeshine. Of course. The guy was born to hunt—it stood to reason that he'd have decent night vision.

"You're not so bad yourself," I murmured, and chuckled as he flushed in turn.

CHAPTER 7

"We're going on break a little earlier than usual today," Maya told me on Friday afternoon as I caught my breath. The lunch rush that day had been particularly hectic, and my feet throbbed in protest when I managed to sink onto my neglected stool behind the counter and shovel down a leftover muffin.

"Too much prep for tonight?" I asked around a mouthful of bran. "Please don't tell me you need me in the kitchen. That'll only end in tears."

"Mm—*no*," she replied with clearly feigned hesitation. "I'm partial to having a working oven. No, I called Rose last night and asked her to get us on the director's calendar, and he's penciled us in at three."

I'd met Pateme ti'Tam a few times, a dark-haired elf with a taste for heavily embroidered dress robes. Had I seen him on the street, I'd have thought him to be my age, though he was actually five hundred years my senior— elven genes were *sweet*. He'd been polite and sympathetic to our circumstances, and as far as I knew, he had yet to refuse to fund any of Maya's café initiatives. The fact that he was Rose's second great-uncle probably didn't hurt on that front. Sure, as family went, the two of them weren't exactly close, but her grandfather had been one of his favorite nephews, and Pateme felt bad about the years Rose had been cut off and kept in the dark about the Pactlands. If approving our beer taps assuaged that guilt, I wasn't going to complain.

"Are we buying something?" I asked. "Expanding?"

She shot me a sly smile. "You'll see."

Though annoyed, I let it go. Between my growling stomach and sore feet, I had enough immediate concerns to occupy my mind...and then there was the matter of Wylan. He'd been back every day that week, newspaper in hand, and though he tried to seem chipper about the search, he was plainly discouraged. I worried about what cash he might have in reserve, even for his crappy little apartment. And while I didn't ask him if he had money for food, by Thursday, I wasn't the only one sneaking him snacks—Maya had emerged from the controlled chaos of lunch prep long enough to say, "Oh, good, you're here. There's leftover breakfast quiche that needs to vanish. Why don't you help a girl out, eh?" Wylan didn't ask for charity, but neither did he turn his nose up at Maya's cooking.

At five to three, we locked up and headed into the DPP lobby. While our access cards could get us into the main building, they wouldn't admit us into any of the restricted areas, and so we knew the drill: wait by the elevators until the babysitter arrived. Right on schedule, the nearer elevator chimed with the arriving car, and out stepped Dup, one of Pateme's aides. The guy was polite to a fault, a blond of sixty or so—pretty young for a sorcerer—and he ushered us into the elevator with a smile. "Ready for tonight?" he asked.

Maya grinned back at him. "Karaoke rematch?"

"You know it."

I chuckled as the floors swept past. Dup had a pretty tenor voice, and he and one of the lab techs were locked in a battle for weekend bragging rights.

The elevator opened on the top floor of the tower, and Dup led us down the hallway that wound through the executive suite. I hadn't seen much of DPP outside of the lab where Maya and I reported for testing, but the executive level was richly appointed: fifteen-foot ceilings with chandeliers hanging well out of antler range, rugs that probably cost as much as a car, and massive windows with fantastic views of the capital. A few of the people we passed gave us second glances, but no one tried to stop us. I might not have been able to rattle off their names and titles, but I recognized plenty of faces around us, usually viewed from the other side of the espresso machine. As their dealers, we merited nods from the robed executive denizens we glimpsed through office doorways.

Dup knocked twice on the door of the director's massive corner office, and with a faint click, the latch opened of its own accord. Poking his head inside, he said, "Your three o'clock, sir."

"Come in," Pateme called from within, and Dup showed us into the room.

Having been upstairs a few times, I didn't gawk, though my eyes still strayed toward the windows behind the beautiful wooden desk. Four chairs with thick blue cushions sat in a semicircle in front of the desk for visitors. Pateme's overloaded bookcase hadn't changed since my last visit—shelves built of anything less than solid wood would have collapsed under the burden he imposed upon then—but if I wasn't mistaken, one of the paintings on the wall looked like Rose's work. And then my gaze landed on what was surely Pateme's favorite office perk: his bar, a long side table loaded with kettles, mugs, and glass jars full of teas and tisanes. The man didn't need the café—he had a stash that put our tea offerings to shame.

"Welcome," said the director, gesturing toward the empty chairs as Dup slipped out. "Good afternoon, ladies. What brings you upstairs?"

Maya, who hadn't bothered to hide her wings, spread them carefully behind her as she took a seat. Though they were tough and flexible, she'd learned the hard way not to sit on them. I watched as she opened the thin folder she'd brought with her, as clueless as Pateme was as to her master plan.

"We know you're busy, and so I'll get to the point,"

Maya began. "The café's had a steady uptick in business over the last six months. I've brought a copy of the financials—"

"Ahead of you," said Pateme with a smile. "The accountants are *very* pleased."

"Great. Well, part of the success of our daytime model is speed: we have some loiterers, but most of the customers pass through on their way to work or run down to pick up a meal. There's only so much the two of us can handle," she continued, cocking her thumb at me, "and since we haven't plateaued yet in terms of average orders per day, I'm concerned that our response time is going to suffer. That would do a service to no one."

Pateme steepled his fingers. "Go on."

"Nights, now, speed isn't of the essence, but I do put a fairly complex menu together, and it sells well. The more we sell, the more I'm needed in the kitchen, and that leaves Annie all by her lonesome to handle the taps and tables."

"You want more help."

"I'd like to hire an additional person," she confirmed. "Not a chef, not a full-on barista, just an entry-level hire we can train. I've got experience on that front."

"What sort of compensation package would you want to offer?" he asked.

Maya glanced my way, then shrugged when I didn't volunteer a figure. "Beats me. I don't even know what minimum wage is around here. Enough for a roof and food, you know?"

He nodded. "That could be arranged. Did you have someone in mind, or would you like for us to advertise?"

"Actually, I've got a prospect," said Maya.

Pateme paused, perhaps considering her sly smile, then propped his chin on his fist and stared at her across the desk. "This wouldn't have anything to do with the Huntsman who's been reported lurking around the café for the last three weeks, would it?"

"Before you say no, hear me out."

"Oh, I'm listening."

She began to tick off her points on her fingers. "Okay, first, Wylan moved out of his dad's place and is trying to make it on his own. I respect that. I've hired plenty of kids looking for that first job so they can finance the crappy apartment that isn't Mom and Dad's house, and the fear of losing the job and thus having to move home motivates them to do well. Second, he's been nothing but friendly with us. He's not a creeper. Right, Annie?"

"Not a creep at all," I said.

"Third, he's a dude, and he's big," she said to Pateme's poker face. "I mean, he's not a troll, but he obviously works out. It would be nice to have someone around to help with the heavy stuff—the big food deliveries, moving the furniture, and so on."

"We do have spells for that," the director reminded her. "You could hire a sorcerer."

"Sure, but unless that sorcerer is Pars Mera, we don't get to my fourth point: security. You heard about the restaurant three blocks away that was freaking *robbed* two weeks ago?"

"I did," he admitted.

"They had sorcerers on staff. Elves, too. But downstairs, it's just the two of us. We're open to the outside, and we're defenseless." Her wings fluttered, betraying her agitation. "Sure, it probably helps that we're attached to DPP, and maybe some potential robbers have caught a glimpse of Annie and thought twice, but Wylan's the real deal. I'd like our odds a lot better with him hanging around on a full-time basis."

Pateme considered Maya's proposal in silence for a moment, his expression barely shifting as he thought. Finally, he leaned back in his chair and sighed. "You understand why I'm not in love with this idea."

"And I'm not afraid to fire people who don't work out," said Maya. "But that guy's been searching for a job for weeks, and no one will give him a chance. I think he'll mind his manners."

The director contemplated the ceiling as that sank in, then grunted. Straightening, he pulled a notepad from his desk, opened a pen, and wrote a figure on the page he ripped free. "It's not a great offer, but the accountants won't poison my tea over this. If he accepts, he's your responsibility, and he works at your pleasure. Be sure that he understands there will be no recourse to me if you terminate his employment."

I couldn't help but smile as Maya stood and took the paper from Pateme. "You won't regret this," she promised.

"Let us hope." With that, he waved the door open and pressed a button on his phone. "I'll send for Dup. Oh, and Maya?"

"Sir?"

"I'm hosting a meeting on Tuesday afternoon with several of my agency counterparts, and these events are typically catered."

She smirked and cocked an eyebrow. "Oh, are they?"

"Yes, and it's my turn."

"Coffee and sweets? Anything in particular?"

"That would be ideal, and I don't know if it's possible, but Rose has mentioned a cheesecake…"

"She'll do it," I interrupted, slinging my arm around Maya's shoulders. "Our new hire can help me while she bakes for you. See, this is working out beautifully already."

He snorted but chuckled as he called his aide to take us back to the lobby.

I didn't know how early Wylan usually went to bed, but I figured he'd forgive us for the visit at eleven that night.

"Shit," Maya muttered as I led her toward his apartment building. "This place has seen better days, hasn't it?"

"Be nice," I said, and rang the buzzer.

It took three tries before I heard Wylan's voice, low and groggy, answer through the tinny speaker: "Yes?"

"It's me," I replied. "And Maya. Can we come up?"

Instantly, the door clicked open, and Maya cackled as I led the way inside.

Wylan was waiting at the top of the staircase as we puffed our way up the final flight. Given his mussed hair, I assumed we'd awakened him. I didn't know how he usually slept, but he'd thrown on his leather leggings to greet us. His shirt was another matter, however, and so I was treated to a view of his...well, frankly gorgeous pecs and abs as we dragged ourselves up the last steps.

"Are your wings not functional," Wylan asked Maya, "or are you merely being supportive of Annie?"

She jumped, flapped madly, but only made it two stairs higher before landing. "Not the best," she said between gasps. "Did we disturb your beauty sleep?"

"I wouldn't go *that* far. Come in."

I'd prepared Maya for the state of the place on the way over, and Wylan hadn't purchased any furniture since our dinner earlier that week. "I would offer you both a chair," he mumbled, rubbing his neck as he slouched to avoid the ceiling, "but, uh..."

"We're not staying long," Maya assured him. "Been on our feet all day. But look, we've got a proposition for you."

His brows drew together. "Oh?"

"Yeah." She took the director's folded piece of paper from her pocket and handed it to him. "Take a look at that figure and tell me if you like what you see."

"In what context?" asked Wylan, frowning at the number.

"Your annual salary, should you come work for us."

He straightened in shock, then crouched as the top prongs of his antlers sent a shower of plaster to the floor. "*Seriously*? You'll hire me?"

"Told the director that we could use the help," she said, grinning. "Hope you like coffee—"

The end of that sentiment was lost to Maya's surprised "*Oof*" as Wylan, overjoyed, grabbed her in a tight hug. By the time he released her, I'd braced myself and patted his back as he hugged me in turn. "Welcome aboard," I wheezed as my lungs reinflated.

"So here's the deal," Maya told him once she'd caught her breath. "We realize that you don't know shit about coffee or baking, but we can teach you. For now, I need someone who can help me with the stockroom, keep the place clean, and do whatever odd jobs pop up, and I'm sure Annie could use a hand taking orders during the crunch periods."

"Anything you ask," Wylan assured us. "I don't care."

"Just curious," I chimed in, "but if someone were to come in and try to rob us, would you have any qualms about, say, punching him in the face?"

He looked at me as if I'd asked him whether he intended to follow the law of gravity. "That goes without saying. Of course. Why wouldn't I intervene in that situation?"

Maya and I traded glances, and she gave him a curt nod. "That'll do it. You're hired. We work six days and two nights per week, and Sunday's yours. Be there at three-thirty tomorrow morning for prep, got it?"

Wylan thanked us again as we headed out, and I lingered at his door as Maya hurried downstairs toward the street and her waiting bed. "She went to the director today to bring you on," I whispered. "It was a surprise to me, too. Maya knows her stuff, and she's got high standards, but she's not an ogre. You'll catch on pretty quickly."

"Will you teach me to work the espresso machine?" he asked with a slightly worrying gleam in his eye. Then again, I reassured myself, it might just have been his eyeshine in the hallway lights.

"Eventually. You'll learn to work the register before I let you near scalding liquids," I replied, and followed Maya. "Get some sleep. Tomorrow's going to be a long day."

When we walked up to the café the next morning in the predawn gloom, we found Wylan already waiting for us by the door, kitted out as always but for the missing newspaper he no longer needed. "Good morning," he said, far too excited for the hour. "What can I do?"

"Well, first," said Maya, scanning in on the pad beside the door, "I've got to get to work in the kitchen, so you'll be with Annie. No planned deliveries today," she said, pushing her way inside, "but we need to finish the cleanup from last night. Think you could sweep and mop?"

"Gladly."

She chuckled. "That's what I like to hear. And, uh…" She flipped on the lights as I locked the door behind us, then gave Wylan a quick study. "I don't pretend to be the fashion police, but I don't think I've ever seen you in anything but a variant of that outfit."

He glanced down at his lace-up tunic and leggings. "Is this offensive?"

"No, just odd. And I'd rather you not have to scrub it out in the sink every night—accidents happen around here." As he frowned in consternation, she went around the counter and opened the register, then pulled out a wad of bills. "Here," she said, handing it to him. "Two hundred marks or so. Emergency petty cash fund. There's a better than decent secondhand shop five blocks south of us. Why don't you stop by this afternoon or tomorrow and see if you can't find a change of clothes?"

Wylan glanced at me uncertainly, and I patted his arm. "I'll go with you, all right?"

"I don't know the styles of dress here…"

"And I'm no expert," I said, "but we can get you something that you won't mind spilling coffee on."

As Maya heated the oven and pulled the previous day's work from the fridge, ready to go as the first batch of the morning, I wiped down the counter and checked the beer in the cabinet beneath it while Wylan tended to the floors. He worked quickly and without a fuss, then cleaned the tables and chairs as I started the coffee brewing. Once he finished, I beckoned him behind the counter to learn our payment system. "Fair warning: be careful of *that* light," I cautioned, pointing out the low-hanging fixture closest to the register as he joined me. "It's easy to snag it without knowing you're getting tangled."

"Really?"

"Okay, it's easy for *me* to snag it," I amended. "Proprioception must be nice."

"What is—"

"Oh, uh…an awareness of where your body is, more or less. Like, if I told you to touch your nose, you could do it without looking in a mirror, right?"

Wylan demonstrated with aplomb.

"Exactly. But my brain's mental map ends about here," I said, tapping the top of my head. "It doesn't account for the antlers, so I tend to be hyperaware of dangling things these days."

He didn't respond. Instead, he considered the hanging light and its thin chain, then hoisted himself onto the counter, stooped a little to avoid grazing the ceiling himself, and held out his hand. "Hammer and nail?"

I pulled the repair kit from the storage closet and passed him what he'd requested. With a few taps on the ceiling to determine the orientation of the support beam, he raised the light and nailed the chain in place, putting the fixture well out of my range. "How's that?" he asked.

"You think it'll hold?"

"I'm fairly confident." He jumped down, landing in a crouch, then reached for the rag to wipe away the evidence of his boot prints. "Wish you'd mentioned it sooner."

I wasn't helpless. I could have adjusted the light with, say, a stud finder and luck, and Maya standing below, begging me not to fall or ruin the ceiling…but I smiled and put the hammer away. "Thanks. Ever worked a register?"

"Never touched one," he declared, planting his hands

on his hips. "Show me."

By the time the first customers dragged themselves in—early Saturday mornings were slow, our customers almost exclusively those poor agents stuck working the weekend shifts—Wylan understood the basics of the register and the payment options, and he was standing behind my shoulder, watching as I slowly pulled a shot of espresso. The agents gawped—if they'd noticed Wylan in the café, they'd surely never expected to see him on the far side of the counter—but I didn't give them time to ask questions before launching into my welcome spiel and taking their orders. While Wylan handled the money and pulled pastries from the display case, I brewed and mixed and poured, and we sent the agents on their way. When the next duo arrived, Wylan took the initiative as I wiped down the espresso machine, punching in their orders and ringing them up. We had them settled in short order…and suddenly, we had a system.

Understandably, the morning rush wasn't without its missteps. I had to void a few orders where Wylan got confused with the buttons, and he had to ask me to point out the correct pastry on two occasions, but by and large, we made an efficient team. Since all I had to do was manage the drinks, I fell into a rhythm, and I even had time to clean up as I went—a rarity during the crunch periods. Sure, people stared at our new hire, but if they had thoughts about Wylan's presence, they had sense enough not to share those thoughts in front of him.

As the rush tapered off, Maya emerged with a fresh selection of pastries and cookies for the case and wiped her brow. "How's it going out here?"

"He's doing great," I said, wiping a few stray crumbs into my hand. "And we don't have an angry mob yet, so all in all, I think we've had worse Saturdays."

"Mm. What happened to my light?" she asked, squinting at the raised fixture.

"Hazardous for Annie," Wylan replied. "We fixed it."

"Oh. Well, okay, then," she said, and retreated to her lair.

Once the door flapped shut behind her, I smirked at him. "*We?*"

"It was your hammer. Now, are you going to let me try to make drinks?"

Baby steps seemed like the most prudent course of action, so I supervised while he started a fresh pot of drip coffee. I was enjoying the down time, even taking the chance to restock our to-go cups and plates, when Syvin walked in.

I'd never seen the chief deputy in anything less than a formal robe, and the fact that she owned a flowy pink blouse left me momentarily speechless. If I wasn't mistaken, the silvery sheen on her hooves was something akin to nail polish.

"Good morning, Syvin," I called, waving as she approached. "What are you doing here today? Working through the weekend?"

"Fortunately, no," she replied, then folded her arms and peered at Wylan. "Pateme told me about your new addition. I thought I'd see for myself."

"Gotcha," I said, hoping the situation wouldn't devolve. "Wylan, you remember Syvin, right? She's the chief deputy, and she'll have a large black coffee and…"

"A bagel," she decided. "Lightly toasted."

To my relief, he managed to split and properly toast her breakfast, and she gave her coffee a test sip as I added two packs of the jelly she preferred to her paper bag. "Wylan made the coffee," I told her. "Decent?"

She grunted, but she also nodded at him as I slid the bag across the counter. "Not bad."

"Do I pass inspection?" he asked with a hopeful smile.

Syvin didn't reciprocate. "Not yet, but…this is progress," she said, lifting her cup. "We'll see. And Annie, I'll have a new book for you Monday," she added, then marched off into the morning sunshine.

I whistled softly as the doorbell jangled in her wake. "She's nice once you get to know her." Wylan seemed unconvinced, but I cocked my head toward the espresso machine and said, "Come on, I'll walk you through a latte."

We closed around three that day, giving Maya time to cook and me time to take Wylan clothes shopping. The proprietor of the secondhand store choked on his drink when we walked in, but I waved and rushed Wylan toward the menswear, and the staff let us be.

An hour later, we emerged with two large shopping bags—I'd added to Maya's funds—and I'd had ample opportunity to appreciate Wylan's musculature. He'd tried on almost everything I suggested, then stepped out from the curtained cubicle for me to vet the result...and once I'd offered my verdict, he'd wasted no time in freeing himself of whatever shirt he'd happened to be wearing. Most of what we found had buttons instead of lacing like that of his familiar tunics—he only owned two, he'd admitted. I'd convinced him to buy a light zip-up jacket, and I'd managed to sell him on the idea of a flannel. As for the other half of his wardrobe...well, I didn't know what went on downstairs, and Wylan had sense enough not to fully strip in front of me. All I knew was that he filled out a pair of well-worn jeans *rather* nicely, and before I shut her up, the part of me that hadn't been with anyone in more than a year wondered what they would look like tossed on my bedroom floor.

When we returned to prep for the evening, Wylan sported a button-down with the sleeves rolled up over his toned forearms, plus my new favorite jeans. Maya gave her approval, but she didn't have time for a fashion show, and I hustled Wylan into the main part of the café to help me clean and move tables around.

Maya outdid herself that night, and our usual crowd of

agents and their friends crowded in for tapas and drinks. If they'd balked upon noticing Wylan, he'd managed to make a few converts to his cause by the end of the evening, as he had a trick in reserve: Wylan knew booze. Sure, I could find my way around a wine store back home, and I vaguely knew the different styles of beer, but most of that was useless information when trying to deal with Pactlands brews and bottles. Wylan had made a point of tasting everything on tap before we opened that evening—well, all but the troll-only beer, which I insisted he leave untouched as a matter of safety—and I discovered that he had a surprisingly good sense of pairings. The man could barely tell an espresso from an americano, but he *knew* beer, and after sneaking a few tastes of the wines we were pouring that night, he functioned as an amateur sommelier. I mean, it's possible that our customers were just too freaked to reject a Huntsman's drink suggestions, but no one complained.

By ten, the alcohol was flowing, the kitchen was running on schedule, and I'd spent a good portion of the evening pouring more complicated drinks from our selection of spirits, which sat on the back counter in place of the microwave and toaster during our weekend nights. I was just filling a pitcher of beer to take to a table near the karaoke stage when I noticed the assholes on the prowl again.

Three of DPP's healers had come out for a girl's night, drinking white wine and splitting Maya's infamous small plates. I knew them from our many trips to the labs upstairs, but also because two of them needed caffeine to function, and we were the most convenient source. They'd been having fun that night—all of them had taken a turn on stage, to general applause—and I, for one, didn't begrudge them an evening without their black lab coats.

The quartet of men was another matter. The guys weren't DPP, but they'd visited us every Saturday night for a month, and inevitably, they'd tried to hit on the women in the room. From where I was standing, their weekly humiliation was almost entertaining, but I felt for our female customers. Still, I couldn't work as both bartender and security, nor was I equipped to handle four tipsy sorcerers at once, so I'd been allowing nature to take its course.

But that evening, the sorcerers—maybe drunker than usual, or maybe just desperate—weren't taking the hint. The healers crowded together at their table, smiling coldly and insisting that they really wanted to spend time with just each other, but the men pressed in around them, even helping themselves to their food. Fed up, I pulled Wylan aside and muttered, "See those guys bothering the three women?"

"Yes…"

"Mind doing something about it?"

A moment later, the men looked up to find Wylan looming over their table, arms folded across his broad chest and head high. "These ladies have no desire for your company," he said, his voice rumbling around the café as other tables quieted to watch the fireworks.

The leader of the sorcerers half rose from his chair and swayed as he slurred, "Who says?"

"They did. Repeatedly," Wylan replied, then caught the man's shirt in his fists, pulled the drunk sorcerer close, and growled, "*Go.*"

The door slammed behind them as they made their ungainly exodus, and they knocked over two chairs in their haste to flee. As Wylan straightened the furniture, Maya, who'd poked her head out of the kitchen in time to see, whispered in my ear, "That's money *well* spent."

Wylan didn't complain during the cleanup late that night, though he looked pensive as he mopped. With Maya prepping for Monday in the kitchen, I dropped my cleaning spray and beckoned him into the bathroom.

"You okay?" I quietly asked. "It's a long day, I know—"

"Oh, no, this is fine," he assured me. "I'm grateful to be here, but I, uh…something came to mind."

"What's up?"

Absently rubbing his elbow, Wylan murmured, "The weather will turn soon. Days are shortening. I never know precisely when Father will ride, but it's often in the fall. And if he summons me to ride with the Hunt…I don't know whether I'll be able to refuse him."

The poor guy looked so guilty that I almost hugged him, but I settled for waving his concerns away. "It's called personal leave. Vacation time. If you need to go for a few days, we'll carry on and see you when you get back."

"You're sure?"

"Look, just because Maya and I never go anywhere doesn't mean that *you* can't. She'll understand if you want time off…" Glancing toward the toilet, I muttered, "Is that a beer on the floor?"

Wylan picked up the can and made a face. "Unfinished."

"Who brings a beer to the bathroom?"

He held it slightly closer and sniffed, then grimaced. "I'm not entirely certain this is still beer, Annie."

"Oh, *shit*."

"Close!" he replied with false cheer, then carried the offending can out to the dumpster.

CHAPTER 8

Over the following three weeks, I noticed an uptick in customers—particularly Interdiction agents. Two or three seemed to linger in the café at all times, doing paperwork with a cup of coffee or taking a long lunch. After seeing Pars four times in one day, I pulled him into the lobby and said, "I know what you're doing. He's *fine*."

"So far," Pars allowed. "Anyway, Chief's orders. We've got an emergency snack budget now," he added, "so maybe we should be thanking you, eh?"

To be fair, had Pars's chief, an eight-foot, razor-tusked, no-nonsense troll improbably named Gentle Breeze, ordered me to take a coffee break, I wouldn't have given her any lip about it, either. While Gentle Breeze had never been anything but civil to me, I suspected that she could end me in a variety of painful ways—a tusk to the gut, claws to the throat, an old-fashioned head crushing—and I respected her people's sense of self-preservation.

But if Wylan was rattled by the parade of agents from the door-busting end of the building, he remained superficially unruffled. He proved to be a quick study behind the counter—sure, he still consulted my laminated beverage cheat sheet, but not every time—and what's more, he exhibited a knack for matching orders and faces. Within two weeks, he knew what our regulars would want with eerie accuracy.

He also possessed an uncanny ability to recognize who was there without even turning around. One afternoon, after seeing him pour Syvin's coffee before she spoke or he so much as looked over his shoulder to greet her, I jokingly asked him whether he had eyes in the back of his head. To my surprise, however, he grew somewhat embarrassed. "I have a good memory for scents," he confessed. "The odor of coffee is strong here, but it's like background noise by now. When people come in, I can smell them, and I, uh…remember."

"You've got super-smell?" I asked incredulously.

"Not super, but it's close to troll level."

Since a trained troll could smell poisons and toxins in blood, that was close enough to super in my books. .which suddenly brought up all manner of concerns about my own stench. As if reading my mind, Wylan hastily reassured me, "You don't stink, I swear. And even if you did, I've lived with *many* men—I can handle it."

I wasn't entirely convinced, but I doubled up on the deodorant and hoped for the best.

By the time August rolled over into September, the bulk of our DPP patrons had come to terms with the fact that the Huntsman in the lobby made a damn good latte and only menaced customers who got drunk and turned into cretins. And on the first Sunday of the month, with much coaxing from Rose, Yven invited Wylan to join the four of us for dinner at his place.

Wylan dressed with care that night, and while his wardrobe offered him only casual or vaguely medieval options, he looked put together in those perfect jeans and a white shirt, its cuffs rolled up just enough to hide the tiny coffee stain on one sleeve. He'd even ventured to the nice wine shop that afternoon and returned with a bottle of something red, allegedly full-bodied, and almost certainly out of his budget. Maya paired one of her usual sundresses with a light wrap as a concession to the evening chill, while I settled for nice pants and a striped green button-down—boring, but then my options were limited.

As the three of us walked toward Yven's building,

Wylan remarked, "I was wondering if the mark on your earlobes was natural."

I reached up and brushed my fingers against the small gold hoops I'd put in for the evening. Seldom did I wear earrings around the café, as no one but the occasional male faun went for pierced ears in the Pactlands. "Just keeping the holes open," I said. "Yven doesn't seem to get grossed out by them, so I thought I'd wear a little jewelry tonight."

"They're pretty. Simple." He paused briefly. "They suit you."

"You're kind."

"I mean it. You should wear them at work. It's not as though you'd be any more upsetting to our customer base than I am," he joked.

"I'll think about it," I replied, and smiled to myself as we rounded the corner.

A few minutes later, I tugged my shirt straight as we rode the elevator up to Yven's apartment. Glancing in the mirrored wall, I noticed Wylan's hand tighten on the wine bottle—a subtle tell, but a sure sign that his calm was only a façade.

"You'll like them," I murmured as the elevator dinged on arrival. "Don't worry."

I had no time to offer further reassurance. Rose was waiting in the hall for us, all smiles, and accepted the wine from Wylan with effusive thanks. "Y'all come in," she said, slipping into English like a pair of well-loved sneakers. "He's made a whole turkey. Who's thirsty?"

I looked at Wylan in time to catch his confusion. "Not to be a killjoy," I told Rose in kind, "but he doesn't speak—"

"Oh...*shit*," she muttered, smacking the heel of her hand against her forehead, and returned to her accented Pactish. "Sorry about that," she said to Wylan. "Old habits, you know?"

"No offense taken," he replied, and pointed to Maya and me. "Perhaps someday one of them will teach me."

"Or there's the potion route," said Maya, and pulled him toward the door.

As worried as I'd been that Yven would feel uncomfortable around Wylan, the problem resolved itself within the first moment of our arrival. Once over the threshold, Wylan stopped in his tracks and turned to the orchid garden in Yven's den, and he actually *gasped*. "Oh, how beautiful!" he exclaimed, venturing a few steps closer to the flowers without touching anything. "Exquisite! Those blossoms..." He crouched beside the nearest cluster of pots, sniffed deeply, then closed his eyes as a look of bliss crossed his face. "Simply superb. What *are* these?"

I turned from him to Yven, who stood by the dining room table with his stained apron and a manic gleam in his gaze. "Would you like the tour?" he asked.

Wylan straightened and beamed at him. "Yes, please. Tell me about your collection."

Behind me, Rose softly groaned. "Let's go ahead and start the drinking," she muttered. "They're going to be a while."

Sitting at the table with a glass of wine—Wylan really had chosen a nice bottle—and halfway listening to Rose and Maya chat, I watched as Yven led Wylan around the room, lecturing his audience of one about orchid cultivation. Yven was cute when he was excited, I mused. His turquoise eyes seemed to sparkle as he rattled off names and stats, and with those dimples and his slightly mussed white-blond hair...yeah, I could understand what Rose saw in him, even if the sharper elven teeth didn't do it for me. But Wylan...

Hell, Wylan was cute all the time. No, I mentally amended, not *cute*—handsome.

Hot, even.

I mean, yeah, if you overlooked the antlers. And the pointed ears had taken some acclimatization. But those amber eyes, so rich that I could sink into his stare, not to mention the torso hiding beneath his shirt...I mean, Yven was no ninety-pound weakling, but next to Wylan, he looked like a reed.

And when Wylan smiled at me...

Sipping my wine, I forced myself to look away and be rational about the situation. I was lonely, nothing more. Suffering through an unexpected bout of celibacy. Guys in the Pactlands never gave me the time of day—except Wylan—so naturally, my pent-up libido was in overdrive, imagining hints that didn't exist.

And they *shouldn't* exist, I reminded myself. I wasn't some sort of stealth elf like Rose—I was a human with a bad potion reaction and a temporary visa, nothing more exotic than that. I liked Wylan, so even if I felt *that* way about him—which I didn't, really, it was just hormones talking—I wouldn't want to put him in danger of falling afoul of the law by sneaking around together. Honestly, I didn't...

Oh.

Oh, *fuck*.

I finished my glass and reached for a refill.

I wasn't falling for Wylan, I told myself. I was absolutely *not* crushing on my surprisingly appealing coworker. He needed friends, I needed friends, and we were seeing a lot of each other because of the hours we kept, but this was strictly platonic. And even if I had picked up the tiniest bit of interest in him, he'd never been anything but a gentleman around me. No accidental feel-ups behind the counter, no soulful gazes when he thought I wasn't looking, no hints that I'd be so much hotter if I unbuttoned a bit of my shirt...

I'd hung out with some *real* winners in the past, but to my relief, Wylan didn't seem to have picked up a copy of their playbook.

Then again, he probably wasn't trying to play the game.

The lack of romance in my life wasn't the only thing getting me down that fall. As the days cooled and the leaves on the stunted Pactlands trees began to turn, my thoughts drifted more and more toward home. While Maya and I were still a few weeks out from marking a year away from the real world, the changing season reminded me of the impending anniversary and of everything I must have missed since the previous November.

I tried not to show my feelings around the café—I wasn't looking for a pity party from the agents passing through—but on Saturday afternoon two weeks after our dinner with Yven and Rose, Wylan pulled me into the bathroom during a lull. "You're upset," he said. "It's none of my business, but are you and Maya fighting?"

"Heavens, no," I insisted, weakly chuckling at the suggestion. "No, we're fine. It's nothing, I'm just..."

He waited for a moment as I let the thought hang, then finished, "Homesick?"

I nodded.

"Did something in particular spark this?"

Leaning against the sink, I folded my arms and looked past him at the basket of spare toilet paper. "Unless the lab delivers a miracle in the next few weeks, this is going to be the first time I've missed deer hunting with my dad since I was *seven*."

A surprised little smile quirked the corners of his mouth. "You didn't tell me you hunted."

"Recreationally. Dad and his buddies have been going out in the woods since they were little kids, and they started taking the next generation along once we were old enough to be taught not to shoot each other," I said, thinking of my first orange safety vest. "A lot of us didn't take to it, but I liked sitting up in the stand, being absolutely quiet and waiting for the deer to come along. Dad's friends knew I wouldn't throw a fit, so they didn't mind me going with the guys. Deer in the fall, turkey in the spring...I mean, are you actually having fun if you still have feeling in your fingers?"

"You're a decent shot?"

I shrugged. "Not going to the Olympics any time soon, but I'm competent with a rifle. Dad taught me bowhunting basics, too. I've killed a buck, if that's what you're asking."

"Just a thought," said Wylan, "and I realize this wouldn't be the same, but you and I could go hunting. I haven't been out in months, and surely you could use a break from this place."

"That's sweet of you to offer, but all my gear is back in Richmond. I didn't come here with more than the clothes on my back."

"I have extra," he replied, warming to the idea. "And I know some great spots with proper woods. *Deep* woods. No one would see us."

My brows knit. "In the *Pactlands*? Aren't the forests around here, like, family recreation areas?" The last thing I wanted to do was shoot an unsuspecting hiker.

His smile turned impish. "Who said anything about the Pactlands?"

"Ooh. See, that's another problem: I don't have portal credentials. I can't get out," I explained. "Officially, it's too risky."

The bell over the door jingled with an arriving customer, and Wylan unlocked the bathroom door. "Tell you what, Annie. You dress for the hunt and meet me here early tomorrow, and I'll take care of the rest."

I waited in the bathroom for a minute after his departure, trying not to let on to the customer that we'd been crammed in there together, and wondered what Wylan had in mind. As exciting as an unanticipated hunting trip seemed, I had no idea where he intended to take us—or how, as he had no vehicle. My van was big but a poor choice for off-roading, and I wasn't sure I wanted to put any carcasses in the back.

But Wylan grinned at me as I slipped out of my hiding place, a satisfied smile that spoke of secrets, and I decided to let him have his fun.

I was nervous as I hurried toward the café at dawn the next morning, still groggy after my short night's sleep but fueled by coffee from our basic apartment drip machine. Wylan had given me no hints about his plans on Saturday, leaving me to hope that whatever he had in mind wouldn't end with me locked in a cell in the DPP tower for my own good. My camo was back in Virginia—or I hoped it still existed back in Virginia, maybe stuffed into a storage unit in case I returned—and so I'd done the best I could with black leggings, a dark green, slightly oversized flannel, and a ratty brown jacket from the secondhand store.

When I walked up, Wylan was outside waiting for me beneath a streetlight. The lace-up tunic and leggings had returned, I noted, and the dark cloak thrown atop his ensemble did nothing to lessen my impression that he'd escaped a Renaissance faire. On the sidewalk by his boots lay a black leather duffel bag large enough to fit a corpse. He grinned like a kid at Christmas and lifted a hand in greeting as I hurried to join him. "Ready? I brought all of my extra weapons, so there should be something in here to suit you," he said, nudging the bag with his toe.

"Sounds great," I replied, smiling back at him—his excitement was infectious—and glanced around the quiet street. "So, uh…where are we going, and how are we getting there?"

"I'll show you." He hoisted the loaded bag onto his shoulder with only the slightest grunt, then held out his hand. "Do you trust me?"

Though the question left me somewhat anxious, I clasped his extended hand. "Sure. Wouldn't go into the woods with you and your bag of fun if I didn't."

"Glad to hear it." Tightening his grip on me, he murmured, "You told me yesterday that you don't have portal credentials. Neither do I."

"Okay…" I said, suddenly wondering if our outing was going to end in a high-speed chase. I didn't know what sort of security the portals had—I'd been unconscious in the back of a DPP van on my one and only time through.

"That doesn't matter," Wylan continued, leaning closer, "because we of the Hunt don't *need* portals."

"What do you mean?"

"Close your eyes, hold your breath, and trust me."

Though my gut protested that this was a terrible plan, Wylan seemed calm about the situation. Taking a deep breath, I screwed my eyes shut and tensed as if expecting a blow from behind.

"I won't let you fall," he insisted, but before I could ask questions, the ground dropped away.

I tried to scream—instinct swore that this was the proper occasion for a good, old-fashioned, blood-curdling screech of terror—but before I could do more than release the air I'd been holding, gravity returned. I stumbled when I felt solid earth rising up to meet my feet, and Wylan steadied me with a hand to my elbow. "That's it," he soothed. "All over, well done."

"What the hell—"

"Open your eyes, Annie."

Trembling, I dared to crack one open, then gasped.

The pristine streets of Beukal were *gone*, replaced by deep darkness, tall trunks, and the musty smell of damp earth. Releasing Wylan, I fumbled with the little flashlight I'd shoved in my jacket pocket and waved the beam in a circle, taking in the night-dark forest, the low bracken, the thin pines, the turning leaves on the hardwoods. Somewhere behind me, a pair of owls hooted at each other. The forest didn't extend far in every direction—a few yards ahead, the trees gave way to grasslands, and I thought I detected mountains in the distance, their bulk black against the star-strewn sky.

A *very* starry sky, I noted. Wherever we were, light pollution was the least of our problems. And given the sudden drop in temperature, we had to be far from the capital.

As I goggled and tried to process what had just occurred, Wylan chuckled. I wheeled on him, perplexed and alarmed, and his eyes shone in my flashlight's glare. "What the hell?" I repeated.

"Are you all right?"

"Where *are* we?"

"I'm not entirely certain," he admitted. "I don't know the name of the place, but I like to come here. The game is plentiful, and I seldom see anyone."

Panic, which had been bubbling below the surface for the last minute, started to push its way to the fore. "You don't know where we are?"

"I know the area, just not its name," he replied, calm in the face of my distress. "Really, I've been here many a time. There's good hunting."

"Just give me a second," I said, stepping away from him, and tried to get my bearings. The scent of the place wasn't altogether unfamiliar to me, though I didn't see the first hint of a landmark. Scanning the ground, I caught a dirty, half-torn piece of paper with my flashlight and plucked it from the drift of old leaves.

"This is a Montana hunting license," I told Wylan.

"Oh?"

I turned to him. "*Montana.*"

He shrugged helplessly. "I'm sorry, I don't recognize the name—"

"Are we out of the Pactlands?"

"Of course. There's little decent hunting in there," he explained, "so when I feel the urge..." He spread one arm as if showing off his tree collection. "As I said, we don't need portals."

Home, I realized. I was home...or back in my world, at least. Closer than I'd been in almost a year. A flurry of half-cocked plans flashed in my mind like strobe lights at a nightclub. Montana was only two hours behind Virginia—

I could find a phone, call my parents, and tell them I'd been kidnapped by freaky government agents. Or I could run toward the mountains and wait for daylight, then try to make my way toward civilization. I could hitchhike...or maybe Wylan could take me home. If he could find his way to freaking Montana, then surely I could guide him toward Richmond...

Or not. If anyone saw me, what would happen next would surely make DPP's treatment of Maya and me look like a spa day at the Four Seasons. Though I was closer to home, I couldn't take that risk, no matter how much I wanted to see my family and friends again.

While I'd been considering my options, Wylan had dropped his bag and now crouched beside it to rummage through his gear. "Here you go," he said, interrupting my spiraling thoughts. "Try this."

I looked down and saw a bow in his hand—not a compound bow like the ones Dad and I had used on our trips, but rather a longbow, a piece of equipment that wouldn't have seemed out of place in a Robin Hood reenactment. "Uh..."

"My spare," he explained, perhaps mistaking my hesitation for fear that I was swiping his good weapons. "Give it a try. We can adjust the tension if need be."

"I, um...I'm not the world's greatest bowhunter," I admitted, taking it from him. "Especially not with one like this."

"No? Well, that's fine," he replied, fishing out a quiver of arrows for me. "We've got hours to practice, yes?"

We moved quietly in the darkness, stopping every so often at the tree line to scan the grassy plain for game. I kept my flashlight off, following Wylan and willing my eyes to adjust to the predawn gloom. After half an hour, they'd acclimated as much as they were going to, and while I could pick shapes out of the darkness, I found myself looking for movement instead of discrete forms or color variations.

Wylan and I had taken cover behind a low screen of branches when he pointed to a mass about twenty yards away. "Elk," he whispered. "See it?"

I nodded. The creature was massive—a bull, certainly, judging by its impressive antlers, and perhaps eight hundred pounds. He seemed to be casually feeding, stopping to graze as he made his way toward the mountains.

"The first shot is yours," Wylan told me.

Though I was sure he meant the gesture as a kindness, I was feeling less than confident about my ability to hit the target with my oversized loaner bow. Still, I took up my stance, nocked an arrow, and let it fly…

…and it landed an embarrassingly long way from the elk, who lifted his head for a few seconds and grunted before returning to his meal.

"Sorry," I muttered, sliding away to give Wylan room, but he gripped my shoulder to stay me.

"Your form was good," he whispered. "May I help you?"

As I couldn't shoot any worse with his assistance, I acquiesced. He told me to nock another arrow, then slipped behind me and subtly adjusted my position. "That should line you up," he said. "Shoot."

That time, the arrow struck home, though not where I'd have preferred. Instead of catching the elk near his chest, it embedded itself in his rump like an overgrown bee stinger, and the wounded bull bellowed and took off running.

"Shit," I muttered, fumbling with my quiver, but Wylan burst through the branches and chased after the fleeing elk.

I was in decent shape, but he was *fast*. Even if I'd been able to see where I was going, I'd never have been able to keep pace with him. Sprinting and praying I wouldn't step in a hole and break my ankle, I followed him as well as I could while he ran down our prey, listening for the elk's cries to guide me through the darkness.

By the time I caught up to Wylan, puffing like I'd just stepped out for an impromptu marathon, the elk was dead in the grass, its throat having been cut to give it a quick end. Wylan pulled my arrow free and handed it over. "First blood was yours," he said—and damn him, he didn't even sound winded. "Do you claim this?"

"What," I managed between gasps, "the elk?"

"Yes. You were the first to wound him."

"I only annoyed him. You brought him down," I replied. "I can't take credit for that."

He didn't argue with me, and I could just make out his smile as he stood. "Perhaps we could split this one, then. Would that suit you?"

"Sure." I bent over, resting my palms on my thighs as my breathing slowed. "How did you want to get him to the Pactlands?"

"Wait here."

Before I could protest, he knelt and gripped the elk's forelegs, and the two of them vanished. I jumped back, surprised and uncomfortably cognizant that I was very much alone in the wilderness, but Wylan reappeared seconds later and chuckled at my expression. "There, problem solved."

"Where did you go?" I demanded.

"My apartment. I left the elk on the roof to be cleaned," he replied. "Brought some tarps up this morning, just in case. He'll be fine for a few hours."

"And your landlord doesn't mind?" I asked as we started on.

Wylan snorted. "He can't mind what he doesn't know about, now can he?"

If my shooting improved over the few hours we spent

stalking the lonely wild, it did so only minimally, even once the sun rose over the frosty grass. I missed my rifle every time I drew the bow. Still, I was having more fun than I'd had in months, a taste of near familiarity. Hunting with Wylan wasn't like hunting with Dad and his friends—compared to Wylan with his preternatural aim and stamina, my old hunting buddies looked like sluggish novices—but when we called a halt that morning, we'd taken down another elk and a pair of young deer.

"I've got to say," I began, pulling Wylan's arrow out of the last deer, "I'm impressed."

Squatting beside me, cleaning his knife in the weeds, he looked up and cocked his head. "With what?"

"*You*, silly. You don't seem tired, and you've been running for hours. You see well in the dark, you shoot pretty damn straight…"

He chuckled. "I appreciate it, but I'm nothing special. You should hunt with some of my brothers."

"That's not reassuring in the slightest," I replied, then grabbed the deer in a fireman's carry and hoisted it over my shoulders. "Think we should head out?"

His eyes widened as he stood. "You're stronger than I thought."

"Yeah, well, my dad toughened me up," I said, and shifted the body to redistribute the weight. "Want to put this bad boy on the pile?"

"Close your eyes," Wylan warned me, gripping my wrist, and I braced myself before the world fell away.

Knowing what to expect, I didn't stumble on arrival that time, and I dropped the deer beside the other three carcasses with relief. "That is a *ton* of meat," I said, eying our take.

"I'll handle the cleaning," Wylan offered, walking around the loaded tarp. "How much of the flesh do you want, half?"

"Honestly, I'm not sure we have the freezer space…"

"Neither do I, but what about the walk-in at work? Do

you suppose Maya would want any of this for meatballs?"

"Ooh. Yes. *I* want her to have this for meatballs," I replied, grinning. "Don't think she'll turn down fresh game. But are you sure about the cleaning? I've never processed a deer, but I'm willing to help…"

"It's no trouble." He smiled and rubbed his elbow, then cleared his throat. "Thank you for the hunt. I haven't had one that nice in a long time."

"Thanks for taking me. Sorry I was such a lousy shot—"

"You were fine," he said, though I think we both realized that was a fib.

Suddenly, I was hyper-aware of the fact that the two of us were alone on the roof. As I massaged my shoulder, I met Wylan's stare…

I knew I wasn't imagining the hunger I saw in his eyes. With the way my pulse was racing, surely he saw that hunger reflected in mine, too.

Before I could lose my nerve, I crossed the short distance between us, reached one hand behind his neck, and pulled his mouth toward mine. I felt his quick, surprised intake of breath an instant before our lips touched, and then his arms encircled me and drew me in as he kissed me in return.

It wasn't the most swoon-worthy kiss I could have imagined—Wylan was far more competent a hunter than a lover, and I briefly wondered whether ours was his first kiss when his antlers almost entangled with mine. We moved away, both flushed and awkwardly laughing at the near-miss, and then I murmured, "Let me."

He held still as I cupped his face in my palms and kissed him, carefully angling myself so as to avoid catastrophe. When I stepped back, Wylan looked dazed but hungrier than ever…

What was I *doing*? We couldn't have this, DPP couldn't find out…

God, I wanted him, but I knew I needed to go before

we crossed a line we'd regret.

"I'll see you later," I said, and hurried downstairs into his apartment. He didn't follow me, and as I let myself out into the stairwell and jogged toward the ground, my face burning, I acknowledged two truths.

Whatever he was, I wanted Wylan. I wanted him to hold me close and explore my face and neck with his fumbling kisses. I wanted to feel his strong arms around me as I took in the sight and sound and scent of him, the curious bouquet of sweat and the perfumed air of wild places.

And there was no way in hell that I was going to breathe a word of this to Maya.

CHAPTER 9

I seldom paid much attention to the TV mounted in the corner of the café. Maya and I left it on low for noise, usually tuned to one of the capital's news stations, which meant that I often ended my day with a vague sense of current events but no real details.

The Friday after my weekend hunt with Wylan was different. The news had been slow of late—dry reports about the latest from the Forum, recaps of fancy parties, puff pieces about smiling children doing volunteer work or winning prizes—but Friday's lineup featured mystery and potential scandal, and the morning television reporters attacked it like sharks heading for a bleeding baby seal. They weren't the only ones. Wylan stepped out just before we opened to grab his usual newspaper, and when he showed me the front page, I found the facts and breathless speculation repeated above the fold.

Wednesday was the last time anyone had seen Fellora ti'Mal. An ordinary missing person might not have ginned up such coverage, but Fellora's mother was the lady of Hall ti'Mal, and Fellora stood to inherit the title someday. What little I knew of elven politics came from snippets of television stories and quick explanations from Yven— who, frankly, seemed embarrassed by much of the social drama—but I'd certainly heard ti'Mal mentioned.

Lady ti'Mal was only a year into the gig, her father having notoriously died after trying to fulfill a lifelong dream of mountain climbing in the Alps. Her ascent having been unexpected, the society reporters had quickly cobbled together profile pieces about the new lady: she'd been married for seventy-five years to a man out of Hall ti'Pon—an attractive guy from a middling Hall like ti'Mal, a good match—and their eldest child was Fellora, a beautiful and *quite* eligible woman of sixty. Shortly thereafter had come the happy news that Fellora was engaged to Camun ti'Grell, a major step up for her. Ti'Grell was a far more prominent Hall, one of the few of the southern bunch that had survived. While Camun was only the third of his parents' children, his father was the lord, making him a prize for Fellora.

The wedding announcement had been beautiful and widely covered, and even I had noted the pictures of the happy couple holding hands and giving each other puppy eyes in front of a floral backdrop. The wedding was less than a month away, a highlight of the fall calendar for the well-heeled elven set.

And now the bride was nowhere to be found.

Throughout the morning, the television jabbered theories and speculation about her whereabouts. Had Fellora come down with a bad case of cold feet? Did she have a hidden lover, someone from a Hall far beneath hers in prominence—or worse, a non-elf? Had she taken the draught and run away with a human? (Unlikely. Given her position as a docent at the capital's fine art museum, she'd probably never left the Pactlands.) Or had she come to harm? No one could say, and as her family and her fiancé's family proved unwilling to speak to the press, the gossip fire burned all the hotter.

By Sunday, when Rose and Yven had the three of us over for dinner again, I probably could have rattled off Fellora's shoe size and perfect date, given the unrelenting coverage. There was still no sign of the runaway bride, and DOL, unsurprisingly, had declined to make a statement concerning whether she'd become the subject of an investigation. I was eager to see whether our hosts had any insider knowledge of Fellora's disappearance. Sure, Rose was new to the Pactlands, but if anyone had dirt, it had to be her great-grandfather, who was the director of the Division of Intelligence on top of everything else.

I tried to be subtle about my digging. "So," I said as we started on the salad, "have you two seen the stories about what's-her-name?"

Rose smiled around her fork. "Could you be *slightly* more descriptive?"

"That elf woman, you know, the blonde all over TV."

"Fellora," Maya offered, reaching for her wine. "The missing bride. Have you not seen the news?"

Rose and Yven traded glances, and both nodded. "Yeah, I've seen it," she said.

"Do you know her?" I asked.

Her face betrayed her incredulity. "Who, *me*? Never met her."

"You haven't had a proper social season yet, either," Yven added.

"What about you, then?" Maya asked him. "Have you met?"

Yven chuckled softly and played with his tomatoes. "Uh, no. Ti'Mal may not be the top of the heap, but they don't socialize with ti'Ansha. We barely make the cut as it is."

From hearing him and Rose talk, I wasn't sure what was more scandalous about their engagement, the fact that she was partly human or that his Hall fell so many rungs below hers. A well-bred ti'Dana girl should never have looked for a partner in a Hall like ti'Ansha, but then Rose had only recently taken on the ti'Dana name, and Diriem didn't give a damn who she chose as long as she was happy.

"Is no one searching for her?" Wylan asked between bites.

"Yeah," I said, "that's pretty weird. I'd have thought there'd be a manhunt by now. Dogs out and drones over the park, or whatever they use here. I mean, if someone pretty and wealthy disappeared back home, I'd expect to see a helicopter and everything."

Again, our hosts locked eyes, holding each other's gaze in a moment of silent communication, and then both put down their utensils. "If I tell you something," said Rose, "then you've got to *swear* it won't leave this apartment."

"Deal," said Maya, leaning over her plate. "Spill it."

Rose sipped her wine, keeping us in suspense for a few seconds longer, but cracked before Maya could lunge over the table at her. "DOL came to me on Thursday. They've asked me to try to find Fellora with farsight."

Not a bad plan, I had to admit. Rose had inherited the ti'Dana wild talent, farsight, though with a twist. While Diriem could look forward in time and other farseers could revisit the past, Rose was uniquely oriented toward the present. If she focused on a particular person and he wasn't protected in some way, she could spy on him remotely—and while her skill with magic lagged in many areas, she'd had months of intensive farsight practice during the past spring. She probably should have followed Diriem to DOI with the future-oriented farseeing bunch. but though she'd decided to hang around DPP for the time being, it seemed that the agency didn't mind loaning her out to Laws.

"Her family's frantic," Rose continued. "They're afraid she's eloped or dead, and since either would be a scandal, they don't want a big DOL manhunt to draw attention."

"Too late for that," I replied. "It's all over the news."

"Right?" she muttered. "But that's not my call, and when DOL came by, I agreed to pitch in. *Quietly*."

"Any luck?" Maya asked. "I mean, considering what you pulled off in June…"

But Rose's mouth tightened, and she shook her head. "Not a blessed thing."

"Seriously?"

"It's not like flipping a switch," she protested, and stabbed a cucumber slice. "And there's ways to hide, you know. I'm not omniscient."

"Blinding potion, right?" I cut in. "Isn't that what they're called?"

"Yeah, but this doesn't feel like a blinding potion." She chewed slowly, then took a long sip of wine before explaining. "If I'm dealing with a blinding potion, all I see when I focus on the protected person is white. It's like stepping into a blizzard. If I focus on someone near them and try to see them that way, they're just a white blotch. I can't even hear them. But when I concentrate on Fellora, I don't see white—I see *black*, like I've just fallen into a void."

Wylan frowned as he listened. "Could that mean she's dead?"

"Pop doesn't think so," said Rose. "He said that when he tries to focus on someone who's dead by a certain point in the future, the gears just don't click. As far as I can tell, my farsight's working, but something's blocking me from seeing Fellora, and even Pop's stumped." She drank again, draining her glass. "I'm worried," she murmured. "This doesn't feel like my idiot great-aunt's elopement did."

"No?" asked Maya.

"Nope. First, if she were going to elope, then why hasn't there been any sighting of her at the Tribunal building yet?"

"We've got an old law," Yven told Wylan. "If a couple marries against the wishes of the lords or ladies of their Halls, then the union can be annulled if one of the pair is brought before a tribunal within a month. Keep hidden until the deadline, and the marriage is untouchable. Rose's great-aunt tried to beat the clock back in March, and we hid her and her husband outside the Pactlands for a time."

"Until she decided she loved Daddy's money more than she did poor Deono," Rose muttered. "Anyway, since Fellora's time wouldn't start running until she was married, why would she be hiding right now? Second, the facts don't suggest an elopement."

I'd been watching her face while she spoke, and I saw the unease in her eyes. "You know more than the reports have been saying."

"Yeah. Let me just bring in the main…"

Yven patted her shoulder as he stood. "Sit there, I'll plate. More wine?"

"I'd better not." As he gathered the remnants of the salad, she sighed and absently rubbed her forehead. "Fellora was last seen at Green Lake."

"Right," I coaxed.

"She's a hiker. *Loves* it. Knows every trail in that park, even the rough ones. She goes out at least every other week. And since the museum is open on the weekends, she tends to take Wednesdays as one of her days off."

"Okay…"

"So she does everything right that morning. Calls her fiancé to tell him where she's going and when she plans to be back. Texts her sister, too, just in case. DOL spoke with one of the park rangers who saw her before she hit the trail, and he said she was carrying a light pack. Allegedly, she always travels with a flashlight, food and water, a first aid kit, and her phone."

"No weapon?" I asked.

Rose shrugged. "Elf, remember?"

"Defensive magic is an option for *some* of us," Yven added from the kitchen. "I'm not so great with it, but—"

"You can freaking start fires," said Rose, turning to give him a look. "Anyway," she said to us, "no, she wasn't armed."

I nodded, cataloguing that fact. "And no one heard from her again after she set off, right?"

"Not a soul. She never called, never texted, and never came home. Her fiancé got worried around nightfall and drove to out there to find her. Her car was still there, locked and untouched. The rangers have combed the trail she said she was taking, but it's like she disappeared into thin air. Abducted by aliens."

I glanced at Maya and exchanged brief smirks. "Know *that* feeling. But is that all DOL has done?" I asked incredulously. "Get the rangers to walk the trail and pull you in to try the farsight angle?"

"Oh, no," Rose reassured me, "they've been busy. They've been trying to trace Fellora using her hair and her parents' blood—"

"That takes a while to set up," Yven offered, carrying out the first pair of dinner plates, "but DOL has the sorcerers to spare."

"Still, no sign of her yet. And ooh, that looks amazing," she told him as he set a roasted quail in front of me.

"Ditto," said Maya, grinning up at him. "Compliments to the chef."

Yven beamed at her praise and hurried back to retrieve the other plates, but I remained focused on Rose. "I get that the family doesn't want this to become a circus, but you'd think they'd be all in favor of a search party."

"I don't know," she replied, "but if *I* ever disappear, please feel free to bring in a clown car if it means I'm found alive. As for Hall ti'Mal...I mean, I'm sure they have their reasons for trying to minimize the press, but I'm not holding out a ton of hope for Fellora."

I pitied the poor thing, especially if her parents were more concerned about bad press than about locating their missing daughter...and as I mulled over the matter, a wild thought came to mind. "If DOL's not doing much in the field, then I could pitch in."

The others turned to me, perplexed. "How?" Yven asked.

"I'm a private investigator, remember? What if I did some groundwork on the sly for DOL? If I go snooping around, no one will ever think I'm doing it at their behest. Maybe the family could have some answers, and they might even save face. And Wylan could help me," I continued, warming to my own plan. "He's fantastic at tracking things, and no one ever bothers him."

Rose perked at the notion, but Yven seemed unsold. "Not to bring up a sore subject, Annie, but you don't exactly have a, um…an *unsubtle* profile."

"Right. So get your bosses to loan me a piece of masking jewelry—"

Maya laughed aloud. "Fat chance, babe. You know what the research team will say to that."

"And someone's life may be in jeopardy, so I really don't give a damn," I countered. "I'll take the risk of a bad cross-reaction. Besides, it's not like I'd be leaving the Pactlands, right? Even if I had a catastrophic mask failure, what's the worst that could happen?"

"I don't know, but when the freaking experts think it's too risky, maybe you should listen."

"Maya has a point," Wylan murmured.

"Granted, but every instinct I have says Fellora didn't run off with a secret boyfriend," I replied, holding his worried stare. "With disappearances, time's crucial, and it's been four days already. The longer she's gone, the likelier it is that she's dead in a gully," I said, ramping up despite the company. "If her family's too goddamn stupid to see that and DOL's too cowardly to cross them, then *someone* needs to step in on her behalf. Doesn't she deserve a chance to be found?"

Coming up for air, I glanced around the quiet table, at the lovely quail and the wine stems, and mumbled, "Sorry."

"Don't be," said Yven. "You're right." Looking to Rose, he began, "Do you think the director would—"

"I'll call Pateme later tonight," she interrupted, and wiped her mouth. "First things first," she said to me, "if you're going to try this, then you'll need a *good* piece of jewelry."

Yven frowned as she went to her feet. "I'm sure we have loaners. Or DOL will…"

"Maybe, but with Annie's complication, she doesn't need to be fooling around with government hand-medowns. Excuse me for a minute, will you?"

Rose rummaged through her purse and disappeared into Yven's bedroom, though she left the door cracked. As we lingered in uneasy silence at the table, I heard her say, "Hello, Teolm. Sorry to bother you, but I need a favor."

I'd never met any of Rose's relatives but for Pateme. Her maternal great-grandfather, Diriem, apparently thought she'd hung the moon. Her paternal great-grandfather probably would have preferred to shoot her to the moon in a faulty rocket.

Rose was an acknowledged ti'Dana, but she had equal claim to Hall ti'Cren, at least on paper. While the great-aunt who'd stepped in as a surrogate grandmother to her was a ti'Cren, the rest of the family viewed her with a...*complex* blend of emotions. The patriarch of the clan, Inade, was a murderous drug kingpin who'd happened to work as a jeweler to keep up appearances. When Rose had testified against him the previous June, Inade had ended up with a *long* prison sentence, and his wife and three of their children had since been sent away for their part in his criminal enterprise. In public, the remaining ti'Cren children claimed to be horrified by their parents' and siblings' actions. But in private, for some of the family, Rose was the half-blooded bitch who'd betrayed them and sent their Hall's reputation into the sewer. Never mind that she'd dared to out herself as the granddaughter of the ti'Cren son who'd taken the draught and exiled himself— her actions had tanked the family's immediate fortunes, and rumor around the café suggested that at least one or two ti'Cren marriages in the cadet branches had fallen through over the summer. Old and wealthy as the Hall might be, Inade's drug ring left an indelible blotch on the family's reputation.

There were, I'd gathered, two great exceptions to the ti'Cren pact to pretend Rose didn't exist. Her great-aunt

Liliol ran a garden nursery in a tiny Appalachian town and didn't give a rat's ass what the rest of her kin thought, and Rose talked about her on occasion. And then there was Teolm, the eldest ti'Cren child and the new lord of the Hall after his father's removal. I didn't know much about him beyond the odd snippet from television. Lord ti'Cren was a short, slight, dark-haired man. Rather than quit his job to manage the Hall's finances, he'd hired an accountant and kept his position as an experimental botanist, which led to the occasional photographer lying in wait outside his workplace to snag a shot of a high-ranking elven lord covered in unspeakable plant goop. If he minded, I never heard about it. Like his sister and their father, Teolm was a floramancer, and he intended to make good use of his talent.

I didn't know why Rose had called him until she directed me through the evening streets to the capital's better shopping district, a five-block stretch of couture, fine housewares, luxury cars, and magical tools that cost a small fortune. Rolling up in my van felt almost like sacrilege, but Wylan and I couldn't fit inside conventional cars. At least Rose didn't seem bothered to be cruising around town in a vehicle one bag of candy away from a search warrant.

She had me park in front of a building with a gray stone façade pocked at regular intervals by square glass windows. Behind each hung a display cube, softly lit and empty but for forms suggestive of necks, hands, or wrists. I glanced over the door at the brass lettering mounted to the stone: TI'CREN DESIGNS.

"What are we doing here?" I asked, cutting the ignition.

"Just come with me," Rose replied, and slid out of the passenger side.

The four of us trooped after her toward the front door, which appeared to be locked fast. A moment later, however, a soft click announced the latch's opening, and Rose led us into the showroom.

With its long glass display cases, dark paneling, and thick carpet, Inade's store wouldn't have been out of place on Fifth Avenue. Most of the cases had been emptied for the night, though a few of the cheaper baubles remained on their cushions, trifles for the shopper on a budget. As I glanced around the shop, taking in the tastefully muted paintings and the faint scent of overpriced candles, a door creaked open, and Teolm appeared at the bottom of an interior staircase. While he wasn't covered in sap and mud that night, he didn't exactly look the part of a prominent lord in faded jeans and a dark green T-shirt.

He took two steps into the showroom, then came to a halt as he noticed Wylan and me. "Uh..." He cleared his throat and stared at Rose. "You didn't mention your...*friends.*"

"This is Maya," said Rose, then went around the room. "That's Annie, who's why we're here, and the big guy is Wylan. And you remember Yven, don't you?" she added, gently nudging her fiancé.

Teolm nodded, though he looked at Yven as if in silent query about just what the hell was happening. "Let me get this straight," he said after a brief pause, and pointed to me. "You need to mask *her?*"

"She wants to help find the missing ti'Mal woman," Rose told him. "And she's experienced...albeit back in Richmond."

Comprehension flashed across his face. "So this is the result of that novel potion?" he asked, spinning one finger as if he could frame my head and antlers.

"Exactly. Maya, too," she replied, and Maya obligingly fluttered her wings. "Which is why I called you. We need something that will mask Annie without interacting with the potion."

"A tall order," said Teolm, rubbing the back of his neck. "Probably impossible...but I have a thought. Come with me."

We joined him on the far side of the store, where a

tapestry hid the safe entrance. Sliding the tapestry aside, he inserted a key and made a few quick, complex gestures, and the safe unlocked. As Teolm ventured inside, I peeked past the heavy metal door and found rows and rows of clear cases stacked ten feet high, their contents glittering in the security light overhead.

"That's a fortune in there," Maya murmured.

"The family money isn't *entirely* from drugs," Teolm called back. "One moment, there's an internal safe…"

As Maya blushed, he dug around, banged his elbow into a metal box, muttered what was almost certainly Low Elvish profanity, and finally emerged holding a thin box in navy velvet. "Let's try this one," he said as he carried it to a counter, then opened the lid and extracted the sort of necklace that looked simple but probably cost as much as my degree had, a convex silver disc on a delicate chain. "Turn around, please," he instructed me, then deftly fastened the necklace in place.

"I thought you were a botanist," I said.

"A botanist whose father forced him into the shop on many an occasion. Step over to the mirror."

Once I was in position, he took a spot at my left shoulder and rubbed his hands together. "Ever worn masking jewelry before?"

"Nope."

"Well, first thing, relax," he said, giving my arm a quick pat. "This won't hurt, and nothing you make with that necklace is permanent. Now, what you want to do is hold the pendant between finger and thumb…right, just like that," he said as I gripped the disc. The tip of my thumb fit comfortably into the depression, and the metal quickly warmed as I pinched it. "All right, this is the fun part," he continued with a slight smile. "Imagine how you want to appear."

"Like…anything?" I asked.

"*Anything*. You can set a default on these once you assemble an appearance you like, but for now, play around.

This is why we start with the mirror, eh?"

I could have spent all night making a thousand minute changes to my face and body, but one alteration took prominence over all others.

Go away, I thought, glaring at my antlers...and in the space of a heartbeat, they vanished.

I gasped and jumped back from the mirror, then dropped the necklace and ran my hands over my unmarred head. "They're gone!"

"Temporarily," Teolm cautioned. "And considering the potion in your system, I wouldn't stay masked for more than an hour or two at a time. If the DPP geniuses are reluctant to let you mask, then they have their reasons—and I know enough about bad magical cross-effects to trust them. This can't be a permanent fix," he said, even as I pushed my fingers through my hair to feel my smooth scalp beneath them.

"How do I look?" I asked, wheeling on the others.

Maya gave me a thumbs-up and grinned. "Good as new!"

Rose and Yven nodded their approval, and even Wylan offered me a weak smile. But though I turned back to the mirror to marvel at seeing *me* in the glass, I knew I couldn't maintain the illusion. "How do I turn it off?" I asked Teolm.

"Just hold the pendant again and concentrate."

A flicker of will was all it took to restore the hated antlers, and I sighed as the mask fell away. "Easy enough," I said as I reached behind me for the clasp. "I'm afraid to ask what I owe you. Or is this a loaner? What sort of collateral do you want?"

To my surprise, Teolm smiled and shook his head. "This one's on the house. Wear it as long as you need."

"I can't—"

"Please." He gripped my arm until I stopped trying to unhook the necklace. "For all his faults, my father is an excellent craftsman. I'd prefer to see his work used for good."

I thanked him profusely, and our party started to leave. As we headed for the door, Teolm said to Wylan, "I'd heard there were only two victims of that potion in the city."

"There are," he replied.

He stopped and cocked his head. "Then——"

"Thanks again, Teolm," Rose interrupted, and hustled us into the night.

CHAPTER 10

Maya was not at all thrilled on Monday morning when Dup appeared in the café shortly after eight and quietly asked for Wylan and me to come upstairs, but she made do, scrawling paper signs asking for patience because we were temporarily short-staffed.

Not having anticipated an audience in the executive suite, we were a bit of a mess—I hadn't even remembered to remove my stained apron before jumping into the elevator, and Wylan, who'd spent a good portion of the morning rearranging the stockroom for Maya, bore streaks of flour down his pants from a slippery bag. Dup had the manners not to comment on our appearance, though he and his formal robe did maintain their distance.

When Dup escorted us into the director's office, I was surprised to find Syvin waiting there as well, sitting in one of Pateme's guest chairs with her arms folded and her hooves dangling a few inches above the floor. "Uh...good morning," I began, looking between her and Pateme for a clue about the summons.

"Good morning, Annie," said Pateme from behind his desk, then paused. "Wylan."

Wylan briefly lifted a hand in greeting.

"Have a seat," the director told us. "We're waiting on one more."

I did as he told me and kept sneaking glances at Syvin, but she remained a closed book.

A few minutes later, as Wylan was admiring the office with naked curiosity, a rap at the door heralded the arrival of the final guest. As an aide showed her into the room, Pateme went to his feet. "Thank you for making the trip. Something to drink?"

The little woman smiled in acknowledgement but shook her head. "Appreciated, but no," she replied in a high-pitched voice. It suited her: the woman was a gnome, barely more than three feet tall and perfectly proportioned, albeit in miniature. Though she appeared to be about my age, I knew that was no help in the Pactlands. She wore her white hair in a simple updo, and as she hoisted herself into the remaining chair, carefully tucking her embroidered robe out of the way, her pale blue eyes studied me.

"Kabno," said Pateme, gesturing toward me, "this is Annie Humphries, the...freelance investigator?"

"Private investigator," I amended.

"My apologies. And, um..."

"This is Wylan," I told the newcomer. "Incredible tracker, also backup in case my impressive muscles fail me."

She snickered at that. "You're not a sorcerer, I take it."

"No, ma'am, not in the slightest. I can throw a mean punch, and I'm quick on the draw with pepper spray, but that's about it."

Pateme took up the reins again. "Annie, Wylan, this is Kabno Erenani, the director of DOL. Kabno, you remember Syvin—"

"Of course, she interrupted, nodding to the silent chief deputy. "Is this a secure meeting?"

He gestured until the room's privacy spell triggered, and beams of red light swept across the ceiling and down the walls, protecting the room from snoops. "It is now. So," Pateme said, turning to me, "Rose called me last night about your offer. I understand that my nephew has loaned you a piece of masking jewelry."

I pulled the necklace from beneath my shirt, then held the disc and concentrated until my antlers vanished. "Works beautifully."

"For now," he muttered. "You're playing with fire, young lady."

"Lord ti'Cren said it would be safe for an hour or two—"

"That's his best guess, and he would defer to the judgment of our research team if pressed. But frankly, your experimentation may be the least of our bad ideas right now."

I removed the mask and tucked the necklace away. "What did Rose tell you?"

"That she brought you up to speed," he replied, and linked his hands atop his blotter. "You've worked a missing person case?"

"Not for law enforcement, but I've worked to locate people who'd rather not be found."

"Any abductions, or just runaways?" Kabno enquired.

"My mentor and I went after a father who'd grabbed his kids and left the country to avoid his ex-wife," I told her. "Fled Canada. He had family in central Virginia, and we tracked him down, then let the sheriff and the FBI do their job. Look," I continued, holding her gaze, "I'm not some grizzled veteran, but I do know the basics. If you're not going to try to find this woman, then I'll do what I can."

Out of the corner of my eye, I saw Pateme bristle, but Kabno remained unruffled. "This is hardly the situation I would prefer, Ms. Humphries," she said. "My preference would be a full manhunt and at least a few interrogations in our tower. Unfortunately, we're dealing with elves. No offense, Pateme, but you people don't make things easy."

"I never claimed Hall politics were simple," Pateme muttered. Turning to me, he said, "Consider Lady ti'Mal's position. That's a mid-ranking Hall, but she's new to the title, and she needs to show stability. If her daughter's been abducted, that's a terrible thing, and no one will hold it against the Hall. But if Fellora has decided to run away before her wedding to a *ti'Grell* boy, not only is that an insult to a higher-ranked Hall, but it shows that Lady ti'Mal doesn't have her Hall well in hand. That wouldn't just affect her standing or her younger daughter's social prospects, but the fortunes of *everyone* else in that Hall."

"So she's willing to take the risk that Fellora's being held by a psycho trying to make a skin suit?" I countered.

The directors flashed twin expressions of shock and revulsion at the notion, but Syvin murmured, "*The Silence of the Lambs*. It's available with subtitles."

"And it's based on real serial killers," I added. "I take it no one has seen Fellora skulking around the Tribunal building with a boyfriend this morning, right?"

"Correct," said Kabno. "I believe that you and I fear the same conclusion."

"Then let me help. I'm not DOL, and I'm not a known investigator. Take the antlers off, and I can blend in a crowd.'

"Unless you begin to have a bad reaction to the jewelry," Syvin interjected, and looked to Pateme. "Sir, you know how I feel about this."

"Your concerns are valid, Syvin," he replied, "and I certainly share them—"

"Then perhaps DOL could put delicate Hall sensibilities aside and do their job," she retorted, cutting her eyes to Kabno. "Our agencies have been relying *far* too heavily on untrained civilians of late. First Rose, and now you want to drag in Annie? *And* a Huntsman?"

"No one's dragging me," I countered. "I'm volunteering."

"Which gives me no less concern for your safety. For all we know, that girl was murdered, and her killer is still on the loose. If you go searching and find him, you have no natural defenses. Come on," she said, sliding forward in her seat to better stare me down, "unless Fellora went willingly, then we're dealing with someone who could overpower an *elf*. Not to be rude, but what chance do you have against that?"

I pointed to Wylan, who'd been listening quietly. "As I said, I'm bringing backup."

Wylan cleared his throat and angled himself toward her chair. "Ms. Deop, you don't trust me, and I understand. But if you have a killer on the loose here, I'm happy to help. Most of my existence has been devoted to hunting— let me put my skills to use."

"Give us a few days to see what we can uncover," I told Kabno. "DOL wouldn't be launching a big investigation, which would keep the family happy. Maybe we'll find something you can use."

She considered that for a moment, rubbing her chin in thought, then asked, "Your price?"

"Nothing. Er, well," I amended, "that is, we're not in this for payment, but if Wylan and I take a break from work to do this and leave Maya alone in the café, she's going to flip her lid. If one of your two agencies could fund some temporary help for her, that's really all we'd ask."

Kabno reached into a pocket of her robe and withdrew a phone scaled down for gnomish hands. "My niece and several of her friends just graduated, and they're raising money to open their own restaurant. Trainable, I would think, and probably not averse to a short-term gig. If this Maya wouldn't mind putting up with thirty-five-year-olds and their still-wet diplomas, I could probably have her sorted by tomorrow morning."

Chuckling, I said, "Maya's only thirty-two, so they'd probably fit right in."

Her eyebrows shot up, but then she remembered her audience. "Humans, yes. I tend to forget about the age thing. And I'm going to hate myself for asking, but you…"

"I'll be thirty in November."

Kabno winced. "Pateme, you didn't tell me she was that young."

"Older than Rose," he replied, but he didn't seem happy about it.

"I'm trained," I told the directors. "Licensed. I had a business before Roulette. And Fellora's still missing—what do you have to lose?"

They might not have liked it, but Kabno and Pateme finally agreed to give me a shot. But before Kabno could call her niece for café assistance, Syvin piped up. "If I may," she said, "let me be the overseeing agent. That way, should anyone look too deeply into the matter, Annie will be linked to DPP instead of DOL."

"That's fine by me," said Kabno, and Pateme nodded. Sliding down from her chair, Kabno asked, "Pateme, is your conference room open? I'd like to make the arrangements before I drive back to the office."

"Of course," he replied, and rose to escort her.

Once the door closed, Syvin stared at Wylan and me. "Here's the deal," she said softly, but in a tone that forbade argument. "I require *daily* updates. I don't care if you've made any progress—I want to be sure you're still alive. Understood?"

"Yes, ma'am," I murmured.

"Good." She stood, plucked a scrap of paper from Pateme's desk, and scrawled across it. "My personal number," she said, handing it to me. "You can call my office with updates, but in case of emergency, don't hesitate."

"Thanks," I replied, touched. "We'll be careful."

"You'd better be, kid," she said gruffly. "No one else is willing to talk *good* books with me."

Soon enough, Dup returned to show us out, but Wylan caught me by the wrist once we were alone in the lobby. "Something wrong?" I asked.

"Just a question," he replied. "You, um…when you told them you were almost thirty…were you serious?"

I laughed in spite of myself. "Yeah. We don't live as long as the folks over here, you know, so I'm a full-fledged adult back home. Why?" I asked, but seeing his face work, I suspected the cause of his sudden unease. "*Oh*…let me guess, you came into existence at some point significantly before I did?"

He looked more uncomfortable by the second. "Yes."

"Dare I ask?"

"Do you really want to know?" he countered.

"Well, now I'm curious."

Wylan folded his arms self-consciously and mumbled, "I'm eighty-nine."

"That's all?" He frowned, surprised, but I just shrugged. "Look, you tell me you're some sort of immortal being who was never even properly *born*, and I have to assume we're playing with different time scales. Come on," I said, and tugged him toward the café. "If Maya sees us loitering here, she'll pull out the deboning knife."

Kabno was better than her word. Around ten-thirty, four strangers walked into the café, all hopeful smiles. They came dressed casually and presented a mixed bag: a dark-haired faun sporting a blue bandana and a gold hoop like a wannabe pirate, a violet-skinned nymph of indeterminate gender—nothing new there—with tied-back locks of indigo blue, an eight-foot troll with a complexion like cement, a black mohawk, and tusks topped with decorative red enamel caps, and at the fore, a gnome in child-sized denim overalls who wore her hair in pink pigtails. "Hi!" she said, standing back from the counter so that she didn't disappear beneath its lip. "My aunt said you might be looking for some short-term workers?"

The gnome, as it turned out, was Dili Erenani, fresh from school and desperate for real-world experience. After watching her and Maya chat for five minutes, I could tell the two would get along like a house on fire. While Dili needed a stepstool to work, she rattled off a number of culinary and food safety certifications she'd achieved during the last years of her education, and the twitching in Maya's wings betrayed her excitement at the new blood. I worked out of duty, Wylan out of desperation, but Dili *wanted* this.

With her had come three of her best buds from school, all similarly certified and eager to pitch in. The troll, a guy who answered to "Frog," was more than willing to handle the heavy lifting if it meant a chance to help in the kitchen, while the faun, Korek Shilg, proudly informed Maya that he'd worked the espresso machine in their on-campus café and could make the standards by memory. And then there was their shy fourth, Makera Gannae, a water nymph who barely spoke above a whisper but explained that her true passion was microbrews.

Maya wasted no time putting them to work, freeing Wylan and me to sneak off with the dossier Kabno had sent to my phone that morning. She didn't give me much, just the names of the immediate family, their address, and Fellora's place of employment, but it was a start. I dropped Wylan at his apartment to put on clean clothes, then drove home, hastily made myself presentable with nice black pants and the lone gray blazer I kept in the back of the closet, and picked up my partner for the trip out of town.

At least there was no arguing over the driver's seat. Wylan had readily confessed that he didn't have his own vehicle because he'd never had occasion to learn to drive one, and he seemed quite content in the shotgun seat, watching the buildings shorten as we left the downtown area and headed for the portal.

There were two sets of portals in the Pactlands. The external portals, the passages home, were off-limits to me and to most citizens. Agents who had business outside were given credentials, as were the growers who migrated beyond the artificial world to better cultivate the exotic plants necessary for potion-making. Apparently, if you had enough money and power, you could buy your own credentials on the black market, but this was severely frowned upon by the higher-ups in the Pactlands government and punishable. Those of the Pact who went outside needed to avoid detection by curious humans, and so, for obvious reasons, casual sightseeing was forbidden as a danger to society.

The internal portals were another matter. Airplanes didn't exist within the Pactlands, but both public and private vehicles could make use of the portals that connected the major cities. Maya and I had each been given a pass in case we wanted to have a look around outside the capital, and we'd employed them on occasion—often enough for me to know how the system worked, at least.

Beukal's internal portal building resembled an Interstate toll facility, ten lanes of inbound and outbound traffic that could turn into absolute gridlock at peak times. Each lane came equipped with a barrier arm, and past that hung an open portal, a hole in space that flashed with colors like a laser show. As the traffic needs changed, portal directions could be switched, and so each lane was topped with a digital sign indicating whether the portal was outbound and where it led. When Wylan and I drove up, half the lanes were steadily disgorging traffic into Beukal, and I maneuvered into the line for the portal to Kelomb.

Wylan read through the notes on my phone while we waited our turn. "I thought we were meant to go to Hiranta."

"We are," I said, inching forward as the lead car slipped past the arm.

"But this is the line for Kelomb."

"Yeah. The portals are on a hub-and-spoke system," I explained. "Big cities connect to other big cities and to slightly smaller places that are close by, and eventually, you make it to your destination. We'll go through to Kelomb, then circle the facility and catch a portal to Hiranta."

"This sounds overly complicated."

"Try catching a flight sometime."

Traffic cooperated, and soon enough, we took our turn and drove straight into Kelomb. A return lane welcomed travelers with other destinations, and I steered us into the lane for Hiranta, which was nearly empty that morning. Within a few minutes, we were on our way through the grassy rolling hills typical of the Pactlands, a giant prairie almost devoid of trees.

"Where to?" Wylan asked.

I reached for my phone, closed the portal guide, and opened the map. "We're about a ten-minute drive away. Watch the directions for me, eh?"

Right on schedule, I pulled off the main road and onto the long brick driveway leading to a home I might have thought to be Georgian in design, though flanked with turreted towers and painted forest green. I parked the van beneath a tall overhang—some of the nicer homes I'd seen around Beukal used them to keep visiting vehicles shaded, as sheltering trees weren't an option—then pulled down the visor mirror and held my pendant until the antlers disappeared. "Are you going to be okay?" I asked Wylan.

He nodded and held up my phone. "I should know this case better than you do by the time you return."

"We'll see about that," I teased, then passed him the keys, slid down, and straightened my shirt. The canvas satchel on my shoulder carried only a notepad and a few pens, and I'd made sure that nothing on my person bore any agency insignia.

When I rang the bell, an elf with dark, worried eyes, a long blond ponytail, and a silk robe that had to cost more than the café's monthly coffee bill met me at the door. "Are you…" he began, waiting for me to volunteer the correct answer.

"Annie Humphries," I said, forcing a polite smile. "Mr. ti'Pon?"

"Yes. Come in, please," he replied, stepping aside and quickly shutting the door behind me. "Did you see any reporters lurking out there?" he asked, peeking through the thin windows framing the door.

"No, sir. No other vehicles."

He sighed softly. "Good. They've been unrelenting, but I think they may be getting the hint by now that there won't be any interviews forthcoming. This way," he said, and strode past me across the foyer and down a corridor.

I scrambled to keep up with his long steps as he led me into a windowless sitting room. Two women waited within on one of the couches, a blonde sporting a dark blue robe and an updo of pinned-back curls, and a younger blonde beside her—a teenager, I saw on closer inspection—in a far more casual knee-length red dress. They looked up eagerly as I entered, and then my guide triggered a spell like the one on Pateme's office to protect us against eavesdroppers.

As he locked the door, I headed for the women. "Lady ti'Mal," I said, nodding to the elder of the pair. I'd seen her enough on television to recognize her face, and so few elves had curly hair that she stood out in a crowd. "I'm Annie. Director Erenani told me about your daughter. I might be able to help."

"Have a seat," she murmured, gesturing to the facing couch, and her husband joined me as I lowered myself to the brocade cushion. "DOL explained your offer this morning. If you believe there's something you can do…"

The room wasn't particularly well lit, but it didn't take a spotlight for me to make out the look of sick grief on Fellora's parents' faces. I knew it all too well from some of my clients back in Virginia, the ones whose kids slipped off in the middle of the night with an unsavory significant other and stopped answering their phones. Much as I wanted to throttle Fellora's parents for their reluctance to throw every public resource into locating their daughter, I didn't think they were faking their distress at her absence.

"This isn't my first missing person, and I've got a decent track record thus far," I told her. "What I'd like to do is get some information from you, then see what leads I can find and follow—all with the utmost discretion," I added. "Sound good?"

She nodded, and I pulled my pad from my satchel. "First question: tell me about Fellora's engagement."

Lady ti'Mal sighed and rubbed her forehead. "Everything's been smooth to this point. Camun is a sweet boy, and Fellora seems deeply in love with him."

"So this *is* a love match?" I prodded. "Not a political pairing?"

"Love," her father insisted. "Noiana and I married for love, and we want the same for our daughters."

"Within reason," Lady ti'Mal amended. "We don't want them running off with, say, fauns—"

"Or ti'Vans."

She grimaced. "Socially appropriate love matches, you understand," she explained to me.

I jotted a few notes as the two of them spoke. "Don't quiz me on Hall standing, but I get the picture. Any reason to believe that Fellora was having second thoughts?" Lady ti'Mal shook her head, and I glanced to her husband. "Mr. ti'Pon?"

"It's Janon," he said, "and no. She's been swept up in wedding planning for months. I've never seen her so happy."

At that, their other daughter finally spoke. "Fell had maybe two days of doubts, but that was way back at the beginning of the engagement, after a few of Camun's aunts told her she wasn't good enough to marry him. He said he didn't care about those old bags—"

"*Keef*," her mother sharply interrupted.

The girl shrank back into the cushion. "Sorry. But they *were* horrible to Fell. Anyway, she and Camun got past that, and she's been excited ever since."

"You're pretty close to your sister?" I asked Keef.

She nodded. "She's always around. Takes me places, lets me meet her friends. She's...pretty great," she mumbled.

Turning my attention back to the parents, I asked, "What does she do for a living?"

"She's at the Museum of Fine Art in Beukal these days," her mother replied. "A docent. She's always had an interest in art, and she gives tours."

"She did one for my class last year," Keef interjected. "Knows a *ton*."

"And she was happy there?" I pressed.

Both parents nodded. "It's a prestigious position, especially for someone without advanced specialization in art," Janon told me. "Fellora has been considering pursing a graduate program, perhaps in conservation. A more practical dimension to her interests."

"But she's been very happy at the museum," Noiana insisted.

I cut my eyes to Keef, who was gnawing her lip. "You don't think so?" I asked the girl.

She hesitated once her parents' gazes fell on her, but she found her courage after a brief pause. "Fell likes it a lot, and she's got some great coworkers, but her boss is a cretin."

Her mother leaned closer, the better to glare at her. "*Keef*, what have we told you—"

"He is!" she insisted. "I don't care about his Hall, he's a creep!"

I waited, but with the parents staying mum, I focused my attention on Keef. "Tell me about him."

"Katoun ti'Lir," she muttered, folding her arms. "His uncle is Lord ti'Lir, so he's not in the main line, but he's close. Fell says he acts like he's a freaking ti'Dana."

Not for the first time, I mused that a cheat sheet of the elven Halls wouldn't be a bad thing to have on hand. Hall ti'Dana was top of the heap, but ti'Lir…

"Forgive my ignorance," I said, "but where does ti'Lir fall, relatively speaking?"

"It's an old Hall," Noiana murmured. "Perhaps on a level with ti'Grell, though ti'Lir claims prominence as a northern Hall."

"Thanks," I told her, and looked back at Fell. "So does

he just think he's better than everyone around him, or does he think he's God's gift to women?"

Despite the tension in the room, Keef cracked a smile. "Both, to hear Fell tell it. He tried to take her out to dinner on her first day there. She rejected him every time, but he wouldn't stop pestering her...and then she and Camun got engaged and he *still* won't leave her alone. Keeps hinting that even if she goes through with the marriage, she'll have thirty days to come to her senses and choose a better man."

I made a face. "Gross. Has anyone else been bothering her?"

The parents shook their heads, but Keef snarled her nose. "She's mentioned arguments with two of her friends from school. I think they're jealous over the wedding."

My pen continued its rapid scratching. "And who would they be?"

"Lunile ti'Van," she said, and I caught Noiana's subtle flicker of distaste. "They've been friends forever, but things have cooled since Fell and Camun made it official. I know Fell sent her an invitation, but Lunile would probably feel out of place at the party."

"Why is that?"

"Ti'Van," her father interjected, "is one of the *new* Halls."

Ah. The elven aristocracy hadn't liked it one bit when their inferiors had arrived in the Pactlands, realized they were all equals under the law, and banded together in Halls of their own, conglomerations of multiple families with perhaps a few common ancestors or adjacent lands. I'd met at least half a dozen ti'Vans in the café, and on asking two of them whether they were cousins, I'd been rewarded with hearty laughter.

"Where could I find Lunile?" I asked.

Noiana's lips tightened. "She...works in hospitality."

"Oh?"

"A bar," Keef translated. "Delight. It's in Beukal."

"And how would you know where it is, young lady?" Janon demanded.

Keef held up her hands to keep him at bay. "Fell told me it's in the capital! I've never *been*, Father."

Mollified, he relaxed back into the couch, and Keef rolled her eyes. "So that's Lunile," she continued. "And then there's Mitti Fanco."

The surname surprised me. "Not an elf?"

"Sorcerer. She and Fell used to compete on the track team together, and she works at a sporting goods store...in Beukal, I think. I *know* she and Fell had a fight recently—I heard Fell yelling on the phone when she was here, but her door was closed, and I couldn't tell exactly what the fight was about—"

"What have we told you about listening at doors?" her mother said with a long sigh.

"Paid off now, didn't it?" Keef retorted. "Anyway, all Fell would say was that Mitti was being a brat. That was two weeks ago."

"Thanks," I said to Keef, and looked back and forth between the parents. "I know this might be painful, but take me through last Wednesday. What do you know about Fellora's movements?"

When the two of them hesitated, Keef quietly said, "She texted me just after seven. I was getting ready for school, and she told me good morning and that she was going hiking at Green Lake..." Keef reached under her knee, where she'd hidden her phone, and scrolled through her messages. "The trail with the blue triangles. I don't know anything about it—I don't *hike*," she said with a grimace—"but Fell always lets me know when she's going out there, just in case. So I told her to have a good time, and I went to school, and, uh..." She swallowed hard. "That's the last I heard from her."

Considering that Fellora had been missing for five days, I understood why Keef wasn't in class that morning.

Janon picked up the thread. "Camun called us around

six when she wasn't at her apartment. They were planning to go out to dinner that night. He came by to pick her up, but the lights were off and the door locked. No one had seen her all day. I told him she wasn't here. About half an hour later, he called us again from Green Lake. Her car was still in the lot…"

I looked down at my notes, giving him a moment to compose himself. "Be honest with me, all right?" I asked once I was relatively sure that Janon wasn't about to cry. "Can you think of *anyone* she might have been seeing on the side? Someone you wouldn't have approved of?"

The parents took a moment to consider the question, and then Noiana said, "No. She had a secret boyfriend when she was fourteen. We found out and forbade it, but she insisted they were in love. It didn't last the year."

"Inferior Hall?"

"No…he's a centaur. Nice young man, married two years ago. His parents are lovely people, and we all agreed that it wasn't a good idea, but we stepped back and let it run its course."

Given the physical concerns such a pairing would raise, I could understand where the parents had been coming from. "No one else?" I pressed.

"No," said Janon. "Fellora has only had a few boyfriends, and we've liked them all."

The two turned to Keef, who shrugged. "Don't look at me. If Fell's hiding someone, she hasn't told me about him."

I wrapped up the interview shortly thereafter, armed with a few names to investigate. Fellora's parents gave me pictures of their daughter, while Keef, who seemed much better informed about her older sister's social life, raided Fellora's room for snapshots of her friends, plus a group photo of the museum staff. "That's Katoun ti'Lir," she muttered when her parents were out of earshot, and pointed to a dark-haired elf in the center of the photo. "Seriously, he's a cretin."

Thanking them for their time, I took my leave and hurried back to the van. "Hi!" said Wylan as I climbed in and buckled up. "Any luck?"

"We've got leads." I glanced at the house, but as no one had come out to see me off, I removed the mask and started the engine. "Three people to look into off the bat. I want to start tonight. Have any plans?"

Wylan's smile turned predatory. "Now I do."

CHAPTER 11

"You look nice," said Wylan as he joined me in the van that evening.

"Wrong season, but thanks." My lone sundress was becoming less appropriate by the day, and I'd only be able to transition with a dark wrap over my shoulders for so long. I'd thrown on black knee-high boots in an effort to make the ensemble slightly more autumnal, but the outfit still felt a bit like laundry-day desperation.

And then there was Wylan. While his wardrobing choices were unpredictable—the leather leggings still made appearances—he looked good in just about anything he threw on, and he happened to be sporting my favorite jeans that night. Pity that I wouldn't get to enjoy them.

I'd easily tracked down an address for Delight, and my plan was to go in, have a drink, and see what I could learn about Lunile ti'Van. With any luck, she'd be on duty and feeling chatty. Even with the antlers masked away, I couldn't quite blend—I'd learned to hide a lot of my natural accent when speaking Pactish, but traces of my drawl slipped through, and the best I could do by way of an explanation was claim to be visiting the capital from some far-flung town. Hardly perfect, but that was the ammo at hand.

The bar wasn't too far from Wylan's place, on the cusp of the uncomfortable side of walking distance, but we needed our ride. As Wylan couldn't go inside without causing a scene, I'd be on my own in the bar, while he'd watch the door and come to my aid if I needed backup.

At least he'd be waiting for my call. I'd realized that afternoon that Wylan had no phone, and after leaving Fellora's family, I'd swung through an electronics store to find a cheap one for him. By evening, he only had Maya's and my numbers programmed in, but he was taken with the camera feature and promised that he could entertain himself while I looked for Lunile.

I parked in an alley with a view of the bar and held my necklace to trigger my mask. "Wish me luck," I said, tossing Wylan the keys, and headed off for my night out.

To my relief, Delight wasn't a strip club, nor was it the sort of venue that specialized in pounding bass loud enough to dislodge fillings. The place seemed classy: decent illumination, two-top and four-top tables of varying heights with tea lights for atmosphere, and an inoffensive instrumental background soundtrack low enough to allow conversation. Roughly half the tables were occupied by couples or groups of friends, and two of the four-tops had been pulled together for a laughing party of young women—mostly sorcerers, though I noticed an elf and a centaur in the mix.

And no one was staring at me. Hell, the other patrons didn't seem to have noticed my entrance. No one was whispering and pointing, no one was going bug-eyed and backing away...

God, I'd missed anonymity. Suppressing the giddy laughter that tried to break forth, I headed toward the action.

The main bar was located at the back of the building, a long, dark wooden counter lined with stools. A massive mirror had been mounted on the wall behind the bar, and translucent shelves almost made the bottles of colorful liquor appear to float. Seeing mostly men at the bar, I girded my loins and pulled up a stool on the far end, the better to observe in peace.

Two bartenders danced around each other, mixing and pouring without so much as jostling a shoulder in passing.

The male of the pair was a sorcerer with a shorn head and short, dark beard, handsome in a hipsterish fashion, while the female was an elf—and *stunning*. Blonde and easily six feet tall, with sharp, perfectly white teeth, she flitted among the men as she made their drinks, seemingly engaging them all in simultaneous conversation.

Her appearance, I surmised, was probably a mask. Oh, elves could be very pretty, but the bartender's proportions were too fantastic to be natural—as thin as she was, her perky C-cup chest couldn't have occurred of its own accord. Elves and sorcerers could mask without jewelry, and since putting together a mask took less time than applying liquid eyeliner, those with a creative streak or good, old-fashioned insecurity masked in public.

As the female bartender was preoccupied with her attentive male customers and the male bartender was busy handling the rest of the bar's orders for the waitstaff, I examined my options and bided my time. I could be patient. But when a few minutes' wait turned into nearly a quarter of an hour without a drink, I found it increasingly difficult to hide my annoyance. Thus, when the male bartender approached, he led with an apology. "I'm so sorry about that," he said, and swept one hand toward the tables. "We're understaffed tonight. Our third broke her arm yesterday, and the healers haven't released her to work yet. What can I get you?"

He sounded exhausted, and I smiled to clear the air. "Glass of wine? I'm not picky."

"And you're my new favorite," he replied, pulling a bottle of pale golden liquid from beneath the bar. "Haven't seen you here before."

"Passing through. Thanks," I said as he slid a half-full glass toward me. "Your colleague seems pretty popular."

He glanced over his shoulder at the elf, then turned back to me with a snort. "Nothing new there. After a drink or two, some of them think they stand a chance with her, and she likes men enough to pretend that one of them might get lucky someday. Truth be told," he continued, leaning toward me and lowering his voice, "she prefers women, but those desperate fools make better tippers." Giving me a once-over, he added, "If you're interested, I'll slip her your number."

I sipped to buy time. "Appreciated," I told him, "but I've got someone waiting for me."

He winked and stepped away to make up a pitcher of a cocktail that would surely give anyone but a troll a nasty hangover.

As I drank, trying to remain conscious of how long I'd been masked, I kept sneaking glances at the elf. After a few minutes of observation, I got lucky. "Hey, Lunile," one of the men slurred, "when do you leave tonight?"

"Later than you do, dear," she replied with an impish grin. "Drink up, now. Don't you like that cocktail? It's my *specialty*," she said, drawing out the word as she bent just enough to give him a hint of undiscovered breast.

The guy might have been drunk, but he had sense enough to throw back his drink and ask Lunile for another one, and she quickly obliged.

When the sorcerer returned to check on me, he seemed tired but pleasant. "Long night, huh?" I said.

He nodded. "Indeed. So, since you're alone this evening, what brings you out this way?"

I segued into a story I'd previously deployed to great effect and tweaked for the occasion. "My boyfriend's parents."

"*Ooh*," he groaned with a sympathetic wince. "They don't approve?"

"No, they seem to like me well enough, but they're...a *lot*. I came to town to spend a week with him—I'm based in Kelomb, and our schedules can be pretty wild, so neither of us is ready to deal with the portals on a daily basis just yet. But his parents also live here, and we spent all weekend with them. Nice people, but they have so many questions, and I feel like I just survived a two-day interview."

The bartender chuckled. "Sounds like my family. My wife almost broke up with me after I brought her home to meet them."

"Fortunately, I got some breathing room today," I continued, "and my boyfriend and I were going to have a nice night out...but he's stuck late at work, so there's my romantic evening gone. His mom called, and I'm seeing an old friend right now," I said through a poker face. "A *very* old friend. Couldn't possibly blow this off to have dinner with his parents. No, that just wouldn't work."

I drained my glass for emphasis, and the bartender reached for the bottle.

"Better not," I told him, covering my glass with my hand. "Maybe some water first. I'm kind of a lightweight," I added, faking an embarrassed laugh.

He obliged. "They really drove you to drink, huh?"

"No, it's just...you know, different city, I don't know many people here, and my guide is still in the office. Honestly, a long walk's usually all I need to recalibrate, but after what happened to that hiker at Green Lake last week..." I took a sip of water, then shook my head. "Silly, maybe, but I just don't feel comfortable wandering around in the dark right now."

To my surprise, he reached across the bar and gripped my free wrist. "You're not being silly at all," he murmured, leaning closer to me, and I moved in to meet him in the middle. "If my wife told me she wanted to go for a walk by herself right now, I'd have her head examined. The monster that grabbed that poor woman is still out there, and until he's found..."

"You think she was abducted, too? That she's not eloping?"

He cut his eyes toward the other end of the bar, where Lunile was still swarmed by her adoring fans. "Come with me," he said, and pointed to a dark corner near the bathrooms.

Curious but on my guard, I followed him, then realized why he'd chosen that spot. The music was softer there, and with the shadows, it was an ideal place for a quick, semi-private conversation.

"The woman who disappeared, Fellora?" he murmured. "School friend of Lunile's. Engaged to a great guy—Lunile's been telling me about the wedding planning. Says she's never seen Fellora so happy."

"Is she invited to the wedding?" I asked, feigning surprise. "That's going to be quite an event, isn't it?"

"I don't know," he admitted. "Things are complicated. Hall politics, probably—I don't understand elves sometimes, I really don't," he added with a sigh. "But Lunile's been a mess since she got the call last week."

I frowned. "The call?"

"From the fiancé. Last Wednesday night. He called everyone he could think of to try to find Fellora, and so Lunile's known she's been missing since before the news publicly broke. She offered to come back early and join the search, but he said not to—there hasn't been a massive search of the park yet, as far as I know."

"Lousy way to end a vacation," I guessed.

The corner of his mouth ticked. "I wouldn't call it a vacation. Old Creek Vodka held a training seminar in Ananila all day Wednesday—it's a little resort town in the Edolis," he added as my brow furrowed—"and our boss sent Lunile and me. Nice trip. Drive out, see the scenery, learn about the new products, get a demonstration from one of their mixologists, and then enjoy a fancy dinner at the hotel restaurant. We'd planned to stay overnight and come back Thursday."

"Sounds weird to have an event like that in the middle of the week," I said.

"Eh, that's practically my weekend," he replied. "Anyway, we were at dinner, and she stepped away from the table to take the call from the fiancé. Came back in hysterics, and I sat with her in her room until she calmed down." He glanced toward the bar, but if Lunile had noticed our departure, she paid us no mind. "She took Thursday night off, and Lunile *never* misses work," he murmured. "She's worried sick about her friend. Been putting on a brave face and doing the job, and she's one hell of an actress. Maybe those guys falling all over themselves at the bar can't see the difference in her, but I can. Anyway," he said, and cleared his throat. "Sorry, didn't mean to unburden on you. Guess I was trying to say you've got good instincts. I wouldn't go walking in the woods right now."

"Thanks," I told him, "and don't worry about it."

We returned to our positions, me to my stool and him to his mixing. He poured me a fresh glass of water without asking, tossing the one I'd left behind before I could give it a taste, then brought me a second glass of wine. I drank it slowly, though I kept an eye on the time, not wanting to push my luck with my mask. Once I'd finished, I caught his eye to settle up, left a generous tip, and started for the door.

I hadn't gone ten feet from the bar before someone grabbed my arm, and I spun around to see Lunile behind me. "Hi, sorry," she said in a rush, releasing me. "Are you leaving?"

"Uh…yeah," I replied, forcing a small smile. "Yeah. Better get home before my boyfriend misses me."

"You came alone, didn't you? Do you have a ride? Are you parked nearby?"

Gone was the laughing, flirtatious blonde, and in her place, I saw a woman genuinely concerned for another's safety. Her eyes had turned serious, and she nibbled on her bottom lip, which, up close, looked ragged beneath her lipstick.

"My friend is here to pick me up," I said, and clasped her shoulder. "But thank you, I appreciate it."

Satisfied, she nodded and let me make my exit, and I hurried across the street to my waiting van. "How was it?"

Wylan asked as I climbed in. "Learn anything?"

"Lunile's working tonight, and she's got an alibi that would be *easy* to check. Out of town last Wednesday, and her coworker says she's taking Fellora's disappearance hard. I don't get the sense that she's involved with—"

"Hold that thought," he interjected, and pointed to the bar. "See that man? The one in the brown jacket?"

I squinted into the darkness. A man—I couldn't tell if he was a sorcerer or an elf—leaned against the brick, watching as one of the women from the big group walked home alone.

"He's been lurking for the last hour," Wylan muttered, "and I know a predator when I see one. Excuse me."

"What are you doing—" I began, but he was already out of the van and jogging across the street. At a loss for a better plan, I ran after him.

Wylan didn't dawdle. The man had barely begun to follow his target when Wylan grabbed him and slammed him into the building. I arrived in time to catch a glimpse of the man's face as he noticed who was holding him off the ground with a hand to his throat, and as he gasped and stopped struggling, his crotch began to darken.

"Leave her be and *go home*," Wylan ordered, and dropped him.

The man fell like a sack of potatoes, then scrambled to his feet and sprinted in the opposite direction of the woman, who walked on oblivious to the danger behind her. Wylan wiped his hands on his pants, and with the crisis averted, we started back to the van.

"You did a good thing," I murmured, nudging him in the arm.

"I don't like sneak attacks," he replied. "Especially on a weaker target."

"She's a sorcerer, remember. Defensive magic is an option."

He grunted and headed for the passenger door. "Not if she's knocked unconscious first."

I slept in on Tuesday morning, and though Maya teased me on her way out the door in the wee hours, she didn't complain. Around six, which felt like a decadent hour for a weekday, I got up, made coffee, and sat down to find my next suspect.

Keef had suggested that Mitti Fanco had fought with Fellora over the phone shortly before Fellora's disappearance, and that Mitti worked at a sporting goods store in Beukal. That left me with a number of options, as the capital and its suburbs didn't lack for shopping. But luck was with me that morning as I dug in on my phone. The Pactlands had its own internet separate and protected from the one I knew, but their search engines were easy to navigate, and a request for Mitti's name turned up several dozen results. I found news clippings about her school track meets and her many victories, even a picture of her and a much younger Fellora with their sweaty arms slung around each other's necks. Mitti was built like a gazelle, with long legs and lean muscle, and a few crooked teeth made her smile all the more endearing. She wasn't a showstopping beauty like Lunile (or Lunile's mask), but she had a friendly, open face.

I was into my second cup of coffee when I found Mitti's employer. Social media hadn't taken hold in the Pactlands as it had back home, which had complicated my search, but the local news pointed me straight to her via a column about a junior running club for kids. The sponsor was a store called Enik & Gemet, which had been supplying the capital's athletic needs for well over two centuries. The story included quotes from the brains behind the initiative—one Mitti Fanco, a manager at the location in Old Farm.

I knew about Old Farm only because so many of the agents with families lived out there. The city center was for the young or single; Old Farm, Beukal's former breadbasket, was close enough to the heart of the capital to make the commute bearable but sufficiently far to allow for detached houses and yards. The area was nice, if somewhat blandly suburban, and like most good suburbs, it offered a modest commercial district.

Wylan surprised me when he showed up around eight, and with breakfast, no less. "I wanted to see if I could be of help," he explained as he stood in the den, taking in the relative splendor of our apartment. Beside his run-down unit, Maya's and mine looked like a Manhattan penthouse. "Figured food was a good place to start."

He'd swung by the café, both for sustenance and to confirm my address with Maya, who, he reported, was in high spirits. Her new foursome of minions ran circles around Wylan and me, and Maya had even had time to step aside and chat during the morning rush. "She looked...composed," he told me as I unpacked our breakfast sandwiches. "Almost relaxed. Wearing less flour than usual."

I filled him in on my snooping while we ate, and then I slipped off to my room for a few minutes to make myself presentable. A button-up shirt and leggings did the trick, and I decided that my hair wouldn't fall out in protest if I went a few hours longer before showering. If Wylan noticed a funk, he was polite enough to keep his observations to himself.

By nine, I'd parked in a free lot across the street from the strip mall where Enik & Gemet's outpost had taken root, and I pulled down the visor to watch my mask coalesce. Once the antlers vanished, I considered my reflection for a few seconds, then willed myself blonde.

Wylan laughed in surprise at my additional transformation. "Dare I ask?"

"What, you don't like it? I'm *teasing*," I quickly said as panic flashed across his face. "Just a precaution. I really don't think Lunile and Mitti are going to be comparing notes about me, but it can't hurt to vary things up a little." Giving myself another look, I shifted my eye color toward brown, nodded, and grabbed my purse. "Let's see about some shoes. I'll be back as soon as I can."

I hadn't thought that Tuesday morning would be a particularly busy time. What my pre-breakfast searching hadn't revealed, however, was that Enik & Gemet had a robust customer loyalty program, and that day happened to be a major early-bird sale for their preferred shoppers. By the time I got inside, no fewer than eight women were demanding attention in the shoe department, all desperate to be checked out before the sale ended at ten, and the two clerks on duty were hustling. One, a faun decked out in a pink tank top with coordinating tape around her ankles, ran back and forth between the stockroom and her antsy customers. The other was in worse shape, a tall, dark-haired sorcerer who hobbled around the department with her left foot in a black medical boot. Sneaking peeks and comparing her to the photos I'd seen online, I knew that had to be Mitti—particularly once her associate called her to the register for a manager's override. She looked a little older than Fellora now—maybe in her late twenties, to my eye—but for a sixty-year-old sorcerer, that was par for the course.

Though my clock was running on the mask, I couldn't cut to the front of the line. The women around me were of the sporty sort, some fairly aggressive in their demands, and I feared that any attempt to come between them and deeply discounted sneakers would end in violence. Instead, I inspected the display shelves and considered the variety of shoes on offer: ordinary-looking running shoes, minimalist options, shoes promising magical blister control or defense against shin splints. Three shelves were devoted to troll-sized options. A round display catered to centaurs with reinforced whole-hoof coverings in a variety of colors and patterns, while the adjacent table offered similar products for fauns…though judging by the measly three shoes on display, the faun hoofwear market wasn't booming. Moving among the displays, I thought I'd stumbled into the children's department until I realized I'd found the selection for gnomes.

Forty-five minutes later, as the faun checked out the last of the sale shoppers, Mitti found a moment to catch her breath and limp over to me as I studied the running shoes. "Good morning," she said with a tired but professional smile. "Something you'd like to see?"

"Do you have any of these in the back?" I asked, pulling a moderately priced pair from the shelf. I did need new shoes, I told myself, and the odds were decent that I could get these on DPP's dime. "I don't know my size, I, uh...fluctuate," I added lamely.

"Not a problem," she said, then whispered and gestured at my feet. Lime-green numbers flashed in the air above my toes, and she considered the shoes I'd chosen. "If I may make a suggestion?"

"Sure."

"Those aren't going to serve you well. You have flat feet, and you overpronate. Something with arch support would be kinder to your joints. Did you like the shape of those shoes? The materials?"

"Uh...the color," I admitted sheepishly.

Mitti grinned and plucked another pair from the display. "How about these? Better suited to your feet and less expensive."

When she returned from the stockroom with a pair to try, I took a seat and slid off my old loafers. "I'm sorry to put you to the trouble..."

"What trouble?" she asked, handing me a ball of socks.

I pointed to her boot. "That can't be comfortable."

"Better than you might think," she replied, pulling out a stool for herself. "I had surgery a week ago today. The healers do wonderful work, but I was off my feet until Saturday. This is a vast improvement."

"Accident?" I asked.

"No, no, this was planned. I was born with skeletal deformities in that foot. Used to run and hike all the time, but the pain got so bad that I had to stop."

I grimaced in sympathy. "No potion to improve that, huh?"

"My problems were more than a potion could fix," she explained with a sigh, "but I've been putting off surgery for years because I worried that something would go wrong and leave me worse than before." She chuckled to herself. "Silly, right?"

"Nah. I hear you about not wanting surgery," I said, and laced up the left shoe. "Hope you have a speedy recovery…"

"Like I said, this is *such* an improvement already, and my three-day postop scans showed remarkable progress. But thank you. How does that feel?"

"Good." I quickly put on the right shoe, then stood to test the fit and marveled at how on the money Mitti's recommendation had been. Better yet, she had another easily verifiable alibi. If she'd been recovering from foot surgery on the day of Fellora's disappearance, then I doubted she'd been involved, much less skulking around a wilderness trail. Still, I decided to pry. "You said you hike?"

"Not lately, but sure. Once this boot's off and the healers clear me, I'll be back at it. Take a few steps, now, check the fit in the toes."

I did as she ordered. "Any suggestions for places to go? I'm new to town, and I've been looking for some nice spots for trail running. Sidewalks are *passable* but not great, you know?"

"Absolutely."

"A friend of mine mentioned good trails at Green Lake, but I haven't been out there yet. Any thoughts?"

Mitti winced at the name, then vehemently shook her head. "No. *Don't.* Haven't you seen the news lately?"

"Been moving and unpacking," I lied, and shrugged helplessly. "Why, what's going on?"

She glanced around the store, but by then, the satisfied throng had taken their lightened wallets elsewhere. "Last week, one of my friends went hiking out there. She disappeared."

I did my best to feign shock. "Oh, my gosh…"

"Yeah," she murmured, her voice suddenly shaky. "No sign of her yet. No body, but…" She hunched on her stool and stared at the floor, then blurted, "She's supposed to get married next month. I was invited, but she's been so busy with wedding planning that we've barely seen each other in ages."

"I'm so sorry," I said, touching her shoulder. "Are you…"

When she lifted her head, her eyes glistened, and her mouth twisted like she was trying to hold back a sob. "No, I…*I'm* sorry, I…"

"Come on," I gently insisted, and helped her off her stool. She allowed me to lead her back into the stockroom, and she covered her mouth with her hand while she pulled herself under control.

"I'm sorry," she mumbled again once her breathing steadied. "I thought I was past the 'crying jags at work' phase, but—"

"Your friend is missing. This is understandable, okay?"

"It's not just that." She leaned against a wooden shelving unit stacked high with shoeboxes and folded her arms. "We had a fight about a week before she disappeared. Stupid shit. I told her I was having my surgery, and she said she'd try to visit but couldn't guarantee anything because of plans with her fiancé's family, and I…I was scared, yeah? And I snapped. Said she'd changed since she got with her fancy rich guy. If I was going to cramp her schedule, she shouldn't bother calling. And she said I was being unfair and she's stressed, and we both said…well, *I* said some things I regret before ending the call. But that was the last time I spoke to her, and now…"

I had a fairly well-tuned meter for bullshit, and Mitti wasn't setting off my alarms. "Maybe she got lost," I said.

"People get lost in the woods, right? Fell down a ravine, twisted her ankle, a little sunburn, but she'll be fine."

It sounded weak even as I said it, and my attempt at reassurance failed. "Not Fellora," said Mitti, shaking her head. "She knows the trails at Green Lake like her own name, and she always travels prepared. For her to vanish like that...." She shuddered, her arms tightening against each other. "Either she had a fatal accident out there or someone grabbed her, I'm sure of it. She wouldn't run off like some of the reporters are speculating. But I wouldn't be caught dead out there right now, *especially* not alone. The trails are nice, but—"

"Not worth the risk," I finished. "Thank you, I mean it."

"Sure," she started, but her control was weakening again, and before she could catch herself, a sob escaped.

Maybe Mitti's shoe department colleague knew what was going on and stayed out of the stockroom to give her some space, or maybe the early sale had done in their customers for the day. In any case, no one bothered us while Mitti cried, and when I tentatively hugged her, she whimpered and squeezed me in turn. But as I held her and patted her back, I noticed a weird itch on my scalp, centered around my masked antlers, and looked around the stockroom for a clock. I'd been masked for about an hour and fifteen minutes, I realized, and the sudden itching told me I needed to get a move on.

By the time Mitti calmed and wiped her face dry, the itching had grown more pronounced, but I did my best to ignore it and focus on her. She checked me out, even giving me a ten percent discount, and I hurried from the store with my new shoes in a paper shopping bag.

Wylan waved as I approached the van, then unlocked the doors and rolled up his window. "Any sign of her?" he asked.

"Oh, yeah. She's broken up over Fellora, and she was on bed rest after surgery most of last week. I don't think she's caught up in this."

Dropping my mask, I turned out of the lot and headed back toward the city center, but to my dismay, the itching didn't subside. If anything, it worsened as we rode along, until finally, I pulled up at a red light and leaned toward Wylan. "Do you see anything on my head?"

"Besides your antlers?" he asked bemusedly.

"Scalp."

He carefully parted my hair around the base of the antlers, then sucked a breath through his teeth. "Red and swollen. Did you use something different on your hair?"

"No, this itching started in the store, and it's not letting up. *Great*," I muttered, and pulled out my phone.

"Who are you calling?"

"Syvin. She'll want an update, and maybe I can distract myself."

The chief deputy picked up on the second ring. "Are you safe?"

"Back in the van with Wylan," I reported. "I've talked to two of Fellora's friends, people her sister identified as folks who might have been on the outs with her. Both have alibis."

"Give me the details, and we'll double-check. Any other leads?"

"Her boss. I'll try to make contact tomorrow."

"Good. How's the mask working out?" she asked.

I thought about fibbing, but the skin around my antlers had begun to burn. "It's doing the trick, but now I have this weird scalp itch, so either I'm allergic to athletic shoes or keeping the mask on for more than an hour leads to side effects."

To my surprise, Syvin sounded sympathetic. "How bad is it?"

"Ever had a mosquito bite?"

"Of course."

"Well, kind of like that, but, say, a dozen of them..."

"Go home, Annie," she ordered. "I'll meet you there."

CHAPTER 12

Twenty minutes after I returned to my apartment and headed to the bathroom to stick my head under the cold shower, Wylan answered a knock at the door and admitted Syvin. Hearing her voice over the spray, I hastily threw my fuzzy robe on and draped a towel around my shoulders to catch the worst of my dripping hair. "That was fast."

"The office isn't that far," Syvin replied, marching past Wylan with a paper bag in her hands, "and the healers keep this around."

I cocked an eyebrow. "You see a lot of folks with itchy scalps in there, do you?"

"Not at all," she said as she extracted an unmarked plastic bottle full of green goop. "The healers maintain a bit of a pharmacy for us—numbing potions, bandages, pills for indigestion. And since anyone who's been around a young faun knows how miserable horns can be when they first grow in, the healers stock this in case someone gets a frantic call from home."

Taking the bottle from her, I watched the liquid ooze around the inside and frowned. "They hurt?"

"It's like cutting teeth. Horn buds stay below the skin until the baby's a few months old, and then they erupt. That's the worst of it, but as the bases of the buds widen, you get some discomfort. Itching, tenderness, occasional burning."

I winced at the thought.

Syvin rapped her knuckles against one curling horn and grinned "No pain now, of course, but I remember how miserable they could be when I was little. This is an *old* remedy. It does the trick, and my mother swears by it, but there's a slight drawback…"

By then, I'd popped the cap and caught a whiff of the stuff, which assaulted my nose with an acrid funk stinking like lake muck, rotting plants, and warm garbage.

"The scent's not great," she said as I recoiled. "I'm sorry about that. A few brewers have tried to neutralize or cover the odor, but in my experience, that only makes the bouquet worse. On the bright side, it'll clear your sinuses."

"But do I *want* them cleared right now?" I countered.

She chuckled. "Trust me, the relief is worth the stench. Rub that in, let it sit, and don't plan to go out for the rest of the day. Plastic wrap over the treated area helps." Gripping my robe lapels to pull me closer to her height, she gave me a zero-arguments-allowed look and added, "*No* masking until your scalp heals, understood?"

"Yes, ma'am," I mumbled.

"Good." With that, Syvin released me, nodded curtly to Wylan, and saw herself out.

As the door closed behind her, I sighed, opened the cap again, and grimaced. "You're not going to want to stick around for this," I told Wylan. "I'll see you tomorrow, okay?"

But he shook his head. "What are you going to do all day, sit here alone and stink? I'm not working—I could at least keep you company."

"You've got freaking super-smell," I protested. "If I'm next to gagging with this stuff, then you're going to be miserable."

"I can clean carcasses," he assured me. "My nose has experienced worse. Come on, sit."

Wylan coaxed me into taking a seat on the edge of the tub, then gently moved my wet hair around until he saw the extent of the irritation. "How bad is it?" I asked, staring at the tiled floor and resisting the urge to scratch my skin bloody.

"Not great. Let's see what this gunk does."

"Hold on," I said before he could squirt it out, then stood and rummaged in my medicine cabinet until I found my bright idea: the half-full pot of Vick's VapoRub that Rose had pulled from my home bathroom for me. It had to be a decade old, but it smelled as potent as ever, and menthol beat the odiferous mixture in Syvin's bottle. I smeared a generous dollop under my nose, and Wylan followed my lead. "Tingles," he said, twitching his upper lip.

"It's harmless," I replied, washing my hands, then sat on the tub again and closed my eyes. "Okay, hit me."

While the Vick's couldn't completely hide the stench, I managed to not throw up while Wylan carefully massaged the goop around my antlers. By the time he returned from the kitchen with a roll of plastic wrap, the stuff was working—the burning had ceased, and the itch had subsided to a less than maddening level. Wylan did his best with the roll, leaving me badly wrapped, damp, and smelly but feeling better.

And yeah, my poor sinuses had never been clearer.

"Do you want a cup of tea?" I asked as Wylan wriggled the plastic wrap back into its box.

He smiled, his philtrum still glistening with its protective coating, and followed me to the kitchen.

I put the kettle on and readied a pair of mugs with teabags and packets of sweetener while the water came to a boil. As I worked, Wylan said, "Tell me more about Mitti. You think there's no chance of her involvement?"

"I mean, never say never," I replied, "but if her alibi checks out, she wasn't even walking on the day Fellora disappeared. Plus, I got a look at her hands and forearms—no scratches."

"It *has* been nearly a week…"

"I know, and healing potions can work quickly, but the fact that she doesn't seem to have wounds weighs against her having anything to do with this."

"Unless she hit Fellora from behind."

"Fair. Which is why Syvin left too quickly," I said, and called her.

She picked up after the first ring. "Did the salve work?"

"Pretty well," I replied, leaning against the counter as the first wisp of steam escaped the kettle. "I should have given you the details on those potential alibis earlier, shouldn't I?"

"Eh, no time like the present. What do you need?"

Wylan poured the water and steeped the tea as I filled Syvin in on Fellora's friends' movements. When I finished, she said, "The hotel won't be difficult to verify. I know Ananila, and it has exactly one property sufficiently large to host an event like this alleged vodka seminar. I'll call DOL and have one of their investigators run it down. Now, medical records are slightly trickier—"

"Privacy issues?"

"Of course. But surgeries and other major procedures are logged and flagged in the reg, so—"

"Huh?"

She chuckled. "Sorry. We have a central register for medical issues. That way, no matter which healer needs to treat you, your history is accessible. Ordinarily, you need to be a healer or have an order from a tribunal to access the reg…"

When she left that thought unfinished, I prompted, "But?"

"But my baby brother is one of the reg's maintenance clerks, and he owes me *several* favors. I should be able to verify the girl's story without a significant headache."

I frowned. "Sounds great, but would that not be illegal?"

Syvin paused. "There's illegal, Annie, and then there's *illegal*, if you understand me. Besides, I got my brother community service when he was caught with enough psychotropic drugs to land him in jail for a decade. He's grown up a lot in the last century, but he still owes me, and he knows it."

With Syvin on the job, I put my phone aside and sipped my tea. "Not bad," I told Wylan. "Have you considered a career in the restaurant business?"

He smiled at my lame joke and joined me when I headed for the kitchen table. "How's your scalp?"

"Much better. Not back to normal yet," I said, prodding at the plastic covering, "but not driving me crazy anymore. It's just…ugh," I muttered, and lifted my mug.

Wylan watched while I sulked with my drink, studying me as I scowled into space. "Are you frustrated about Fellora or about something else?"

"Both, I guess." When he didn't rush to fill the silence, I explained, "I wish one of the two friends had given us a clue. Tomorrow, assuming I don't stink like sewage, I can look into Fellora's boss, but a short suspect list makes me nervous."

"Mm. What else is on your mind?"

I puffed my cheeks and exhaled slowly, looking away. "The mask."

"It works—"

"Only for an hour at a time! Keep it on too long, and I end up like this," I muttered. "I know, I *know*, everyone said there might be side effects, but…"

"You were hopeful," he murmured.

I nodded. "Maybe the experts would be wrong, and I'd be able to mask well enough to go home…or at least look like myself around here. Guess not."

He hesitated, and I could almost see him selecting his words before he spoke. "How does it feel when you mask?"

"Before the itching starts, you mean? Feels great—"

"No, not physically," he amended. "You feel, uh…normal?"

"Yeah," I said softly. "For a little while, it's like Roulette never happened. That's *me* in the mirror. And people don't stare at me when I walk in a room. They don't whisper or cross the street, they're just...nice. Polite. Friendly. In the last day, I've gone out to a bar and gone shopping in a normal store where no one knows me, and I haven't done that in *so* long, and it was freaking amazing to be ordinary. Guess I'd forgotten what that feels like." I drank my tea while my half-formed thoughts coalesced. "But now I know I can't have that feeling all the time. I'm still cursed. And yeah, it was stupid to pin so much hope on the mask, but..."

"You're disappointed."

"That's a mild way of putting it," I said, and raised my mug again to hide the quivering in my chin.

Wylan had the grace to glance away while I pulled myself together, then said, "I noticed your television. Want to see what's on?"

All afternoon, Wylan stayed with me on the couch as we stared at the finest weekday programming the Pactlands had to offer: game shows, a marriage counselor, and a talent contest for teenagers. Syvin called to confirm both alibis—Lunile was seen at the hotel multiple times on the day in question, while Mitti wasn't even discharged from recovery until early that evening, when her brother drove her home with heavy pain potions. But other than that, the two of us vegetated for the rest of the day.

As dinnertime approached, Wylan called Maya at the café to suggest that she stay out late. "Annie's fine, but the apartment stinks right now," he explained. "It's Syvin's doing. Perhaps a leisurely dinner elsewhere would be a good thing." When I assured Maya that I wasn't about to combust, she agreed to go out for a while—after all, a coat was all she needed to hide her thoroughly inoffensive wings.

While Wylan picked up dinner for the two of us, I unwrapped my head and showered, scrubbing and shampooing until the bathroom smelled like coconut-scented pond muck. I was drying off when he returned, and I sat on the edge of the tub, wrapped in my towel, as Wylan inspected my head again. The swelling had almost subsided, but the area around my antlers was an angry red and raw, and so Wylan gamely reapplied the salve for me.

"Thanks," I said, holding my towel closed as he worked. "You know, I never expected antler care to be part of my regiment."

"The good news is that they mostly take care of themselves," he replied, squirting another dollop of the foul gunk into his palm.

"Mind if I ask a dumb question?"

"Go ahead."

"Do you ever shed yours? Like, you know, deer lose theirs in the winter…"

I fell silent, hoping I hadn't offended him with the comparison, but he kept massaging my head. "No, they don't drop. They grow and can break, and I've had to file down broken prongs on occasion, but they're always with me." His fingers rubbed lightly around the most irritated places. "I don't know what I'd do if I woke up one morning without a rack. Panic, perhaps," he said, chuckling. "It's difficult to imagine my antlers not being there. *Weird*."

"No masking for you, then," I said, glancing up to catch his eyes.

He sat beside me on the tub, his hands still slick with salve. "I was born like this, Annie. Or, uh…well, I came into being like this, if you prefer," he amended. "You didn't. If our positions were reversed, I'm sure I'd be as unhappy as you are with a reflection you don't quite recognize."

I sighed. "Don't mean to be a downer…"

"I don't mind. But, um…" He paused, then blurted, "May I say something without getting punched?"

One of my eyebrows rose. "Okay…"

Wylan slowly exhaled as if steeling himself. "Annie…I

realize you feel uncomfortable with your antlers," he said softly, "but I think you're beautiful—with or without them, that is," he hastily added. "What I'm trying to say is that you don't look monstrous. At all. And yes, perhaps I'm somewhat biased, but—"

I darted forward and silenced him with a kiss, catching a faint whiff of Wylan's scent beneath the omnipresent stench of Syvin's cure-all. As he deepened the kiss, his hands sought my shoulders and pulled me closer...and then I yelped and retreated as I almost lost my towel.

"Sorry, sorry," he mumbled, then groaned. "Shit, I forgot that my hands were dirty..."

Glancing in the mirror, I noticed fresh greenish patches glistening on my bare skin and laughed in spite of myself.

With that, the moment was well and truly past, and Wylan slunk out to let me clean up in peace. I rinsed off, plastic-wrapped my head, and emerged in my far more secure bathrobe for dinner.

He didn't try to kiss me again as we ate, and I made no overtures—honestly, it's difficult to feel sexy when your head smells like rot and resembles a plate of leftovers secured for the fridge. But I caught his small, secret smile once or twice, and he lingered in the kitchen after we'd cleaned up.

I didn't want him to go. We had the apartment to ourselves, and regardless of whether it was wise, I was developing feelings for Wylan. I'd just decided to try to ignore my less than lovely appearance and shoot my shot with him when I heard the front door open, and Maya swept in. She made it three steps into the foyer before she stopped in her tracks, covered her nose, and gagged. "What the hell is that *stench*? Did something die in the vents?" she demanded.

"Try the Vick's. It helps," Wylan suggested, and nodded to me. "See you in the morning, Annie."

He slipped out as Maya, coughing, hurriedly opened every window in our apartment and ran to the laundry room for the bottle of imported extra-strength air freshener.

One week. Fellora had been gone without a trace for a full week, and that boded nothing good.

With the pit in my stomach making sleep an impossibility, I rose around two and hit the bathroom. I'd allowed my head to stew in the goop for hours, and I cringed as I picked away the wrappings to see the damage. Tying up the refuse in a garbage bag for quick disposal, I jumped in the shower and stood under the hottest water I could muster, willing my pores to open and accept the coconut milk shampoo instead of the funk. After a second shampoo for good measure, I stepped out, toweled off, and wiped the steam from the mirror to inspect my scalp.

Not bad. A little red around the base of the antlers, but I'd had worse sunburns.

I threw on my robe and tossed the stinking trash, then caught Maya coaxing the coffeepot to life and shuffled into the kitchen. "Smell my head, will you?"

Sometimes, if you're very lucky, you find a friend who'll do weird, stupid shit for you. Maya and I had reached that point of familiarity after nearly a year together, and she stuck her nose between my antlers without hesitation. "Better, but nope. Wash it again."

I groaned. "Maybe my shampoo's not strong enough. What do you think, vinegar? Tomato juice? Vinegar *and* tomato juice?"

"Skunk removal solution."

"You've got a bottle of that floating around?"

"Nope, but I know the formula. Got sprayed on a Girl Scout trip one summer, and I made myself memorize the ingredients, just in case. Get the bottle of hydrogen peroxide from under my bathroom sink, will you?"

When I returned with the goods, Maya had measured out dish soap and baking soda in a plastic pitcher, and she added the full bottle of hydrogen peroxide and mixed it up. "Go shower *now*," she said, shoving the pitcher into my arms. "While this stuff is fresh. Work it in and leave it for at least five minutes, and try not to get it on any fabrics."

Hydrogen peroxide wasn't the most soothing liquid I could have put on my scalp that morning, but I washed as directed, then conditioned heavily. When I emerged and presented my head for a second smell test, Maya deemed me fit for polite society, then headed out to open the café. "Got to see about my minions," she said, grinning.

"Still working out?" I asked.

"Delightfully. You and Wylan may be out of a job."

"You're a real pal," I called as the door closed behind her, and Maya laughed as she took her leave.

Clean but up far too early to go snooping, I settled in for some online research to see what I could learn about Fellora's job.

The Museum of Fine Art was part of an educational complex just north of downtown, four buildings around a grassy quadrangle with picnic pavilions and a small stage for outdoor performances. Flanked by a history museum and one devoted to the history of magic, the Museum of Fine Art was open daily from nine until six and offered four sprawling levels of galleries: landscapes, portraiture, sculpture, textiles, jewelry, paper, glass, metalwork, and even ceremonial items. One gallery was devoted to pieces of art that moved or shifted colors with the aid of magic, and while ambulatory sculptures seemed neat in principle, I decided to avoid that room unless I brought backup. The museum's information portal offered biographies of its founders and primary patrons, and I noticed Teolm ti'Cren's name in the list—apparently, not all of Hall ti'Cren's charitable giving had ceased with its former lord's arrest. After a few pages of biographies of the major artists represented came the staff listing: the executive director, artistic director, educational director, and a host of other people with their names in large, bold type, followed by the smaller names of the people who presumably did more of the hands-on work. In the left column, about two-thirds of the way down the page, I found my target—Katoun ti'Lir, Assistant Director of Education, Visitor Relations.

The museum didn't offer photos of its staff, but given Hall ti'Lir's prominence, Katoun wasn't difficult to locate online.

The luminaries of Hall ti'Lir had their fingers in a number of pies: a foundation supporting artistic residencies and retreats, several musical associations, a publishing house, an anti-bulling initiative of middling success. Lord ti'Lir had what I'd come to think of as a typically elven look: straight brown hair to his mid-back, loosely tied and tucked behind his ears, impossibly high cheekbones, a clean-shaven chin, and a parade of expensive, heavily embroidered formal robes. He never seemed to wear the same one twice. His eldest daughter, the presumptive heir, was her father in feminized form, but other family members appeared in the occasional picture with their lord: his wife and younger children, his siblings, an aunt who colored her blonde hair various pastel shades, and a number of cousins, nieces, and nephews.

Katoun stood out in a crowd. Tall and slender, he wore his black hair relatively short, though it often cascaded over one eye when he tilted his head and grinned for the camera. His robes tended to be less ornate—he liked dark solids, tasteful without too much flash—though he accessorized with rings and the occasional gold necklace. But what I noticed after the third photo was the pattern in his companions at social events. I couldn't have named any of his dates had there been a gun to my head, but they fit a physical mold: pretty blonde elves tall enough to rest a cheek against his shoulder and fix the photographer with a plump, playful smile. The women all wore their hair long and loose, and most had large brown eyes fringed with thick lashes.

Fellora would have fit right in.

I waited until sunrise to call Wylan, who chirped a greeting far too chipper for the hour when he picked up. "Boss has a type. No wonder Fellora's sister thinks he's a creep—he never seems to go out without a leggy blonde on his arm."

"Hm. Think we could bait him?"

"You read my mind," I replied, swirling my third cup of coffee. "But I'm going to need a little help on that front."

Fortunately, Rose had set aside the morning for painting instead of practicing magic with her tutors, and she didn't mind driving in from the ti'Dana mansion in Viratta.

"Pop says hello," she reported as she breezed into the apartment around seven-thirty, "and he wanted to remind you to be careful out there. Ooh, do I smell coffee?"

I'd kept a pot on for hours, hoping the scent of French vanilla would mask the lingering odors of air freshener, artificial pine candles, and that godawful salve. To my relief, it seemed to be working. "Want a cup?"

"Please."

"Did you tell him what we're doing?" I asked, heading for the mugs.

"Didn't have to. Pop and Pateme had a long talk after we visited Teolm. How's the masking necklace working out?"

"Decently," I said. "There's a definite time limit on how long I can use it—"

"Is it shutting off?" she asked.

"No, my head just turns into a swollen, itchy mess if I go more than about ninety minutes."

"*Annie*—"

"It's fine," I insisted. "No luck on the farsight end, huh?"

A frustrated huff answered *that* question. "I was going to try drawing again today, see if I can't get past the block, but that's almost certainly not going to work."

Wylan sat beside her and offered a reassuring smile. "You might surprise yourself."

"Unlikely. I took Awakening yesterday, and no luck."

He cocked his head. "Awakening?"

"It's a potion kind of like magical LSD—a drug," she clarified as his brow creased—"but it can be helpful for beginning farseers when used sparingly. Pop authorized it for me in the first place, but he doesn't like it, and he babysat me while I tripped."

"So you didn't start licking the walls?" I guessed.

She snorted and accepted her coffee from me. "Not quite. When you come down, you're left with an excruciating headache…which would have been worth it, had I been able to see anything. No dice. So," she said, raising her mug, "what's so sneaky that you couldn't discuss it over the phone?"

I pulled out the chair opposite hers and steepled my fingers. "Need to pass for an elf. My target's more likely to talk to me if he wants to get in my pants."

"Uh-huh," she replied with a dubious frown.

"You could help me put together a mask, right? I mean, hell, you live with elves—"

"Oh, sure, but the mask isn't the problem. How's your Low Elvish?"

I stared at her for a few seconds as the realization sank in. "*Shit.*"

"They're all perfectly fluent in Pactish, but they default to the 'old speech' around each other. Now, we could find you another of those language potions, but there's no way of knowing how you'd react. You might get a moment's dizziness, or you might lose consciousness for a few days."

"Don't have time to risk that."

"I figured. Plus, as I'm sure you've noticed with your Pactish, it does nothing for your accent. Even if you could speak Low Elvish, you'd blow your cover the moment you opened your mouth." But as my shoulders slumped, she asked, "What if we got you close? Do you know his preferences?"

Wylan nodded and slid her the stack of waiting papers. "Here, Annie printed reference photos."

Rose flipped through them and whistled. "Yeah, I'd say he has a type. We can work with this...but we're going to need more than a mask."

"What else?" I asked.

The smile she flashed showed entirely too many teeth. "I'll know once we've been shopping in Maya's closet. Come on."

The world looks different from atop platform heels.

I'd seldom seen the need for extra height. At five-foot-eight, I wasn't a basketball star, but neither did I need stripper heels to get my money's worth at an amusement park. While I'd learned to walk in heels—my mother had insisted—I hardly ever wore them unless I was in a wedding party and couldn't get away with ballet flats.

But Maya was three inches shorter than me, and when she wasn't baking in sensible shoes, she loved to give her feet a little panache. Spikes, peep-toes, strappy sandals that made one think of bondage gear—she'd built quite the collection, and Rose had sneaked into her closet back in Richmond to bring over her favorites. Maya's feet were dainty little things, sixes beside my solid nines, and so I'd never dreamed of rummaging through her shoes before that morning. But I had masking jewelry now, and that meant I could disguise my foot to Cinderella my way through Maya's stash.

It also meant that I'd had to leave the apartment masked, as I'd have been driving barefoot otherwise.

Rose, operating on the theory that Maya would forgive the intrusion, had directed me to give myself a couple extra inches, turn my hair platinum blonde and wavy, and flip my green eyes to chestnut brown. She deemed my chest passable—I wasn't particularly endowed, and elves skewed flat—but she fussed over the rest of my curves until I could have strutted down a runway in feathered wings and a diamond-studded bra. After a few additional touches—raising my cheekbones to the top range of normal human levels, removing my moles, thinning my eyebrows, and puffing up my lips like I'd paid for a minor injection, or maybe just suffered a bad bee sting—she zipped me into one of Maya's soft green dresses, which looked flirty on her and dangerously short on my augmented body. A brown bolero and a knotted purple scarf made the ensemble slightly more seasonal, and I'd have thrown on boots and been done with it had Rose not returned from Maya's room with three-inch platform pumps in brown suede and a twinkle in her eye.

When she dragged me out of my bedroom, tottering on the carpet and tugging at my barely-there hemline, Wylan just gaped.

We took it as a good sign.

With the clock ticking, I burned rubber getting to the museum, and Wylan cracked the windows as I slid out. "Happy hunting," he said, opening one of Syvin's paperback mysteries. "Try not to fall, eh?"

I stuck out my tongue and slammed the van's door.

Sashaying up the green marble steps and into the museum, I did my best to remain upright and paused once I'd reached the vaulted entry hall. Between the plentiful windows and the translucent glass ceiling, the building was filled with light, and I stood off to the side for a moment, taking it in. But I didn't have long to linger—I needed to find my target, and if I wanted to avoid another night in plastic wrap, I had to get a move on.

While I knew virtually nothing about Pactlands artists, I could feign appreciation for a painting as well as the next schmuck, and I decided to take a tour in hopes of spotting

Katoun. Unfortunately, the first tour didn't leave until ten, but the smiling gnome behind the desk was happy to give me a fold-out guide and recommend the special exhibits. I thanked her and set off on my slow trip through the galleries, pausing on the pretense of admiring the sculptures and trollish folk instruments to cast my eyes around the room for my elusive assistant director.

As luck would have it, however, he spotted me first.

I'd stopped just inside a gallery of nautical landscapes—an odd subject for the Pactlands, a place with no sea to speak of—to watch a group of schoolchildren on a tour. The kids couldn't have been more than ten, and while the docent, a sorcerer, had the patience of a saint with them, some of the boys ignored him in favor of playing a game of surreptitious tag. I smirked as they slipped around the room's support pillars, trying to avoid each other and their teacher's attention, but when one started to run a little too quickly, the teacher, a naga, struck out with her muscular serpentine tail and grabbed him around the waist as he passed, yanking him off his feet. With a firm squeeze and a stern look from her, he slunk back to the pack, and his fellows quickly did likewise.

"They're so rambunctious at that age, aren't they?" murmured a low-pitched voice near my ear.

I twitched and spun toward it, only to find myself inches away from Katoun. He dropped a wink at me and grinned as the docent led the children onward. "There's a reason that *he's* giving that tour instead of me," he added.

Recovering, I tried to play along. "If that were me, I'd be requesting combat pay."

Katoun's smile widened. "I'll see if I can't slip him a bonus."

"Oh!" I took a step back and pressed my fingertips to my mouth in mock surprise. "I'm so sorry, I didn't realize you were in charge here..."

"Mostly just for tours and talks, I assure you." His eyes quickly traveled from my chin to my toes, then landed on the pamphlet in my hand. "First time here?"

I *hated* playing the dumb chick—it wounded my professional and personal sensibilities. But my mask had been on at least half an hour by then, and to be fair, I really knew nothing about the art on display. "I'm new in town," I said, flipping my hair over my shoulder. "My friends said I should check this place out, but..." I let slip what I hoped came across as a helpless little sigh. "I am *so* bad at art. And the tour isn't until ten, so I thought I'd try to make the best of it while I have a free hour..."

"Well," he said with an exaggerated glance at his watch, "I have nowhere to be until ten, as it turns out, so might I be of service?"

I tried to add extra wattage to my smile. "You're sure you wouldn't mind?"

"Not at all. Katoun," he said, and took my hand.

"Namia—oh, my," I replied with a giggle as he kissed the backs of my fingers. "This is a real treat."

His blue eyes twinkled. "The pleasure's mine. Shall we? Let me show you the highlights."

Giving credit where it was due, Katoun knew his stuff...or if he didn't, you couldn't have proven it by me. He stopped in front of paintings and sculpture and display cases, rattling off interesting facts about the art's provenance and meaning without so much as glancing at the informational placards, and I smiled and nodded as my scalp began to tingle. Sure, there were better ways of seeing an art museum—hustling through the galleries in platform heels and a short dress with the guide's hand creeping toward my elbow or the small of my back wasn't exactly *ideal*—but I made a note to return once I was off the clock and tried to ignore the warning signals of mask overuse.

As Katoun wrapped up the whirlwind tour, I offered him a little golf clap, and he took a bow. "I do hope you'll visit again when you have more time to browse," he said, walking with me toward the elevator. "We barely skimmed the surface of the offerings here. I admit that I'm *slightly* biased, but I promise you this collection is worth savoring."

While we waited for the car to arrive, I nibbled my oversized lower lip. "Listen," I said in a flustered rush, making a point to twirl my hair, "I never do this, and I know we just met, but...like I said, I'm new in town, and you seem really nice, and...any chance you might want to get a drink sometime?"

The elevator chimed, and he offered me his hand as I tottered aboard. Once the doors closed, he said, "I'm flattered, Namia, *sincerely*, but my girlfriend might object."

Girlfriend?

"Oh, my gosh," I said, hand to my chest, "no, of course, I didn't mean—"

"No, really," he hastened to reassure me, flashing his perfectly white smile once again, "I'm flattered. Forgive me if I'm overstepping, but a woman like you should have no trouble making, uh...*friends* in Beukal."

Faking embarrassment, I glanced away and bit my lip once more. "You're kind to say so. In any case, thank you so much for the tour."

"No, it's I who thank you. I seldom have the chance to give them these days, so I appreciate the opportunity."

The elevator opened on the ground floor, and we headed down the long, sunlit hall toward the main doors. "Too bad. You're really good at them. Why don't you give tours more often?"

Katoun chuckled softly. "I oversee the docents, and that's a job in itself. But we're down a docent right now, so I'm giving a full tour at eleven. I'm taking a few minutes to meet my girlfriend and buy a baby gift for her brother first," he whispered. "This way, we can't stay out shopping all day."

"Sneaky. I like it," I replied. "And I'm sorry, it's such a

pain when people quit unexpectedly."

I let the thought hang, and Katoun paused before he spoke again. "She hasn't quit. Have you, uh…have you seen anything about the woman who went missing at Green Lake?"

I stopped in my tracks, feigning shock. "The hiker? She works here?"

He nodded, but his expression hardened. "She's been missing a week, now. Seems like DOL is sitting back, drinking tea and hoping she comes wandering out of the park on her own."

"I heard she ran away from her wedding—"

"That's *nonsense*," he scoffed. "Fellora adores that lunk she's marrying. She could do so much better—she's so much brighter than he is—but that's love, I suppose. There's no way she'd have fled, and if she had a boyfriend on the side…well, the docents talk. I'd have heard rumor of it by now." He cleared his throat and smiled again, though it seemed strained. "I apologize, that's not your problem—"

"No—*no*," I insisted, gripping his arm, "no problem at all. I'm sorry to hear she's still missing. Hope DOL finds her safely soon."

"Hope they start looking," he muttered, but his mood brightened in an instant as a stunning elf stepped through the door. Statuesque, leggy, blonde, brown-eyed, wearing a simple dress that probably cost more than my rent back in Richmond—check.

Katoun hurried over and kissed her, and though she smiled at him, she looked askance at me as I headed for the exit. "You must be Katoun's girlfriend," I said, putting on my friendliest face. "Just as lovely as he was telling me." Her expression softened, and I nodded to Katoun, who looked relieved. "Thank you again for the quick tour. I'll be sure to come back another day and do the rounds with a docent."

I slipped out and hurried toward the van, my head

itching like I'd picked up a bad case of hives. Jumping into the driver's seat, I unbuckled Maya's shoes and removed the mask, making my borrowed dress ever so slightly more modest but at a real risk of seam splitting.

"Did you find Katoun?" Wylan asked as I ran my fingernails over my scalp and sighed in relief.

"Yeah. He's got a gorgeous girlfriend—I don't think he's caught up in this."

His eyebrows rose. "Didn't you say the sister thought he was a creep?"

"Sure. He's handsy, a little flirtatious, and he thinks Fellora's making a mistake, but he seemed happily involved with another woman. Frankly, I think she's prettier than Fellora. And if he's sneaking off from work to go buy baby gifts with her, then he's probably somewhat serious. We can keep an eye on him, but I'm not getting kidnapper vibes."

Wylan mulled that over as I drove us out of the parking lot. "How's the head?"

"Itchy, but not as bad as it was yesterday. If I leave the mask off for a bit, maybe it'll settle down without the salve."

He grunted, which was fair—I feared that my salve-free plans were wishful thinking. "So, now that you've rejected the three people the family named, what's our next move?"

The logical answer to that, as I saw it, was the fiancé.

As I sat on the edge of the tub, letting Wylan slather my head with salve, I called Fellora's mother and relayed my findings. She passed along Camun ti'Grell's number without hesitation. Lady ti'Mal explained that he worked as an accountant for a large firm in the capital, which made me question either the firm's hiring choices or Katoun's conclusion about the man's intelligence, but at least Camun took my call. Having already been filled in about my work on the case by Fellora's parents, he offered to clear his schedule, but I begged off until five, giving my scalp time to calm and me time to deodorize.

When Wylan finished his ministrations, I offered to make us brunch and retreated to the kitchen with my wrapped head, putting on coffee for the scent as much as anything. As the bag of refrigerated hashbrowns—one of Rose's special deliveries—fried in the skillet, I glanced out in the den to find Wylan pacing and scowling to himself. "Are you all right?" I asked. "Something bothering you? I'm sorry, the smell's still gross—"

"Just tense. Nothing to worry about."

"Are you sure?"

"Absolutely," he replied, and smiled.

His smile didn't reach his eyes, but I left Wylan to his thoughts, hoping food would cure whatever ailed him.

CHAPTER 13

I wasn't completely whole by my appointment time with Camun, and my head started tingling as soon as the mask went on. Even though I did nothing to augment my appearance other than hide my antlers, whatever magic was at work didn't care. Popping aspirin and raiding Maya's bathroom on the off-chance that an antihistamine would help—hell, maybe I was just allergic to masking—I headed out with Wylan riding shotgun to see what the fiancé could tell me.

Cofa Sisters occupied four floors of a skyscraper on the edge of the downtown district, a vaguely brutalist structure of pale concrete and thin windows. It wasn't what I'd have chosen, had I needed to house a wealthy company, but the building did overlook a large park and presumably cost less than the offices closer to the center of the action—probably a responsible choice for an accounting firm to make. I parked on the street across from the main entrance, giving Wylan a view of the joggers and the children's playground, then masked up and walked inside.

Camun met me when I stepped off the elevator and hurried me past the double row of closed doors into his office. Brushing off one of his pair of padded guest chairs for me, he took the other, which was then doing double duty as a clothes rack for a spare robe. I studied him briefly as he sat: about six feet tall, blond hair held in a braid falling halfway down his back, hazel eyes that were pretty even with the shadows beneath them. While elves in general didn't get my motor revving—I liked my men with a bit more meat on their bones—Camun was handsome, the sort of fellow for whom crackers in bed would *not* be a problem. He also looked like he hadn't slept in a week, so I could only imagine what the effect would be if he'd walked out fully rested and dressed to kill.

When he spoke, his voice was so soft that I had to lean closer. "Thank you for coming. Lady ti'Mal told me you were pursuing several leads…"

"None of which have panned out yet, I'm afraid," I replied, and his shoulders slumped. "But I'm not giving up—not by a long shot," I hastened to reassure him. "I've talked to Fellora's family, but I bet you know her circle even better than they do. What can you tell me?"

He paused, drumming his fingers on his knees as he considered the question. "You know about her job, yes?"

"Sure. I visited the museum this morning."

"Have you spoken with any of her colleagues? She and I go out with a group of docents once or twice a month."

"Just her boss as of yet…Katoun ti'Lir, right?"

Camun made a face.

"You don't like him, huh?" I prodded, trying to sound casual.

"Katoun…is very good at what he does," Camun replied with evident diplomacy. "He's smooth, knows how to work a crowd…excellent at small talk…"

I couldn't disagree.

"Fellora says he's highly knowledgeable about art, and I have no reason to doubt her. He certainly steers the conversation in that direction whenever he joins our outings. Personally…" He hesitated and raised an eyebrow.

"Go on, please."

He huffed with distaste. "The man's a snob. Thinks I'm some sort of drooling idiot because I can't debate the merits of every major portrait painter for the last half millennium. They're *portraits*," he continued, rolling his eyes. "Fine, very nice, but you can obtain a better representation far more readily with a camera—" A knock at the door, cut him short, and he excused himself to answer the summons.

As Camun sent the visitor on his way, I glanced at the framed papers on the walls of his office. Diplomas and certifications, almost certainly. Maybe he didn't know art, but the guy was no fool.

When he returned to his seat with an apology for the interruption, I said, "Keef hinted that Katoun might be upset that she's getting married."

"Oh, he's not thrilled," Camun replied with a weak chuckle. "I'm not good enough for Fellora, to hear him tell it. I'm sure he'd prefer that she find love with one of their patrons, someone wealthy *and* cultured."

"You don't think he has feelings for her, do you?"

Camun mulled that over, then said, "Not anymore. Perhaps once—she's a beautiful woman, and Katoun wouldn't be the first man to admire her. But he's been dating Remia since before our engagement..." His voice drifted off, and he regarded me sharply. "Why, did he say something?"

"No, that was just Keef's impression. Katoun is worried about Fellora—I could tell that much—but I saw him with his girlfriend, and he looked very much taken."

He relaxed slightly. "If I may ask, who else did her family suggest you pursue?"

"Lunile ti'Van and Mitti Fanco."

"*What?*" he scoffed. "No. They're her friends, they'd never hurt her."

"Then who would? Does she have any enemies? Rivals?"

"No, and that's the problem: I can't think of *anyone* who would want to hurt Fellora."

My next question would be difficult, but I tried for tact. "There's been a, uh...a suggestion made that Fellora might have run off. With someone, perhaps. I'm not saying that's the case, but do you think—"

"Never," he insisted, staring into my eyes. "I've never had a moment's doubt of Fellora's faithfulness. She loves me, and I...I can't imagine life without her," he said, his voice cracking. "She's the best thing that's ever happened to me..."

I glanced away while he took a few deep breaths, bringing himself back from the brink of tears.

"Fellora's brilliant," said Camun. "Funny, kind...I couldn't ask for more in a spouse. I can't keep up with her half the time, and she tolerates so much of...well, this," he said, flopping one hand toward his document-covered desk. "I'm not the greatest at parties and such, but she doesn't mind. And I..." Again, he stopped to struggle with his emotions. "I don't want to think of what life would be like without her. I've refused to consider it to this point, but with every day that passes..."

I reached out and took his hand, and he squeezed as he wrestled with himself.

"Thank you," he murmured. "For what you're doing. I understand why Lady ti'Mal has been trying to keep the investigation quiet, and my father agrees with her, but...that's *Fellora*. She hasn't run away, I know it."

"And I'm not giving up on her," I told him, squeezing his hand in turn. "All right? I'm going to keep searching."

"I appreciate that, but it shouldn't be you alone. Her parents should have insisted on a manhunt by now. I know their reasons for avoiding one, but if Fellora dies and they could have saved her by acting sooner, then I swear I'll never forgive them." Releasing me, he cleared his throat and stood. "I'm sorry, could I get you something to drink?"

"Water, if you have it."

He pulled two glass bottles from within a minifridge behind his desk, and I sipped while he drained his drink and stared into space. Once Camun seemed calmer, I asked, "No enemies that you can think of, right?"

"None."

"In that case, could you walk me through the route she took? Or point me toward the right trail, at least," I said, pulling a rough map of the Green Lake paths from my purse. "I'm not familiar with the park, but I'd like to retrace her steps, if possible."

"I can give you the detailed version," he replied, and pulled his phone from his robe pocket. "Fellora sent me her route before she went hiking. I've done it a few times with her, and I've been out there ten times in the last week, looking…"

"Maybe we just need fresh eyes on the problem," I said—trite, but Camun was so low that even that sentiment made him fractionally brighten. Passing him my map, I asked, "Could you draw it for me?"

He pulled a highlighter from a novelty mug on his desk—an incongruous hot pink cup printed with red text that read *Accountancy Adds Up to FUN!*—and carefully traced Fellora's route. "She loves this part right here," he said, pointing to a bend in the trail. "There's a bluff, and when the trees give way, the view is lovely…"

I hoped he wasn't picturing his fiancée's crumpled body at the bottom of the bluff.

With that thought, my memory dredged up an unpleasant scene from my childhood. My dad had taken me hunting in the Blue Ridge, but on our first day out, we'd been flushed from the woods by a pack of trained searchers looking for a missing kid. Dad had hugged me too tightly as we stood by his truck and watched the searchers unload a pair of bloodhounds, who were given the little boy's shoes to smell and set loose on long leads. I hadn't had to ask Dad what they were doing—I was old enough by then to understand how search dogs worked—but that was my first time seeing them in action. That night, as Dad and I sat in a diner eating cherry pie to make up for the disappointment of a lost day in the woods, I looked up at the old TV in the corner in time to see the somber reporter deliver the bad news. The dogs had done what they'd been sent to do, but by then, it was too late for the boy.

I hadn't eaten cherry pie for four years after that night.

But that sudden, unwanted trip down memory lane gave me an idea. "By chance, do you have any of Fellora's clothes here?"

Camun looked up from his work, frowning. "Her clothes?"

"Something that smells like her. I'm working with a troll," I improvised.

His face lit at the news. "You think you can track her by her scent?"

"It hasn't rained in the last week, so it's worth a try, right?"

"Absolutely." He bent over to open a drawer, then extracted a small gray duffel bag. "This is all Fellora's. We go jogging across the street at lunch sometimes," he explained, passing the bag to me. "She changes her workout clothes once or twice a week."

Once Camun finished with the map, I folded it up and stowed it away, fiddling with my purse's clasps so as to avoid the temptation of scratching my itchy head. Camun saw me to the elevator, and as it arrived, he murmured, "You'll keep me informed, won't you?"

I gripped his elbow with my free hand, and mustering more conviction than I felt, I said, "We're going to find her. Don't give up hope."

He watched me silently with a polite smile and weary eyes until the doors closed between us.

When I hurried out to the van, to my surprise, it was empty.

"What's going on?" I asked, finding Wylan staring out across the park with his hands in his pockets.

He jumped at the sound of my voice and spun, and I wondered just how lost in his own world he'd been before

I interrupted him. "Annie! Hi. Sorry, just, uh…restless. Wanted some air." His brow furrowed as he noticed the duffel I'd brought with me. "Souvenir?"

"Something I'm hoping you can help me with." I paused, trying to get a read on him, but his expression betrayed nothing unusual. "Are you really fine? You've been twitchy all day."

"Thinking," he replied with a brief smile. "Nothing to worry about. Now, what can I do to help?"

He followed me to the van, and I dropped the mask and explained my plan on the way back to my apartment. If we were going hiking, I damn sure wasn't going to do it in nice shoes.

"Do you think it's possible you might be able to smell a trace of her after this long?" I asked. "I mean, I've heard some crazy stuff about the trollish sense of smell, but I didn't know."

"It's possible," said Wylan. "The weather's been cooperative. Of course, considering how many people have surely been on the trail in the last week, that might complicate the search, but I think it might be done. Won't know until I try, will I?"

Once I'd changed into more woods-appropriate apparel and packed a small bag of necessities—water always came in handy, and I'd need the flashlight soon enough, as the sun was sinking—I plotted the portal route to Green Lake and set off with Wylan. While Green Lake was considered close to Beukal, it was accessed via the portal for Tanaar, which I'd learned would have been roughly atop Nashville, had the Pactlands collapsed. Central Virginia to central Tennessee wasn't *close* by any of the metrics I used, but distances were different in the Pactlands, and the portals turned a nine-hour haul into a quick jaunt to the countryside. Still, one had to navigate the portals—seldom fun during the post-work rush—and by the time I turned off the main road at the Green Lake welcome sign, the sky had shifted to the deep, glowing blue of late twilight.

Driving into the recreation area after spending nearly a year surrounded by the high-rises of Beukal was bizarre: a narrow, gravel road winding away from the paved street, wooden signage reminding visitors to go slowly and remove their litter, the absence of streetlights but for the occasional red lamps keeping guard over the emergency telephones. But what was strangest of all was the fact that we appeared to be driving through a mature forest—the park might have been taken straight from the Blue Ridge if not for the relative flatness. Trees didn't grow well in the Pactlands, so to find myself creeping down a tunnel of arching branches felt almost wrong.

"It's quite wooded here," Wylan remarked as we neared the parking lot. "Curious."

"Some of the DPP folks told me about this place," I said, braking as a possum scurried across the road. "It's hard to grow more than grass in the Pactlands unless you anchor the area to the outside world, and since that's a pain, it's mostly reserved for farms. But somebody woke up and realized that people like to visit places more interesting than rolling prairies, so they created Green Lake and a few other nature parks to give folks a taste of the great outdoors." My headlights caught the eyeshine of a raccoon in the middle of the lane, and I honked until it scampered off, half-eaten sandwich in its mouth. "Ah, trash pandas. Cute little assholes."

Wylan laughed aloud. "*What* did you call that?"

"Joke from back home," I replied, and sighed with relief as we rounded a bend and emerged into the deserted parking lot.

I had my pick of the spaces—Green Lake wasn't a popular destination after dark on a random autumn Wednesday, quite probably due to the chance of a serial killer on the loose. We pulled up beside another red security light and stretched our legs, and then I dug out my flashlight to examine the map. "Okay," I muttered after a moment, "if we're *here*, then the path should be…" I shone my light around until it illuminated the trailhead signs. "Bingo. We follow the blue triangles."

Wylan nodded as he returned to the van for the duffel bag. Unzipping it, he pulled out Fellora's gray T-shirt, which she'd left wadded in a ball.

"Good enough?" I asked.

"This thing is stiff with sweat. If it's not good enough, I'll be having my nose examined," he replied, then squished the fabric against his face and inhaled deeply.

"Yeah, that's gross."

"Still not as bad as that damn salve." With that, he tucked the shirt away and slung the bag over his shoulder, I supposed in case he needed a refresher. "Which way did you want to walk, again?"

I pointed to the sign with the blue triangle. "That way?"

He closed his eyes and took a deep sniff of the air, then grunted. "The smell is strongest in that direction. Let's go."

"You can *still* smell her that clearly?" I asked, training my light on the ground so as not to fall on my face.

Wylan, whose sensitive eyes could keep him out of trouble without the flashlight's aid, nodded again. "It's faint, but she was here. Another week, and I might not catch her, but I guarantee she took this trail. Ah, watch it." He grabbed my arm as I tripped and tried to go flying. "Why don't you stay with me, Annie? Just in case."

Taking a hike in the dark wasn't the best idea I'd ever had, I mused, sticking close to Wylan's elbow. I'd undoubtedly have seen more of the park had I bothered to wait for daylight. But while I flailed, Wylan seemed to come alive, pausing every few yards to sniff the air and continue stalking onward, his footfalls nearly silent on the dirt. With no one around to disturb us, we were free to take as much time as we wanted on the path, and so Wylan made stops to sniff the brush on either side of the trail, occasionally reporting that Fellora had been by.

I kicked myself as we walked. The guy was better than a freaking bloodhound, and yet I'd kept him riding along as standby backup for two days while I ran down rabbit trails. I should have hauled Wylan out to Green Lake as soon as we'd received clearance to take the case. But if Wylan took offense at having ridden shotgun, he didn't let on. He said little beyond what was absolutely necessary, instead focusing his attention on the scent.

After fifteen minutes, he pulled out Fellora's shirt for an olfactory refresher while I tried to see the path ahead by flashlight. The trail was clear and decently smooth but for the odd root, but the trees closed in on either side and grew thickly overhead, blotting out the stars.

"You're blind out here, aren't you?"

I swung back to Wylan, and his eyes glowed like the raccoon's had in the flashlight's beam. "Yeah. Our night vision is pretty terrible."

"It's not just you, then? It's a human thing?"

"I mean, sure, but not only us. Sorcerers seem pretty bad at it, too, and I don't think elves are any better. I can't exactly give you a comparative rundown—"

"No, thanks, that's not necessary. I…" He paused, frowning in thought. "I'm sorry, I wish you'd said something. We can come back in the morning."

"But we've got the place to ourselves right now," I pointed out. "And I'm fine, really. Not my first time wandering in the dark."

"If you say so."

He didn't sound convinced, and when we started off again, I felt him inching closer as if he feared I'd walk into trees if left unsupervised. I didn't mind. No, it wasn't my first time in the woods at night, but these weren't the familiar woods of home, and…well, Wylan was six feet of lean muscle, not counting the antlers. If he wanted to keep me within easy reach, I didn't feel a burning need to protest

Slowly, we hiked through the darkness, stopping only when Wylan needed to take a good sniff. His impressions of where Fellora had been continued to correspond to the blue-marked trail, which somewhat reassured me. The odds that Camun and Keef had faked Fellora's message about her hiking plans had always been long, but Wylan's nose suggested that she had, in fact, intended to come that way.

We'd been hiking for perhaps forty-five minutes when Wylan called a halt, inhaled deeply, then pointed to a thick oak just off the path. "Bring your light over here, would you?" he asked me.

As he circled the tree, sniffing and frowning, I stood in the weeds and aimed my flashlight at the trunk. Nothing odd that I could see—no missing bark, no deep gouges— but as the beam descended toward the roots, I noticed an odd, discolored splotch on the fresh leaf litter. Crouching, I pulled away some of the newest fallen leaves to find that the splotch extended across a whole layer of debris, as if someone had poured out a cup of coffee.

But there was no way in hell that was a coffee stain.

"Wylan? Could you come here, please?" He quickly joined me, and I stood and moved aside to give him room. "Any thoughts about what might be on those leaves?"

He squatted before them and took a few sniffs, then moistened a fingertip, stroked it over the stain, and popped it in his mouth. Before I could protest at the unsanitary practice, he looked up and grimaced. "Blood. Absolutely blood. I'd know it anywhere."

"An animal's?" I asked, though the sick feeling in my gut told me what a stupid question that was.

"No. Fellora's scent is stronger here than anywhere we've passed. This is hers," he said, rising. "I'd stake my life on it."

I sighed and stared at the bloodstain. "Shit. It's not much blood, though. Or is there more hiding under the leaves?"

"You're right—there isn't much. Not a clear sign of fatal blood loss, I'd think. Had something torn an artery, I'd expect to see blood all over the place, but this…" Wylan shrugged. "Maybe she scraped herself. A cut on the leg, something superficial but bloody…" He sniffed again, then said, "Wait here. I'll be right back."

My flashlight followed him as he walked a few yards down the trail, sniffing all the way. When he returned to me, he was scowling in thought. "Her scent stops. This is where she disappeared."

I shone my light into the trees, looking for a place where she might have tripped and fallen, but we were nowhere near a bluff. "If I were back in Richmond, this is where I'd point out that people can't just vanish into thin air, but now we've got freaking magic to consider. Any thoughts?"

"Actually, yes," Wylan muttered.

"Care to elabor—*hey!*"

Without waiting for my question, he'd shimmied up the oak like a squirrel with a dog on its heels. I stood at the bottom, scanning the shaking branches with my flashlight, and screamed a moment later when Wylan jumped down and almost landed on me. "Sorry, *sorry*," he mumbled as I caught my breath. "Are you all right?"

"Fine," I panted. "Why'd you go up there?"

"Because I thought I smelled this," he replied, and extended his hand.

In his palm was a scrap of off-white cloth—rough cloth, possibly homespun. When I picked it up and rubbed it between my fingers, I realized where I'd seen it before. "This is like your lace-up shirts," I said. "The ones you used to wear all the time before we went shopping. Isn't it?"

"It is."

I cocked my head, puzzled. "Did someone steal your clothes?"

"No. This isn't from my shirt."

"Then—"

"It belongs to one of my brothers. Smells like him." He took the cloth back and held it to his nose. "Cralf. I can smell his sweat."

As my mental tumblers fell, I stared at Wylan in horror. "You think your *brother* ran off with Fellora?"

He nodded. "Abducted, I would assume, considering the blood."

"But *why?*"

Wylan glanced away before answering me. "I'm...not certain yet. But this makes sense," he continued, focusing on me again. "If he grabbed her, he could take her from this place just like I took you to...uh..."

"Montana?"

"*Right.* But I doubt she's outside the Pactlands. He probably took her to the lodge—and since no one outside the family can find the place," he continued, accelerating, "that would explain why Rose's farsight is blocked. Maybe the protections that hide our home are hiding Fellora as well."

I considered that briefly, then whispered, "Fuck. What do we do?"

He extended his hand, and I gripped it, bracing myself as the ground disappeared. Barely a second later, we landed by the van, and Wylan nudged me toward the driver's seat. "Let's get back to Beukal. Did you bring your phone with you?"

"Uh...yeah," I said, willing my stomach to stop flopping. "Who do we need to call?"

He jumped inside and was buckled up before I climbed into the vehicle. "Start with Syvin. We don't have much time."

CHAPTER 14

Shortly before eight that evening, I pulled into a street spot in front of the DPP tower. While I certainly didn't have after-hours access to the building, Syvin did, and I spotted her waiting by the front door with her arms folded. She'd foregone a formal robe for the night and slipped on a hooded lilac sweatshirt instead. As we hurried to join her, I noticed that her curly hair was dark with moisture—both atop her head and covering her lower half—and inwardly winced. My frantic call had pulled the chief deputy from a relaxing soak, and that was a *lot* of hair to quickly towel-dry.

"They're waiting," she told us in lieu of a greeting, and scanned us into the lobby. "Kabno only just arrived."

They were taking us seriously, then. When I'd told Syvin what we'd found at Green Lake, I'd insisted that DOL needed to hear this information as well, as the odds that Fellora's disappearance had been of her own volition were roughly equivalent to my odds of winning Mega Millions.

We rode the elevator to the top floor, Syvin and Wylan leaning against opposite walls and staring across the car as if sizing each other up. For once, however, Syvin didn't seem hostile toward him, and she said nothing as she led us down the long corridor toward Pateme's corner office.

The director was standing by his tea bar with his DOL counterpart, talking softly as their drinks brewed, and both turned to us as we showed ourselves inside. "You two made good time," said Pateme. "Something to drink?"

Wylan shook his head, and I replied, "No, thanks. Did Syvin fill you in?"

"Yes, but I want this from the top." As Kabno hoisted herself into a chair, Pateme engaged his office's anti-eavesdropping protection, but then he put his phone on his desk blotter and gestured over it. Once a small, bright bubble appeared around the device, he made a call.

Curious, I glanced at Syvin, who muttered, "The spell on the room normally blocks phones. That's the workaround."

The man on the other end picked up on the second ring, but I couldn't understand him. Pateme answered him in kind—or so I assumed—then switched to Pactish. "I'm here with Kabno and my chief deputy—"

"Kabno, Syvin, good evening," the man interjected.

"I've seen better evenings, Diriem," Kabno replied, leaning on the arm of her chair. "Too far away to join us on short notice?"

Lord ti'Dana, I realized. If DOI was involved in this meeting, then Syvin really had pulled out all the stops.

"Alas," he replied with a sigh, "I agreed weeks ago to host a party for one of my sister's granddaughters. She's to be married in two months. Lovely girl, but the timing of this little event could be better. I've sneaked away to my office, but leaving the premises would endear me to no one in the family. Has our investigative team arrived?"

"Both present," Pateme reported. "Now, Annie, Wylan, what the hell is going on?"

Wylan and I glanced at each other, and he nodded in encouragement. He looked anxious, I thought, rubbing his knees, one leg bouncing as if he were trying to expel nervous energy.

I cleared my throat and sat on the edge of the chair I'd selected, inching closer to the phone. "So, um…I spoke with Fellora's immediate family on Monday, and they gave me three leads to consider. I've ruled out all three."

"Two have solid alibis," Syvin volunteered. "The third,

I haven't heard about…"

"Fellora's boss. Her sister thinks he's a creep who's still carrying a torch for her…" Catching Kabno's bemusement, I tried again. "She thought he might be in love with her. Turns out he's in a committed relationship with someone else. I met with the fiancé this afternoon to see what I could learn from him, and he's upset at the lack of investigation."

"I wouldn't call it a *lack*," protested Kabno, bristling. "A quiet investigation, perhaps—"

"He's more concerned about Fellora's well-being than with Hall politics, but it looks like he's the only one," I said.

When I paused, I noticed that neither of the elves in the meeting rushed to contradict me.

"Anyway," I continued, "the fiancé had a bag of Fellora's dirty workout clothes, and since Wylan's got a nose to rival a troll—"

"Wait…really?" Pateme interjected.

"I've heard as much," Diriem offered.

Wylan coughed to claim the floor. "It's not quite as good, but we're close, I believe. I mean, I've had little experience with trolls, but that's what Father says."

"We can test this later," said Kabno, and waved toward me. "Go on, Annie."

"Well, Wylan and I went out to Green Lake tonight," I resumed, "and he tracked Fellora's scent along the trail she told her fiancé and sister she'd be using. We got a good ways in, and then the scent ended at this tree. We found some blood at the base, and Wylan says it's Fellora's—"

"How much blood?" Kabno asked.

"Nothing fatal," Wylan told her. "Probably defensive wounds, not proof of an injury designed to kill. Anyway, I went up the tree and found this," he said, pulling the scrap of cloth from his pocket. "It belongs to one of my brothers."

The gnome's blue eyes widened. "Your *brother?*"

"One of them. I have forty-six, but you live with someone long enough, and you learn his scent."

"I'm sorry," said Diriem, breaking the brief silence that had fallen on the office, "but... *how* many siblings?"

"Forty-six, all older than me," Wylan replied. "We're a large family, I suppose, but I'm quite confident that I could point to the correct brother. And that's a real problem."

"Our working hypothesis is that Fellora's with the Hunt," I said. "Wylan says there are protections on their home to keep strangers out, so maybe that's blocking Rose's efforts to find her with farsight."

The two directors and Syvin looked to the phone, and I heard Diriem suck his teeth. "That makes sense," he murmured. "I've not experienced a block like the one she's described, but the Hunter is *very* well protected. We've never been able to pinpoint the location of his lodge, and that's not something I readily admit outside my agency. Since attempting to locate a person who's dead at the point of the timeline you're considering looks rather different than what Rose has shared with me, I assume the girl's still alive."

"And with the damn Hunt," Kabno replied, rubbing her forehead. "So what am I supposed to do with *that?*"

"Uh...what about a search warrant?" I suggested. "If someone could test Wylan's nose and verify that he's not making things up, then wouldn't that give you enough cause to go searching for her?"

"Sure," she said with a smirk. "I could get a warrant. But how would you suggest my people *serve* it? You heard Diriem—no one can find the lodge, not even the team of sorcerers who keep the Pactlands intact. It's not like the Hunter put an address on file down here."

"And he wouldn't take kindly to a visit from your agents," Wylan told her. "Father likes his privacy." He hesitated, gnawing on his lip, then said, "I could probably get a small team close. Not like I don't know my way home," he added with a weak chuckle. "If I dropped them near the lodge, then perhaps—"

"Absolutely not," Kabno interrupted. "I appreciate the offer, but something tells me your father would perceive a DOL team as a hostile force on his doorstep, and I'm not risking the casualties of sending my folks against the fucking *Hunt*. No."

"Besides," Syvin added to Wylan, "that would drag you into this mess, wouldn't it? I won't pretend to be familiar with your family dynamics, but I suspect you'd rather not be on your father's bad side."

Before Wylan could weigh in, Diriem said, "We're talking about trying to serve a warrant on a Pact signatory. This wouldn't be a simple undertaking even if we could *find* the man…"

Kabno scowled into space. "The wisest course of action would be to bring this matter to the Forum. A closed-door session, naturally—wouldn't be the first time I've gone this route. If the Forum backs us, then maybe that would be pressure enough to convince the Hunter to open his residence for inspection. *Without* violence."

"I don't disagree, but you know as well as I do that convening the Forum would take time," said Pateme. "Not to mention the political ramifications of going after a signatory—"

"We're not immune from prosecution," Diriem interrupted. "If anything, we should be particularly bound to the agreement we made."

I must have looked perplexed, as Syvin leaned toward me and whispered, "He's a signatory, too. Brought all the elves in."

"Understood," Pateme told Diriem, "but let's think of this in practical terms. Say the Forum authorizes a search by DOL. What happens if the Hunter refuses to comply? How do we force him to let the officers in, much less tell them where to go?"

Diriem grunted. "Time and patience? Diplomacy? If

we're careful with this—"

"We don't have time."

The room turned to Wylan, who rose and began pacing the length of Pateme's plush office rug. "We don't have *time* for the Forum or negotiations or...I don't know, public shaming. Not if you want Fellora back alive."

Pateme started to speak, but Syvin held up a hand to stay him. "What's going on?" she asked.

After another moment of agitated stalking, Wylan paused and tightly folded his arms. "I, uh...I've been feeling increasingly restless for the last two days," he muttered. "Finally understood why in the park tonight. I'm being called home."

"You mean—"

"The Hunt is about to ride. Probably not tonight. Maybe tomorrow, perhaps the next day, but soon. I...I have to go. Father commands it."

Again, Pateme attempted to ask a question, but Syvin shot him a look, stood, and joined Wylan. "Hey, kid?"

He slumped, the better to see her upturned face.

"I need you to be honest with me, all right?"

Wylan nodded miserably.

"Do you think Fellora's abduction is at all related to the ride?"

"I..." he began, then took a deep breath and slowly exhaled. "I fear that it is."

"What are you suggesting?" Diriem demanded from the phone. "You're not saying she was taken as *prey*, are you?"

When Wylan said nothing, Syvin reached up and gripped his arms. "We need answers. Please."

He turned to me, then reddened and glanced away as if embarrassed. "It's the only conclusion that makes sense," he said softly. "We don't keep random people stashed around the lodge."

"Maybe your brother wanted a girlfriend," Pateme suggested.

Wylan shook his head. "I can't recall any of us doing something like that. Father doesn't like outsiders, remember. But if farsight suggests that Fellora is still alive, she's been at the lodge for a week, and the Hunt is about to ride…surely Father has plans for her. She's young and fit, so perhaps…"

He left that thought unfinished, but my stomach clenched at the picture he was painting.

"But the Hunter's never abducted any of our citizens like this," said Pateme. "Has he?"

"Not that I know of."

"And he's not allowed to," the director continued. "That was one of his concessions in signing on to the Pact—he can't hunt us, for obvious reasons, and he's not permitted to pursue humans as a safety measure."

At that, Wylan looked him in the eye and arched a brow. "You've just shown me here tonight how little power you have over Father. You don't *know* that you can enforce your laws against him. So if he's violated the terms of your agreement, then how do you plan to stop him?" When no one raced to volunteer a suggestion, Wylan said, "If you want to find Fellora, you can't afford to wait. I can get your people to the lodge, but they'll need to go in prepared for a fight with the Hunt—and if I know my brothers, with the time almost upon us, at least half of them are currently eager for blood."

As quiet fell once again, I turned to Kabno. "Not to insult DOL or anything, but maybe this isn't a matter for law enforcement just yet. Do you have an army here?"

"No," she muttered. "We've never needed more than DOL before now to maintain order…"

While the directors and Syvin contemplated the problem in silence, I considered the facts. If Wylan was right—and God, I hoped he wasn't—then his father and brothers were about to stage their interpretation of "The Most Dangerous Game." Fellora was an elf, sure, but they'd presumably overpowered her once, and that wasn't with the whole Hunt chasing after her. I'd seen what Wylan could do with a bow, and I didn't like the woman's odds. As Yven had made clear, elves' strengths varied, and I didn't know what sort of defense Fellora might be able to mount, but something told me that if the scenario Wylan predicted played out, the Hunter wouldn't be arming her.

The only way to the lodge was via Wylan. If Kabno sent a strike force with him, her people might be slaughtered—and even if the Hunter let them in, Wylan would be on the hook. None of the farseers had any clue as to where Fellora actually was or whether she was hurt, though she was probably alive.

For now. But since the Hunt was poised to ride...

"What if I went?" I asked.

"Absolutely not," said Wylan. "I'm not taking you anywhere near—"

"Hear me out." I stood, the better to stare him down. "You bring me home with you. I'll hide, and while you're with your family, I'll sneak around and see if I can find Fellora."

"Annie—"

"There isn't a better idea! DOL doesn't want to risk it, and I'm guessing you can't just waltz in and ask to have Fellora back. I'll stay out of sight and try to get her out of there."

He sighed, scrunched his eyes closed, and massaged his temples. "You're overlooking the glaring problem."

"Which is?"

"Our senses are so much better than yours. You're blind in the dark, and you can barely smell. Turn the lights out in here, and I can track you by your scent alone. If you somehow managed to sneak into the lodge, you'd be noticed within minutes. We *know* each other's scents— yours would raise an alarm. And if Father found you..."

"Look at me and tell me she's not going to die if we don't try something."

His amber eyes locked with mine, and I saw the unease

there. "I...can't say that," he grudgingly admitted, "but let's be reasonable. If you go with me, I won't be able to protect you, and you'll never escape with Fellora."

Interrupting our argument, Pateme said, "Wylan has a point, Annie. But if scent is the problem, DPP might have a workaround."

"And I'll call in a favor," added Diriem before abruptly hanging up.

Wylan seemed poised to object, but Syvin slipped into the opening. "Tell me something," she said to him. "Does the prey ever escape when the Hunt rides?"

He hesitated, then muttered, "Rarely."

"This isn't a catch-and-release situation, is it?"

"No. Never."

She grunted and turned to Pateme. "I hate every bit of this idea. That said, a stealth operation is probably our best chance."

"That may be," said Kabno, "but you recall that I'm bound by the law, yes? I can't send my people to break into the Hunter's residence without a warrant, and *getting* that warrant, even under these circumstances—"

"Which is why *I'm* going. I'm a civilian," I said as Kabno started to protest. "Hell, I'm not even a citizen here—if I do something crazy, you can always claim that I acted alone or it's the damn Roulette messing with my head, or whatever you like." Looking back at Wylan, who appeared to be even less enthusiastic about this plan than Syvin was, I said, "We're her only chance. Take me with you."

"But Annie—"

"You were willing to bring along a whole squad of DOL officers, but you won't take little old me?"

"I don't want to put you in danger!"

"You're not. I'm choosing this," I replied, silently daring him to deny me.

We stared at each other in a brief standoff, neither blinking.

And though Wylan sighed, he didn't say no.

Several floors below Pateme's swanky office and behind two sets of locked doors lay one of DPP's research labs. Only a few brewers were on duty in the potions wing that night, and they watched us but didn't protest as Pateme, Syvin, Wylan, and I trooped past the glass-walled clean rooms.

Down the tile hallway—a precaution against spills, I assumed—the director paused before yet another restricted access point and scanned us in. As he opened the thick gray door, a blast of frigid air rushed into the corridor, and I peeked inside to find an oversized walk-in cooler, the sort of storage Maya might have needed were she cooking for a thousand starving people. The cooler was lit from above with a red light and filled with metal racks, which held labeled plastic bins packed with potion tubes.

"Wait in the hall. There's nothing to be gained by all of us freezing," said Pateme, and slipped inside the cooler. He rummaged among the shelves, peering at labels and occasionally rubbing his bare hands together against the chill, then found what he was looking for and extracted two tubes of a bright green potion.

"This," he told me as Syvin locked the cooler door, "is a scent neutralizer. Expensive and difficult to make, so we don't guzzle the stuff, but it's effective enough to fool a troll. You'll have about twenty-four hours' protection once you drink it," he said, handing me one of the tubes, "so go ahead and swig it—"

"Are you sure about this?" Syvin interrupted before I could take a swig. "With the Roulette…"

"I'll take the risk," I replied, and threw back the potion before I could get cold feet.

It wasn't horrible, like I'd feared, just a cold liquid that tasted of lavender. I felt it trickle into my stomach without making me want to vomit, which seemed like a promising beginning.

"Give it five minutes or so to take effect," said Pateme, then pointed toward another door down the hallway. "Clean suits in there. We're careful with detergents so as not to upset the trolls in this division. Wait for the potion to kick in, then strip *completely* and suit up. Everything that smells like you needs to be removed."

Syvin patted me on the back and nudged me toward the dressing room. "I'll assist. Come along, Annie."

While I sat in a cubicle and waited for the potion to work, Syvin put on a pair of disposable gloves and bustled around the room, finding a black jumpsuit in my size, fresh underwear, socks, and booties. She hesitated as she considered a rack of what appeared to be sports bras, then said, "Do you really need, erm…support? I don't see anything here that isn't pullover."

"I can do without," I assured her.

"Thanks. I'm sorry," she said as I remove my trail-soiled shoes, "I don't think there are any fauns currently in this lab, and since we're the only ones who share your pullover problem…"

I drew the curtain and continued to undress. "Antlers are so *freaking annoying*."

"Oh, I hear you." The bench outside my cubicle squeaked as she took a seat. "Horns aren't so bad if you grow up with them, but we all go through awkward phases as they come in and start to curl back. Boys, especially. There's always one in the class who's a late bloomer, and underdeveloped horns get about the reaction you'd expect from other children, those most *sensitive* of creatures."

"Guess we're not so different," I said, snickering to myself.

"Children are universally terrible to each other, which is why I'm quite content to spoil my siblings' offspring and return them. How's the suit fitting?"

I zipped it and flapped my arms, testing the range of

motion. "Pretty well. I can work with this."

A few minutes later, having donned my new shoes and left my stuff in a bag for Syvin to return to my apartment—even the masking necklace, which, to be frank, I wasn't entirely sorry to remove—I emerged into the corridor and did a little twirl for Wylan and Pateme. "All right, come and smell me," I said.

Wylan approached, but as he neared, his face creased with concern. "Um, Annie?"

"Yeah?"

"Are you hot?"

"Not really, no...why?"

"Your face is red. So's your neck."

I glanced at my bare hands, only to find my skin reddened from my fingers to my wrists. Pushing back one sleeve, I saw that the rash extended up my arm. "Great," I muttered. "It doesn't hurt, though, so give me a good sniff."

He was polite but thorough in his examination, sniffing around me before almost shoving his nose into my armpit and taking a deep whiff of my hair. "Nothing," he finally declared. "All right, I'm impressed."

"Good," said Pateme. "Annie, stay here and try not to touch anyone. I need to go downstairs and wait for Diriem."

"He's coming after all?" I asked. "What about his party?"

Pateme smirked. "Frankly, knowing him, he might thank you for giving him an excuse to flee."

By the time he returned, I was growing stiff from standing in the middle of the hallway, avoiding even the walls and benches. Pateme hadn't come alone. Diriem followed on his heels—a man with loose red hair and gray eyes who bore a strong resemblance to Rose, assuming one overlooked the ears—and to my surprise, Teolm walked beside him, carrying a small white box. As they pushed through the final set of doors, the two newcomers took one look at me and stopped dead. "Annie!" Teolm cried. "What's wrong with your skin?"

"Potion side effect," Pateme explained. "She says it doesn't hurt."

"And here's hoping the redness fades once this stuff wears off," I weakly joked. "Syvin has your necklace with my belongings. It's safe, I just can't touch it—"

"Forget the necklace." He stepped closer and frowned at my unfortunate ruddiness. "She's *unstable*, people, and you're making it worse. We don't know how she'll react to the ring."

"What ring?" I asked.

He opened the box, revealing a thick gold ring covered with etching. While I was sure the symbols meant something, they might as well have been chicken scratch to me. "It's adjustable, I assure you," he said, perhaps mistaking my expression for concern about the fit. "Grants invisibility when triggered."

"An incredibly complex piece," Diriem offered. "Rare, expensive—"

"Father spent months perfecting it," said Teolm, and closed the box. "I don't mind loaning it out for a good cause, but I don't want to worsen your condition."

I smiled and shrugged. "Really, this doesn't hurt. Masking is a hundred times worse—"

Realizing my mistake, I snapped my mouth shut, but the damage was done.

"What happens when you use the pendant?" asked Teolm, fixing me with a stare that demanded an answer.

"It's only when I use it too long. Bad scalp itch. Syvin gave me a salve that fixed the problem right up."

My reply seemed too breezy even to me, and Teolm was no fool. "How long is too long?"

"About an hour and a half."

He looked at Diriem and Pateme. "And you want her to go invisible for an undetermined amount of time? What if she passes the maximum safe period and…I don't know, loses her sight? Grows scales? Everything with her is unpredictable, and…" He glanced at Syvin. "This salve she mentioned—that's the horn goop that can clear a room?"

Syvin nodded. "The same."

Turning back to the directors with an exasperated huff, he continued, "If she had to resort to *that* to treat the side effects of an hour and a half of masking, what do you think this ring will do to her?"

"We're trying to save Fellora's life," I cut in. "Tight schedule, no good options."

"And I'd happily see that girl home," said Teolm, "but let's think about your safety as well."

"*Thank you*," Wylan muttered.

I glared at him but quickly returned my attention to Teolm. "Is there an alternative to your ring? A potion or something? I can deal with a rash."

"Oh, there's definitely an invisibility potion," said Pateme, grimacing, "but it's nothing you want to put in your body."

"Potion of last resort," Syvin agreed. "It's short-acting, you have to be naked to use it effectively, and within an hour, it wears off and leaves you with the worst vomiting of your life."

It didn't take a genius to see that appearing nude and puking my guts out might jeopardize my plan for stealth. "What if you gave me something to deal with the nausea?" I suggested. "I could just keep dosing myself with invisibility potion and taking drugs—"

"We've tried any number of anti-nausea remedies in conjunction with that potion," said Syvin, shaking her head. "Nothing counteracts the side effect."

"So what does the ring do, then?"

"It creates a full-body mask that works with the background, leaving the wearer virtually invisible," Teolm replied. "An observer might see a shimmer like a heat mirage in the right light, but if you can stick to the shadows, you'll be virtually undetectable. But as I said, it's a full-body *mask*, and given your prior reaction, that worries me."

"And another wrinkle," Wylan murmured. "We have *excellent* low-light vision. A mass of shadows to you might look quite different to us."

Teolm arched an eyebrow. "Do you keep spotlights on in the house?"

"No…"

"Then she'd probably be safe…unless she's turning purple or sprouting another set of legs."

"I appreciate your concern," I told Teolm. "Really, I do. But we're running out of time. May I at least try it?"

Reluctantly, he slid it onto my finger and showed me how to engage the ring. I took a few steps closer to the wall, where the overhead lights weren't so bright, and turned it on. When I raised my hand to check out the effect, I could feel my muscles moving, but I couldn't see my own body.

Unfortunately, I could sense the side effect within seconds. My theretofore painless rash burned like the worst sunburn of my life, the horrible lobster-complexioned result of a teenage Saturday at Virginia Beach in July with far too much tanning oil, and the sensation of my soft jumpsuit against my skin chafed like razor sandpaper. But I didn't let on. I couldn't afford to.

"Well?" I asked.

Wylan stared at my hiding place for a long moment, then sighed. "It's probably good enough if you stay in the shadows and keep still. Feel anything weird?"

"Not at all," I lied through my teeth. "When do we leave?"

CHAPTER 15

For smell purposes, nothing I carried could be my own. The ring Teolm brought me was soaked in the scent-neutralizing potion and handled with gloves thereafter. DPP also managed to rustle up a switchblade and a canister of a self-defense spray that Syvin explained was heavy on the capsaicin, both of which were also soaked before I was allowed to take possession of them. I had no room for a more substantial weapon—the jumpsuit was designed with only two shallow pockets, and I kept my tools separated for fear that they'd bang into each other and give away my position. Personally, I'd have preferred to go skulking around the lodge with at least a semiautomatic pistol or three, but that wasn't in the cards.

By one o'clock Thursday morning, as Wylan and I prepared for departure, our small crowd had grown. In my rush to tell all on Wednesday evening, I'd neglected to leave a note for Maya, only realizing my mistake once the phone buried in in my clothes bag began to ring incessantly. Syvin dug it out and tried to talk Maya down, but my roommate was no more pleased with this plan than was the chief deputy, and she insisted on coming upstairs. In the end, it wouldn't have mattered had Pateme tried to stop her—Diriem had conveyed the details of the situation to Rose, as we'd need her on standby for this to work, and she'd marched through the lab doors with Maya and Yven flanking her. At least Pateme was able to stop Maya from grabbing my arms and trying to drag me out of the building, though she scowled at any authority figure in range.

The plan was, in theory, simple. Wylan had told us that while the area around the lodge was inaccessible to anyone outside of the Hunt, their territory *did* connect to the rest of the Pactlands. He was sure of it…but he didn't know exactly where that connection occurred or how far it might be from the lodge. He would covertly get me inside and then go about his business, while I, invisible and deodorized, would skulk around the lodge in search of Fellora I carried a well-padded tube of the scent-eliminating potion in my pocket with the mace cannister. When I found Fellora, I'd give her the potion to drink, then sneak us both out of there. We'd run for the border while Rose watched for me with farsight. Once we got far enough from the lodge, the protections that blocked Rose's talent should fall away, and she'd be able to send help to retrieve us.

Simple. Assuming, of course, that I wasn't captured, that Fellora was still alive, and that the lodge wasn't at the center of a hundred miles of hidden territory.

While Rose had rehearsed with me, making sure she could quickly focus on my face, Yven had driven my van back to Wylan's apartment to let him collect his baggage. Wylan had returned with his full gear bag, dressed in his old tunic and leather leggings, his dark hair tied back with a thong.

As we went over our final checklist and Pateme took Rose to a lounge to make her comfortable, Wylan murmured, "You don't have to do this, Annie."

"Come on," I teased, "this is better than making lattes forever. You get a little male bonding time, I try to save Fellora's life—"

"*Annie.*"

Judging by the look on his face, he wanted to grab me by the shoulders and shake me, but he resisted.

"I'll be okay," I insisted with unearned assurance. "And if things go horribly wrong, I'll run. Promise."

He nodded, then shouldered his bag and held out his hand. "Ready?"

Clasping it, I gave the others what I hoped was a confident smile before triggering my ring. The burn began immediately, but I tightened my grip on Wylan and said, "Let's do this."

I screwed my eyes closed just before the floor fell away.

When I hit the ground again, I was slapped in the face with the smell of pine and opened my eyes to find that we'd landed on the edge of a coniferous forest. The air smelled colder than it had in Beukal, assailing my nostrils with the dry, crisp edge of a freeze, but the ground was clear of snow. Turning to look behind me, I saw what seemed like acres of real pines, not the stubby Pactlands version, a wooded belt laced with narrow trails.

Ahead of us stretched a massive complex made of logs and stone, simple in design but gargantuan in scale. Ringed with a covered porch and lit with flickering blue lanterns, the lodge was the size of a nice resort, the kind of place where one might spend five hundred dollars a night for horseback rides and massages with locally grown botanicals. Here, however, instead of a manicured front lawn, the cleaning in front of the lodge was pocked with targets of all shapes and sizes—bullseyes pinned to hay bales, a dummy atop a horse, even a fake deer cleaved in two. Shooting was clearly on this lodge's itinerary, but I doubted the Huntsmen had much use for skeet.

Wylan had released me upon arrival but remained standing by my side in silence, giving me a moment to get my bearings and survey the area. After a final look, I whispered, "Go," and he strode off without so much as a twitch of acknowledgement. I followed as closely as I dared, taking care not to bump into him and trying to keep silent. He mounted the wide front steps, then held the door open while he made a show of adjusting his bag, allowing me to slip in ahead of him. Once over the threshold, I darted into a dark corner, letting the lanterns' flickering shadows swallow me while I held my breath and waited.

Inside, the lodge featured high ceilings, plastered walls, and polished wooden floors. Weapons hung between tapestries of hunting scenes, continuing the theme of the place. And unsurprisingly for a home holding forty-eight men, it smelled rather like a frat house, a mixed funk of sweat and booze. Considering the raucous laughter coming from somewhere down the corridor deeper into the lodge, I suspected that the beer was still flowing that night.

Wylan headed for the wide staircase at the back of the entry hall, but before he could reach the first step, another man called his name. He turned and noted the newcomer: another Huntsman, judging by the antlers, slightly pointed ears, and tunic-and-leggings ensemble, but blond, bearded, several inches taller, and considerably broader. "Derat," Wylan replied, beaming, and dropped his bag to embrace him.

Derat thumped him on the back and released him, grinning like a kid. "The wanderer returns! Did you just arrive?"

"I was going to unpack," said Wylan, gesturing toward his discarded bag. "You're up late."

"As is the rest of the Hunt, as I'm sure you can hear." With that, he stepped into the hallway, cupped his hands around his mouth, and bellowed, "Wylan's home!"

I shrank further into the corner, trying to ignore the burning pain while I watched a handful of Wylan's brothers appear to greet him. The first wave were as welcoming as Derat had been, offering a parade of hugs, backslaps, and smiles. They were also, to a man, notable larger than their youngest brother. Syvin was right, I mused—Wylan *was* small for a Huntsman. Putting aside the issue of their father's virtual indestructability, I could see why a DOL team might balk at the notion of taking on the whole crew.

Fortunately for me, the others were so caught up with

Wylan that they ignored my quiet corner. Well, caught up with him, plus inebriated—having seen my fair share of drunk guys, I surmised that the boys had been having fun *all* evening. Some of the happiest of Wylan's brothers appeared glassy-eyed and just this side of sloppy, and while no one was staggering into the walls, a few slurred their words. I thanked my lucky stars. Drunks were easy to track because they weren't alert to their surroundings, and I hoped that even if my scent-killing potion wore off, the smell of beer would distract them.

But not everyone was in such good humor. After a few minutes, the second wave ventured into the hall to see the newcomer, and the mood chilled. "Well, well," said one of them, a redhead built like a bull, "if it isn't the runaway. Slunk home with your tail tucked?"

The men behind him guffawed, but Wylan stood his ground. "Father gave me leave to go to the capital, Cralf, and you know it."

Cralf. The one who'd grabbed Fellora. That Wylan had addressed him by name had to have been for my benefit.

Cralf spread his hands. "And yet, here you are."

"Wouldn't miss the ride, would I?"

He snorted and gave Wylan's shoulder a quick shove. "Just stay out of my way, boy. I'd hate to shoot you in error."

Cralf's crew started to laugh again, but they quickly fell silent and slid to either side of the hall as something massive marched toward us.

Some*one*, rather.

Back at the café, the biggest person I knew who wasn't a troll was Pars. At seven feet tall and maybe three hundred pounds, the sorcerer looked like he could hurt almost anyone, but I only ever saw his softer side. Quick to laugh, he guzzled coffee by the quart, tipped well, and never seemed to mind answering my dumb questions.

The Hunter made Pars look like a teddy bear. Another seven-footer before tacking on the antlers, I estimated, but probably four hundred pounds. He sported a sleeveless tunic, and his arms, swollen with muscle, were at least as thick as my thighs. His dark hair hung unbound over his shoulders and down his back, though he'd added a pair of decorative braids to his beard. I couldn't see his eyes well from my hiding place, and something told me that I didn't want to. Every deep warning system in my body screamed that I was in the presence of a predator, and since I couldn't run, my best bet was to freeze and hope for the best.

For the first time, my determination to solve the case and the frantic planning of the night gave way to the cold realization that I was in danger. This wasn't a game. This wasn't trailing a surly teenager to her boyfriend's house or taking covert photos of a horny old guy stepping out on his wife. If the Hunter noticed me, there would be no appeal, no help from Wylan—I'd be on my own and probably doomed. I was in *way* over my head, depending on potions and jewelry to keep me alive, and in constant pain, but I couldn't even afford to whimper.

As the rest of his brothers moved out of the way, Wylan nodded to him. "Father."

The Hunter stood there for a moment, sizing Wylan up, then grunted and went on his way without a word.

The brothers quickly dispersed—most followed the Hunter back toward the noise and the smell of booze— but Derat remained and patted Wylan's shoulder as he deflated. "You weren't expecting a warm welcome, were you?" he murmured. "He always did the same to me when I went roaming."

"Honestly, I was expecting worse," Wylan muttered.

"No matter. I'm glad you came home."

"Didn't have much choice, did I? Father called. I take it the ride's upon us, is it not?"

Derat nodded, but he didn't seem enthusiastic about the preposition. "Come with me to the kitchen, eh? Let's raid the leftovers from dinner. My thirst has been slaked for the moment."

Wylan followed him deeper into the lodge, and I tiptoed after.

A hallway opened onto a kitchen that looked straight out of a medieval castle—giant fire, iron spit, blackened cauldron, and all—but for the trio of gleaming stainless steel combination refrigerator/freezers along one wall. Derat opened the doors of the nearest and withdrew a platter, and the two of them stood at the wood-topped kitchen island, eating cold slices of ham with their fingers. They chewed in companionable silence for a few minutes, working their way through the pile of meat, and then Wylan wiped his hands and poured a glass of water from the tap. "So," he asked, "where are we going for the ride this year?"

"I don't know precisely, but Father says he has a good location selected," Derat replied. "Nice and remote, challenging terrain."

Wylan considered Derat as he continued to eat. "You don't look pleased."

Derat said nothing while Wylan slowly drained his drink, then sighed and pushed the ham away. "The prey this year is...different."

"Oh?" Wylan cocked his head. "How so? Something exotic?"

"You might say that." He washed his hands, put the meat back in the fridge, then leaned against the island with his arms folded. "Before the Pact, before we came here, Father led us after all manner of prey. Nothing was forbidden."

"So you tell me."

"He's been limited by his agreement," Derat continued, "but he's grown bored, you might say. He wants challenging prey. Something sufficiently intelligent to do more than just run."

"What's he chosen, then?" asked Wylan, feigning ignorance.

His brother moved closer to him and lowered his voice. "An elf."

To his credit, Wylan played his role with aplomb. "But…elves have magical abilities," he replied bemusedly. "Won't an elf be able to escape? I've seen what they can do in Beukal…"

Though Derat smiled, his expression suggested he'd taken a bite of something bitter. "Father has trapped her in the form of a wolf. She's no more powerful right now than any other beast. I've checked on her—she chewed through her first ropes, so Father switched to chains. Bloodied herself pretty badly trying to open her cage, but it's held fast."

Wylan grimaced. "Poor thing."

"Don't say that too loudly, youngling," Derat muttered, "but I know what you mean. At least her time with us is almost over."

"Oh? When do we ride?"

"Dawn. Can't you tell by the revelry?"

"Now that you mention it," said Wylan, "the others do seem to be in fine humor tonight."

"Father wants a celebration, so that's what we'll give him. And speaking of which, you and I should join the party before anyone comes searching for us. A beer or two will do you good before we ride," he said, slinging his arm around Wylan's shoulders, "and once the ride concludes, you can tell me all about your time in Beukal. Meet anyone interesting?"

"Mildly," he replied. "A shopkeeper at a used clothing store, my landlord…"

I lingered in the kitchen as they wandered off in search of merriment, listening until I was certain that no one was dropping by for snacks, then quietly released the breath I'd been holding.

A wolf. A freaking *wolf*.

Where the hell had they hidden a wolf?

I don't know how long I sneaked around the massive lodge, praying that the wrong person wouldn't hear me breathing and trying not to cry with the increasing pain of my burning rash. I had no watch to check, and with no daylight coming through the windows, I lost track of time. Maybe I skulked around the place for thirty minutes or three hours—I couldn't say.

Aside from my discomfort, my search for Fellora was hampered by two problems. First, the lodge wasn't just a house, but rather a hotel-sized complex of bedrooms, bathrooms, storage spaces, indoor training rooms, dining rooms, and what I dubbed the "Great Hall," where the family had gathered at long tables with a roaring fire and *way* too much alcohol. Second, while no one seemed eager to retire, the Huntsmen kept getting up and slipping out by ones and twos, running to the kitchen or a toilet, or just stepping outside for a breath of air, and I never knew when one of the brothers would come marching by. I crouched behind furniture as I could and cupped my hand over my mouth, willing myself to become one with the shadows even as my heart hammered against my ribs. Learning the floorplan of the house was hard enough without the constant threat of interruption.

Finally, *finally*, I peeked through a window and found a pair of barns sitting perhaps fifty yards from the lodge. I waited until the men started up yet another drinking song, double-checked for witnesses, then eased the nearest door open and let myself out. The hinges, at least, didn't squeal, and I made a clean getaway as I hurried toward the outbuildings.

The wide door to the first structure was open, and I peeked inside to find that it was actually a stable. Long, lit with flickering lamps, and smelling of warm flesh and dung, it was lined with dozens of stalls, and I sneaked into the room for a better look. As I crept past the first doorways, I found horses sleeping or snuffling quietly, but no sign of a wolf. Deciding not to risk a chorus of alarmed neighing if one of the horses sensed me, I tiptoed out the way I'd come and paused in the grass to catch my breath.

The second barn was also open, but this one was a storage space filled with weapons, training dummies, and saddles A forge had been constructed in one corner of the barn, insulated from the wooden walls by a stone shell, but the fire was cold that night, and only a single lantern hung near the door, a lone blue flame flickering in the dark. I stood on the threshold, trying to let my eyes adjust before I could step on a rake or into a pit, when I heard a faint whining deep within.

With a last glance outside to be sure none of the Huntsmen had come down for a walk, I slipped the lantern off its hook. Unfortunately, as soon as I did, the lantern turned invisible, throwing the barn into complete darkness.

Great.

I proceeded slowly, shuffling to avoid danger. My feet crunched on the old straw littering the floor, and as I neared the source of the whining, the sound shifted toward a growl. Hesitantly, I put the lantern down. As soon as my hand released it, the light returned, and I saw what I'd come to find.

The cage at the back of the barn was maybe eight feet in all directions, a cube of metal lattice bolted to the wall. Within, backing up with her hackles raised and teeth bared, stood a small, light brown wolf. An iron collar locked around her neck connected to a thick chain anchored to the floor. Her captors had given her a few creature comforts—a small pile of straw for bedding, a bowl of water, and an untouched plate of raw meat—but no one had bothered to let her out of the cage, as one of the back corners stank with stale urine and feces. The wolf retreated as far as the chain would allow, and I noticed a few patches of dried blood crusted in her fur.

The wolf was afraid, and a disappearing and reappearing lantern surely wasn't helping the situation.

When I turned off my ring, she started at my sudden appearance, then resumed her low warning growl.

"Fellora?" I whispered, crouching in front of the door. "Fellora ti'Mal?"

The growling ceased.

"Hi. I'm Annie. DOL sent me to get you out of here."

The wolf didn't come any closer, but her attitude seemed to shift from outright hostility to guarded curiosity.

"It's the antlers, right?" I continued, pointing to my rack. "I'm not part of the Hunt. Did you ever hear about the Roulette mess last fall? Weird potion, rogue sorcerer, bunch of humans dosed, some died?"

Her head cocked, and her eyes, dark brown but glinting in the lamplight, considered me.

"I'm one of them. Woke up with antlers instead of dead. I'm not going to hurt you, I swear. I...uh..." Suddenly noticing my hand, which had progressed from a simple rash to a blister-covered dermatological nightmare, I groaned. "Shit. I look like a mess, don't I?"

The wolf nodded.

"It's the invisibility ring. Potions and magical jewelry interact badly with whatever Roulette did to my system, but look, we can deal with that later. The Hunt rides at dawn, and we need to make tracks." Lifting the lantern again, I examined the cage until I found the locked latch. "Any idea where they keep the key?"

Again, the wolf—Fellora—nodded, then looked up at the wall.

Following her eyeline, I spotted a small iron keyring hanging from a nail about six feet above the floor. I pulled it down and set to work on the cage, and though the lock resisted for a heart-stopping second, it gave way. Putting the lock aside, I undid the latch and slipped into the cage with the lantern. "Here's how this is going to work," I told Fellora, pulling the extra vial of scent neutralizer from my pocket. "You need to drink this. In about five minutes, the

Hunt won't be able to track your scent. But before we leave, I need you to pee *everywhere* in here."

I didn't know it was possible for a wolf to look offended.

"Really, I don't mean to be crass, but if we can leave a strong scent of you in here, then maybe, if someone comes by to check in the next few hours, he'll smell you and not bother to look closely. I'll turn my head," I promised, "but if you could, you know…empty everything, that would help."

She huffed but didn't try to bite me as I unlocked her collar, which I took as a positive sign.

Once Fellora was free, I uncorked the potion tube and told her to tilt her head back. She obliged, and I, grateful to not be faced with the prospect of forcing a pill past those teeth, poured the potion straight down her throat. She licked her muzzle but appeared unharmed, and as promised, I exited the cage and turned my back while she left traces of herself all over the bedding straw. Trying not to listen to the activity behind me, I allowed myself to enjoy the faintest twinge of hope. I'd made it out of the house. Fellora was with me. We'd run to the trees, then just keep going until we reached the border of this weird place…

And then, as I rubbed my borrowed ring, it hit me.

I had no way to render Fellora invisible. Maybe she could have done it to herself, were she not stuck in lupine form—honestly, I didn't know what elves were capable of—but no one had thought to send me with extra invisibility jewelry. Could she even use it after what the Hunter had done to her? Maybe the Huntsmen would be so distracted by their drinking that they wouldn't notice us, but what if someone stepped out back to take a leak and spotted their quarry making a break for it? Or noticed we were gone and came riding after us? We had to stay unseen…

Could we share the ring somehow? Take turns?

I tried to think through the possibilities. The ring masked me...but not just my body. It masked my clothing as well, plus anything I had on me—my knife, my mace, the potion tube, the lantern I'd carried...

The lantern.

Soft padding behind me announced that Fellora had finished her coverup, and when I turned, she looked at me expectantly. She didn't carry herself like any dog I'd ever seen—understandable, as she'd been quadrupedal for only a week at most—and I wondered just how well she could run if pushed to it. Given our limitations, I hoped we wouldn't have to find out.

"Here's the problem," I said as I locked the cage. "I don't have more invisibility jewelry for you, and the ring only hides things on me. Which is why this is about to get *awkward*," I continued, stretching to put the keys back on their nail.

Fellora sat and waited until I'd finished my tidying, though her ears kept turning toward the open door and the sounds of the night beyond the barn.

"I'm going to have to carry you," I explained, "which means this could be pretty slow. I'll do the best I can, but...well..."

She bumped her head against my leg, and I resisted the urge to scratch her behind the ears. Something told me that the heir to Hall ti'Mal wouldn't appreciate that in the slightest, wolf or not.

"Stand up on your hind legs and put your paws on my chest," I whispered.

Fellora did as I asked, wobbling as she tried to balance in her unfamiliar body. Quickly, I grabbed her around the lower part of her midsection and hoisted her onto my shoulder. The pain of her weight on my blisters was immediate and excruciating, but I bit my lip and shifted Fellora until I had her draped around my neck like an ungainly fur stole. My muscles complained almost as loudly as my skin did—Fellora wasn't huge, but she probably weighed about seventy-five pounds, which was far more than I'd ever carried long distance slung over my shoulders. I bent forward and slid her into a more secure position, holding her legs to steady her, and she whined.

"I'm sorry, this is miserable for us both," I muttered, "but you've got to be quiet and help me."

At least she didn't struggle. Gripping Fellora's legs with one hand, I carried the lantern back to its hook by the door and replaced it, then gritted my teeth and engaged my ring.

My skin *burned*, and I almost screamed in spite of myself, but I turned it into a soft whimper and took deep breaths until I'd acclimated to the agony. Clothing rubbing against my blisters had been bad enough, but Fellora's bulk pressing against my steadily increasing skin irritation brought tears to my eyes. Still, when I looked down, I saw no trace of my body or of the wolf on my back, and I said a silent prayer to any friendly deity who might be listening.

"Ready?" I whispered.

Fellora whined.

"I'll take that as a yes." When I peeked out and saw no one around the barn, I headed for the woods as quickly as my overburdened legs could carry me. The laughter of the drunken Huntsmen filtered out of the lodge, but by the time we were a few yards down the closest trail into the deep woods, the trees swallowed the sound.

Back in Richmond, I lived in an apartment complex with lovely, quiet neighbors…except Dennis, who lived above me. Oh, he was nice enough, but he was a rabid fan of CrossFit, the sort of person who'd somehow make it to the gym before the snowplows had cleared a path. When Dennis wasn't working out away from home, he resorted to doing sets in his den, and so I was regularly treated to hourlong sessions of grunting, jumping, and the thuds of falling weights on my ceiling. He'd invited me to come along with the fervor of any good disciple, but I'd declined, as pulling sleds or flipping tires before sunrise was low on my bucket list of life experiences.

But as I forced myself through the dark woods, dodging branches to the face, trying not to trip over snaking roots and debris, fighting my tired, shaking muscles, and worrying that my burning skin—which seemed to be oozing beneath Fellora—would slough off, I began to reconsider my general fitness plan. Moderate cardio was great, and I'd made plenty of time for strength training in the DPP gym over the last year, but I'd never planned for *this*. Sure, I could haul a deer over short distances, and I'd taken day hikes with a twenty-pound backpack, but Fellora's furry ass seemed heavier by the minute.

Still, it's amazing what the human body can do when the alternative is death, so on I pushed, hoping my adrenaline could carry us through.

It would have helped had I known just how far away safety lay. Did I need to make it one mile or twenty? Would this be a multi-day expedition? I had no map, no landmarks, and no way to call for help. My ticket out of that nightmare was Rose, who wouldn't even know where to send a ride until she could see me again.

Time was meaningless in the woods, and distance was difficult to compute, but I estimated we'd covered perhaps half a mile when the trees began to thin. The forest didn't end, but I noticed that the pines around us seemed smaller and more widely spaced. One near the trail had grown twisted and stunted, and hope leapt within me.

That was a *Pactlands* tree. Never had I been so thrilled to see one of those messed-up little weirdos.

"I think we're getting close to the border," I told Fellora, and pushed forward, momentarily buoyed by the sight.

Even still, I couldn't go on forever. I walked as far as I could with my aching legs and back, hunched over, my jumpsuit adhering to my tacky shoulders, but as the woods finally gave way to grassland, I had to rest. "Putting you down," I warned my passenger, then crouched and helped her slide off. "No bathroom breaks. Don't leave your scent here."

Once again visible, she stretched her legs and snuffled in the direction of the lodge, then bumped into me where I knelt in the grass and whined. Disengaging my ring, I muttered, "Sorry, forgot. I'm okay, I just need to rest for a minute..."

Fellora backed away from me, her eyes wide.

"Is it that bad?" I asked. Though I still couldn't see well in the dark, perhaps whatever the Hunter had done to Fellora had improved her night vision.

She nodded.

In a way, I was glad she couldn't speak. I kept my hands well away from my face and made no move to peel my clothing from the burst blisters, pretending that if I ignored the problem, it wouldn't actually exist.

I wanted to keep moving. We *needed* to put more distance between us and the lodge—after all, what I'd labored to cover on foot could be easily matched with one of the Hunt's horses. But my muscles trembled, and the pain in my raw skin had settled into a dull, constant full-body ache that flared into fresh spikes every time I shifted position. I needed rest. I'd been up for a full day, my last meal had been before our Green Lake trip, and as I'd carried no water with me, my parched throat joined my litany of physical complaints.

Still, the alternative to continuing our escape was in all probability *death*—at least for Fellora—so I hoisted her back onto my shoulders, turned on the ring I'd swiftly grown to loathe, and kept walking.

At first, I told myself that help would come. Surely we were back in the Pactlands by that point. Rose would find me and send our rescuers...

Unless she couldn't see me. Unless we were still within the borders of the freaky little bubble the Hunter had carved out. Unless the ring I wore to save our lives was hiding us from Rose's sight, too.

My stops became more and more frequent as the sky paled and pinkened toward morning. Every time, once I was sure no one was on our heels, I disengaged the ring for a few minutes, hoping Rose was paying attention. But the world was a monotonous prairie in all directions, unbroken by so much as a signpost. I aimed my steps slightly away from the rising sun and headed north, but even if I'd been able to call Rose, I couldn't have given her the first clue as to where we were.

A soft voice in a shadowy corner of my thoughts whispered that we were going to die together out there, and I tried desperately to ignore it.

On I plodded, thinking of reasons to keep going.

Life—that was pretty basic. Getting Fellora home to her family, perhaps so she could chew them out about not employing the full might of DOL to find her. Finding a way back to my own family. To the life I'd known. To the Annie I remembered.

Home.

I could walk through fire if it meant a chance to go home again. What were a few blisters and the dead weight of a wolf by comparison?

But positive thinking only lasts so long, and my strength was failing. With the sun fully above the horizon, I finally stumbled over my own feet and fell, though I managed to release my passenger before I could take her down with me. Sprawling in the tall grass, I lay still and breathed the warm aroma of fresh soil, forcing my lungs to bellow out and in even though my skin felt like it was ripping with every inhalation.

A wet nose nudged my ear, and Fellora whined.

"Sorry," I mumbled, and turned the ring off, but that

brought only minimal relief. By then, I'd so damaged myself that I barely noticed a difference when the ring was working.

She whimpered and nudged me again, rocking my head with her insistent touches.

"Got to rest," I croaked through cracking lips. "I'm sorry. I...I've got to rest."

Instead of pushing me onward, Fellora flopped down beside me with a huffed sigh. She wriggled closer as if trying to keep me warm. Had I not been so exhausted, I'd have told her not to bother. While I was flushed with my exertion, my sweat had run dry, leaving only traces of salt to sting my raw wounds. The cool morning air wasn't terrible, but the real draw at that moment was the ground, the wonderful, unmoving ground, which asked nothing of me and didn't worsen my pain. I sucked the dew off of the grass closest to my mouth, but by then, I didn't have the energy to go in search of more. Searching required movement. I didn't have to do that. I could just lie still in that endless field and close my eyes and sleep.

God, I needed sleep.

Maybe I could sleep and wake up and realize this whole thing had been a nightmare. Our flight, the lodge, the investigation, Fellora, the café, the Roulette, Maya's Halloween party...maybe this was all just a bad dream. Maybe I didn't go to the party after all—maybe I was asleep on my couch in my pumpkin-print pajamas, the ones I'd bought on a lark that turned out to be *ridiculously* comfortable. Maybe I'd left the TV on, and I'd wake to an infomercial for moissanite jewelry or nonstick skillets. If I lay very still and very quiet, then perhaps I could wake into a world in which none of this mess ever happened.

But what about Wylan? asked another voice in my head—not the one predicting a painful death, but a new voice that sounded almost wistful. *You don't want him to be just a dream...do you?*

Did I?

Shit. No.

But if Wylan existed, then everything else came with him…and in that case, I really had splatted into the grass in the middle of nowhere, aching and burning and so desperate for water that I was licking strange plants.

"Fellora?" I whispered.

She scooted a little closer.

"I'm not sure I can get up again."

To my surprise, she just whimpered. Maybe she was weak, too. Maybe the Hunter had done something to her that I couldn't see, something that would kill her once we were far enough from the lodge.

"Can we rest for a little while?"

Fellora didn't complain.

I closed my eyes and allowed myself to drift, hopeful that unconsciousness would mean a respite from pain. But I didn't sleep deeply, as I was startled back to awareness when the light changed.

Something was blocking the sun. I could sense it through my closed eyes…

The ring. The fucking *ring.* I'd forgotten to turn it on. We were visible, they'd found us…

I forced my eyes open, expecting to see a circle of pissed-off Huntsmen standing around us. Instead, hovering overhead was the strangest looking helicopter I'd ever seen. It had no rotor, and it didn't make a sound, but from below, it was vaguely helicopter-shaped.

And it was descending.

Shortly before the landing skids hit the grass, I made out the big *DOL* painted on the side, violet against a silver background.

Laws had found us. They'd actually found us. Had I energy enough to stand, I'd have jumped for joy and run to meet them. Instead, Fellora took the lead, climbing to her feet and waiting beside me as the side hatch opened.

The pair of women who leapt out of the vehicle wore all black and carried satchels on their shoulders—healers, I thought, two sorcerers of middling years. They paused a few feet away from us, and then one touched her earpiece. "Are we sure about the wolf?" she asked. She frowned, perhaps waiting for a response, the nodded curtly. "Right. Are you Fellora ti'Mal?" she continued, crouching and pointing to my companion. "Can you understand me?"

Fellora whimpered.

"Make that sound again. Once for no, twice for yes."

She gave a positive response, and the healer engaged her earpiece. "Ti'Dana was right, it's our girl. Come on," she said to Fellora, beckoning as one would to a friendly dog. "Hop aboard, and we'll see what's been done to you."

But Fellora didn't budge. Instead, she rocked slightly into me, and I cried out at the contact.

The other healer stepped closer. "We're not leaving Annie, Ms. ti'Mal. Go make yourself comfortable while we stabilize her, all right?"

Sufficiently convinced, Fellora trotted off toward our ride, and I closed my eyes again...only to fling them wide open and scream when one of the well-meaning healers patted my shoulder.

"*Oh!*" she cried, jumping back. "Oh, my...I'm sorry, dear, I didn't—"

"Look at those blisters," the other interrupted. "Poor kid. How do you want to do this?"

The first whistled softly. "I'm not sure." Squatting beside me, she said, "Annie, we need to secure you to a gurney for your safety aboard the transport. How badly are you hurting?"

"This is at least a solid nine out of ten," I muttered.

"Good to know. Be still, now."

I could have laughed—I sure as hell wasn't going anywhere on my own steam—but the healer didn't seem to realize the absurdity of her order as she dug in her bag. After a quick search, she extracted a loaded syringe inside a plastic tube, which she broke open and readied.

"We need her awake for questioning," the second

healer cautioned. "You heard the director—"

"Screw that," my new favorite person interrupted, and jabbed the needle into my arm.

I cried out, but only for a second. Before I could worry about what she'd just stuck in me, darkness descended over my vision, and I knew nothing more than blissful oblivion.

CHAPTER 16

The light was wrong.

My eyes, gummy and heavy-lidded, struggled to process the change. I'd last seen morning sunlight, but this seemed paler, cooler, less aggressively present...

The realization that I was no longer on my stomach in the middle of a godforsaken prairie came as a shock, but when I gasped and tried to sit up, a firm hand on my sternum pressed me back into what I quickly recognized as a bed. "Easy, now," said a low-pitched female voice, reassuring but most insistent. "Be still, Annie."

Forcing my eyes open, I blinked until the blur of light and color resolved into the familiar contours of a medical room. I'd been through DPP's in-house hospital on plenty of occasions, as the Roulette research team often brought Maya and me over for physical testing, but I'd never actually needed one of the beds before. The last of the film in my eyes cleared to confirm my impression: cream paint with a teal accent wall, recessed lighting around the ceiling, slate-colored tile. I was tucked into a surprisingly comfortable bed with a soft white sheet and thin blanket pulled up to my chin.

The healer with me was one of my favorites of the bunch, a blue-skinned troll with a black mohawk who went by Dove. She loomed over my bed, which would have been a terrifying awakening before my introduction to the Pactlands—the tusked trollish smile took a little acclimatization—and when she saw that I was returning to consciousness, she gently patted my forehead. "Rest, little one. Your body needs it. How are you feeling?"

Good question. I stopped focusing on my changed surroundings and took stock of my condition. Shifting one leg beneath the covers brought with it a deep twinge of pain, so muscle soreness was on the list. My skin itched, more like awkward scabs than like poison ivy, but that was a marked improvement from the burning and the blisters.

"Better, I think," I rasped.

Dove slowly raised the bed so that I was sitting up and held the straw of a water glass near my lips. I sipped, first with hesitation, then more greedily as my body demanded liquid.

"Don't choke," she cautioned. "It's not going anywhere. We gave you fluids intravenously yesterday, but I'm sure you're thirsty."

I paused and frowned at her. "Yesterday?"

"It's Friday afternoon. You've been sleeping it off for more than a day, but my goodness, you needed it. That was one of the worst non-fatal cross-reactions I've ever seen."

"The blisters?"

"Forget the blisters—your *kidneys* were shutting down." She shook her head and held the straw closer to me. "I realize humans are delicate, but that was awful. Gave the research crew plenty of fresh data, and I'm sure they're grateful," she added, rolling her eyes. "Still, they did have the decency to wish you a speedy recovery."

The sudden dryness in my mouth undid all the good of the water. "Am I going to be okay?"

"All signs point to yes," Dove reassured me. "Kidneys are working again. You're probably still dehydrated, but we can fix that. We've been giving you healing potions since DOL transferred you in. You're showing marked improvement, but the potions aren't working as well as we'd expect."

I made a face. "Fucking Roulette?"

"Exactly. At least the sleeping potions work well. And

speaking of which, I want you to try to sleep once you've drunk your fill and we change your bandages. The more you can rest, the faster you'll be back on your feet."

"What bandages?" I asked, feeling like an idiot.

"You've got heavy wraps on your shoulders. We called a dermatologist in from the trauma center to look at the damage. The patches on your face have healed nicely," she said, bending closer to peer at me, "and the salve he brought has been wonderful, but you had more severe tissue damage that needed intensive treatment. It's nothing to worry about," she insisted as my expression shifted. "He'll be back to take another look tomorrow, but you've been progressing well. Now, once you've finished drinking, let's put you flat again and take a look at your bandages, eh?"

I dutifully sipped until my straw gurgled with air. "So…I can't go home today?"

"Absolutely not." Putting the glass aside, Dove lowered my bed, and I gingerly rolled onto my stomach. "Glad this gown clasps in the back," she said as she pushed aside my covers. "Try to be still. If this hurts too badly, let me know, and we'll find a way to numb you."

Clenching my teeth, I tried to prepare for the worst, but the bandage removal was swift and hurt far less than my average rip job. Dove grunted as she inspected the progress. "It's coming along. You may have some slight scarring, but I can think of a few potions to help those fade."

"Did anyone mention that the scent-neutralizing potion gave me a massive rash?" I mumbled into my pillow.

"Repeatedly. But we've worked with the research team and found a set of healing and painkilling potions that you seem to tolerate well. Just do us a favor, will you?"

"What's that?"

"No more masking. For the love of all that's good and holy, don't make things worse on yourself."

I laughed weakly. "Don't worry, Syvin took my

necklace with her. And this ring…" I paused as my thumb rubbed against my fingers and didn't hit metal. "Oh, shit, where's my ring—"

"Your friend Rose came by to collect it," Dove soothed, holding me flat as I started to flail. "She said it was a loaner from Lord ti'Cren? Uh, the new Lord ti'Cren, I mean."

"Oh…yeah. Good. That's…that's great, actually," I said as my heart slowed from a gallop. "I *really* couldn't have afforded to replace that ring."

"Believe me, girl, the ring is the last thing anyone in this agency has worried about of late. Don't move until I get the fresh bandages on."

Never one to argue with trolls, I cooperated with Dove's ministrations and allowed her to help me flop right side up once she'd finished. "That's much better, isn't it?" she said as she raised the bed again. "All right, I'm sure your bladder could use a little relief. I'm going to support you, so I need you to swing your legs over the side, and I'll just come around here…"

A sharp rap at the door heralded Syvin's arrival and cut short my bathroom trip. "You're awake!" she said, surprised.

I grinned. "More or less. Dove's been fussing over me."

"And she's excellent in that capacity," said Syvin, staring up at the healer, "but I need a few minutes of the patient's time. Is she stable?"

"For now," Dove allowed, "but can't this wait until tomorrow?"

"I'd rather not."

Though she seemed poised to argue, Dove backed down, but only to a point. "You get *ten minutes*, ma'am," she told Syvin, then closed the door behind her.

Syvin waited until Dove's footsteps on the tile faded, then sighed and shook her head. "You have no idea how lucky you are, Annie."

"Dove mentioned my kidneys…"

"That not a minor ailment! I've never claimed to be an expert in human physiology, but I assume you need those. Not to mention your skin damage, the dehydration, and the fact that you carried Fellora for…how many hours?"

"I have no idea," I admitted.

"Neither does she, but she said *hours*, plural."

I perked at the comment. "So she can speak again? Is she, uh…not a wolf anymore?"

"It took two elves, five sorcerers, and a conference call with several experts in theoretical magic, but she's been restored. Physically fine, aside from some cuts and bruises, but I suspect you noticed those."

Nodding, I said, "There was blood in her fur. Did she say what happened?"

"Just like you and Wylan predicted: she was hiking, then she felt someone grab her and hit her in the head. The next thing she knew, she was in a cage on all fours. Poor kid's ravenous—they only gave her raw meat, and she wouldn't touch it. Vegetarian."

"Oof."

"Yeah." Syvin glanced around the room, spotted a rolling stool, and pulled it closer to my bed. "I suspect she'll be in therapy for a while. No one's leaving her alone right now."

"Staying with her fiancé?"

"No, she's back in the bosom of Hall ti'Mal…though not without some *choice* words for dear old Mother and Father Fellora is rather peeved at their decisions about the investigation—oh, no, not with you. She's eternally grateful," Syvin hastily added as my face fell. "As is the family. A token of their thanks," she added, pointing to the window across the room.

Following her finger, I found a massive spray of tropical blooms that I'd been too groggy to notice. "That's nice of them."

"That's the least they could do," Syvin muttered.

"Anyway, Fellora may reach out in the next few days—she'd like to thank you personally. I gave her your contact information."

"No worries." I ran one hand through my oily tangles, which had, as usual, snarled around my antlers. "Dove said I have to stay here tonight."

"*Absolutely*. You're stronger than you look," she said, giving me a once-over in my hospital gown, "but you need more potions and plenty of rest. I'll ask Maya to bring you your own clothes, if you'd like, or reading material. She'll be thrilled to know you're on the mend."

"Any word from Wylan?"

Syvin paused, and one hoof absently kicked back and forth against the stool's steel foot. "Not yet. We've had no sign of him. DOL has people monitoring his apartment, but there's no indication that he's returned to the city."

My guts clenched. "You don't think his dad figured it out, do you?"

"I don't know, and I don't want to speculate without a basis for doing so. But I'll keep you informed," she promised, then pushed herself to her feet. "Once you're discharged, DOL wants an official statement. Pateme has told Kabno that she can't bother you until the healers say so, but just know that they're building a case. Do you want some more water?"

As she refilled my glass at the room's tap, I asked, "Is DOL going after the Hunt?"

"They haven't shared any details with me," Syvin replied, putting my drink on the table beside the bed, "but if what Fellora has said is true, this cannot be tolerated." With a tight smile, she turned to go. "Rest well, kid. At the rate this is going, you might be before the Forum before all's said and done."

Late Saturday afternoon, after a long sleep, a generous nap, and another visit from the dermatologist, I was almost dozing when a burble of voices in the hallway roused me—disturbed, alarmed, even slightly aggressive voices. Curious, I sat up just in time for Dup to knock on my doorframe…though to my surprise, he looked more disheveled than usual. "Ah, good, you're awake," he said. "You have a visitor—"

Wylan shoved past him, still sporting his tunic and leggings from Thursday night, though the tunic bore a splash of dark red against the white. "Annie!" he cried, relief flashing across his face. "You're whole?"

He threw his arms around me before I had a chance to warn him, and I yelped as his embrace tightened around my healing shoulders. Releasing me instantly, Wylan stepped back, startled and guilty. "I'm sorry, did I hurt you?"

"Still a little messed up back there, but I'm improving," I replied, then opened my arms. "Come here. *Gently*. Aim lower."

He managed to hug me that time without paining me, and I held on to his neck, feeling his four-day stubble against my cheek and smelling his curious bouquet of sweat and soil and horse and the coppery hint of blood.

"Glad you're okay," I murmured. "I was worried."

"*You* were worried? I didn't know if you were alive or dead, and I couldn't tell anyone…" He pulled back enough to see my face and shook his head. "I wasn't able to leave until about half an hour ago, and I went straight to your apartment. You weren't home, so I ran to the café, and Maya said you'd almost killed yourself. You *carried* Fellora out?"

I nodded. "Only way to hide her. It wouldn't have been so bad had the scent potion and the ring not reacted like they did…or maybe it was just the ring. I don't know, but if I ever try to wear that thing again, take me to get my head checked."

When I reached for Wylan a second time, strangely comforted by his touch, he didn't hesitate.

"She's safe," I told him. "Back with her family now. You did good, my friend."

He snorted. "I was merely transportation. How did you find her?"

"You guys were too busy carousing to notice me sneaking around the house. How were you all not completely hung over in the morning?"

"Alcohol has never been a problem for us."

"*Men.*" I released my grip, and he withdrew and sat beside me on the bed. "But yeah, I unlocked her cage and carried her out through the woods. What happened when your dad saw she was missing?"

"He…was not pleased. In the slightest," said Wylan, which, judging by his tone, was a gross understatement. "But we rode after wild wolves instead. Shot a few. Not me—I rode at the back and let the eager ones have their fun."

I pointed to his stained shirt. "So this…"

"Stood too close when a throat was cut. Sorry."

"Do you think anyone suspects us?"

"No." Smiling, he brushed the backs of his fingers against my cheek, which had almost faded to its normal color. "They never noticed you were there, and I was with someone from the moment I walked through the door until Father discovered the empty cage." He hesitated, then joked, "We make a good team. I sit around drinking and singing all night, and you wander through the woods with a wolf on your back. Perfect teamwork."

"I'll let you carry the wolf next time, eh?" I replied, grinning.

"Deal. I—"

He paused as a healer poked his head into the room and began to object, but a sharp look from Wylan sent him scurrying on his way.

"Suppose no one told the staff on this floor that I've not come to abduct you," Wylan murmured.

"You can probably imagine why they're a little on

edge," I said, trying to be gentle. "Fellora's given a statement, and word spreads."

He grunted. "Fair. But we're not all like Father and Cralf. You know that, right?"

The sudden fear in his voice made me reach for his hand to reassure him. "I know *you* aren't."

"You'd like some of my brothers," he insisted. "I don't know if you saw Derat—"

"In the kitchen, yeah. He seems decent."

"We're close. But I swear to you, we're not all like…*that*."

Lacing my fingers through his, I said, "I trust you, Wylan, and that's all that matters. Okay?"

He gave my hand a brief squeeze before releasing me, and then, ever so cautiously, he scooted closer and wrapped his arm around my back. I couldn't exactly lean my head against his shoulder—damn the antlers—but when I pivoted and kissed him, he accepted the change in plans without hesitation. Closing my eyes, I pressed myself against the warmth of his body, smelling him, *tasting* him, and when I paused, he cupped his palm against my face and held me near him. "Annie," he murmured, his voice strangely husky, "do you think…I mean, someday, might you consider—"

The sound of Pateme's voice in the hallway cut his question short, and we hastily parted before the director popped his head in. "Made it back, I see," he said, nodding to Wylan. "Dup said you were rather insistent about coming upstairs."

Wylan cocked his head. "He's unharmed. Are you expecting an apology?"

"Should I anticipate one?"

"No."

"I see," said Pateme. "In the future, do me the kindness of not assaulting my staff, won't you?"

"Wylan!" I protested, trying not to laugh. "What did you do to him?"

He shrugged. "Dup told me I couldn't come upstairs without Pateme's express permission. I suggested he reconsider."

I cocked an eyebrow. "You *suggested*?"

"Strongly."

"Just don't leave this wing of the building," Pateme ordered. "If Annie wants you here, then I suppose there's no harm, but let her rest."

"I should be getting up, anyway," I told the director. "The healers said I can leave after dinner, and Syvin told me she's made the arrangements with Director Erenani."

Wylan frowned. "*Now* what are you doing for DOL?"

"Giving a statement about what happened to Fellora." Holding his gaze, I murmured, "If you don't want to talk about your dad, I understand, but DOL wants to push this case and prevent another incident. If you're willing to help…"

He barely hesitated before turning to Pateme. "What does Laws want to know?"

The Division of Laws, like its sister agency, the Division of Plants and Potions, claimed a tower downtown for its needs. But DOL's tower was ten stories taller than DPP's, a seemingly flawless glass spire with an *excellent* security team in the marble-adorned lobby.

Though Wylan and I were expected and Syvin accompanied us into the building, the waiting officers took no chances. Six of them piled into the elevator with us—two sorcerers, an elf, a pair of trolls, and a nymph who made a point of playing with a brushed-steel cigarette lighter. While I didn't know much about nymphs, I *did* know that they were innate masters of elemental magic, and I suspected that the officer's unsubtle gesture wasn't mere fidgeting.

We gave them no cause for alarm, however, and our escort marched us to the director's corner office—a space slightly larger than Pateme's and with a better view of the city, though curiously, with furniture proportional in size to his. Though Kabno was tiny, she made do using an office chair with an automatic lift, and she offered guest chairs designed to accommodate the majority body type.

She wasn't alone when we arrived. Despite the weekend meeting, Kabno was neatly attired in a purple robe, but she was the only one who'd received the dress code memo. I didn't know the others already sitting around the room—three elves, a centaur, a sorcerer, and a nymph who'd put hot pink highlights in his blond shag—but they'd come in Saturday casual at best, leaning toward grunge in places.

Kabno introduced her associates—her chief deputy, two other executives, and the small cadre of well-seasoned counselors who'd been tentatively assigned to the case. "Now," she said as I shifted in my overstuffed chair, "I need you to start from the beginning. Take us through your investigation."

For the next hour, Wylan and I laid forth every step we'd taken, every witness I'd considered, every clue that led us to the Hunter. We described how he'd brought me there and how I'd hidden myself from detection. I told them about overhearing Wylan and Derat's conversation in the kitchen, then about skulking around the lodge until I could slip outside to hunt for Fellora. And I concluded with what I could recall from our long walk out: Fellora's weight on my shoulders, branches in my face, the cold darkness of the woods, the sunrise over the unbroken grasslands. Syvin cut in to detail my injuries, and the DOL personnel winced in sympathy.

When we finished, Kabno turned to the sorcerer, a middle-aged woman with bobbed brown hair streaked with gray, and the centaur by her side, a blonde wearing a sweatshirt and green-striped leg warmers. I suddenly realized where I'd seen them before—they'd prosecuted Inade ti'Cren, though without their formal robes, they appeared to have been pulled off the couch that evening. "Remari, Cennis?" she asked.

The two traded a look, and the sorcerer took the lead. "That meshes with Fellora's story."

"Do we have any idea how far the lodge is from the pickup point?"

Remari shrugged. "No. Fellora was uncertain, and given everything else she'd been through, I'm not surprised. It sounds like Annie here wasn't counting her paces."

"Which is *understandable*," Cennis cut in, as if afraid that I'd mistake Remari's dry statement for criticism. "She's lucky to be out of bed."

"She's lucky to be alive," Syvin retorted. "As is Fellora."

"Which is why we'll be bringing this to the Forum," said Kabno as the elf who'd been recording our statements read over his work. "We're building this case. I don't want to move until we're certain of success."

"We'll get one shot at this," Remari added. "The Forum will be loath to authorize prosecution of a signatory, so this needs to be airtight." Turning to Wylan, the sorcerer asked, "Are you willing to be involved?"

"We do understand if you're reluctant," said Cennis. "Familial matters are inherently touchy, and I think we could do this without your testimony. Annie and Fellora cover the necessary ground. Still, the case would be stronger with your input."

Remari nodded. "And I don't think it's inaccurate to say that no one in this room knows more about the Hunt than you do. But you don't have to decide tonight. Give it some thought, let us know—"

"I'm in," he murmured.

The counselors glanced at each other again, then back at Wylan. "You're certain?" asked Cennis, her tail flicking.

His mouth tightened, but he answered her with a curt nod.

Given the hour and my continued recovery, the meeting adjourned soon thereafter. Cennis and Remari promised to be in touch, and the waiting officers escorted the three of us from the building. Syvin, who'd borrowed a high-ceilinged van from the DPP fleet to drive us over, offered us a lift home, and I gratefully accepted.

Wylan helped me up to my apartment. When I scanned the door open, I found Maya waiting with sparkling wine and one of her legendary cheesecakes—medicinal, she assured me with a wink—and we lounged around the den eating and drinking until I no longer noticed my residual pain. Maya had closed the café early that night in honor of my homecoming, and her wings fluttered as she rose to bring seconds and refills. I smiled to myself while she fussed over us. She seemed happy, and if she had plans to chew me out for what I'd done, I trusted she'd save the chastisement until the morning.

By the time the cheesecake was gone and two bottles of wine had been drained, it was nearly eleven, and my eyes could barely stay open. Maya coaxed me into bed, and Wylan, who lingered outside the room until I was decent, asked if I'd be okay overnight.

"I'm fine," I told him through a yawn. "Get some sleep. You need it."

"Seriously," said Maya, elbowing him in the side. "I'm expecting you two back at work on Monday, so rest up."

Wylan grinned. "You mean your substitutes can't keep pace with the fabulous job Annie and I have been doing?"

She laughed aloud. "Uh, no. They run circles around you both—no offense, Annie."

"'S okay," I mumbled as I pulled the covers under my chin.

"But I want my full staff back, and that means you," she continued, pointing up at Wylan's face. "Got it?"

"I'll see you then," he told her, and waved to me. "Sleep well. Let me know if you need anything."

I didn't even hear him leave. By the time the front door

closed, I was sound asleep.

On Sunday morning, I awoke shortly after dawn, feeling closer to human than I had in days. My face was still blotchy, and my shoulders still itched beneath their bandages, but if I ignored the antlers, I no longer had an appearance likely to frighten children.

Good enough. The masking pendant had made its way to my dresser, but I didn't want to so much as touch the thing until I saw the dermatologist again.

I showered, dressed, and wandered into the kitchen, but the only sign of life from my roommate was soft, muffled snoring through her closed bedroom door. No matter. I put on a pot of coffee for Maya, a little something nice to wake up to, then left her a note and slipped out of the apartment.

I stopped by my much-loved hole in the wall and found both owners on duty. The husband smiled and asked if Maya had fallen ill—I'd never come in for breakfast—but I assured him that she was getting her beauty sleep and I'd need two of the house breakfast specials. While he fried eggs, I paid his wife, then glanced at the television mounted in the corner in time to catch a quick story about Fellora's safe return. All that DOL would confirm was that she'd been abducted, and the reporter seemed peeved that no details were yet forthcoming. The wedding, I was sad to see, had been postponed. I had yet to speak to Fellora, but I'd found a message from her on my phone that morning when I'd finally checked it: *I can't thank you enough. Looking forward to meeting you properly...and without fur. Choose your massage therapist.*

As the husband packed my takeout boxes, his wife smiled knowingly and asked, "Work friend again?"

"Maybe…" I drawled.

Chuckling, she took the boxes from her bemused

spouse and passed them across the counter in a bag. "Enjoy, dear. Bring him by sometime, hmm?"

I promised I would, then hurried off toward Wylan's place.

Early October was milder in Beukal than it was back in Richmond, but the nip in the air heralded the arrival of sweater weather. I'd been in the Pactlands for eleven months.

Eleven *long* months.

But as much as I wanted to go home…well, I was surprising Wylan with Sunday-morning breakfast, wasn't I? Imagining him still bed-mussed but grinning—and shirtless, with any luck—I pressed the buzzer for his unit and waited.

No one answered.

Putting the food on the step, I fumbled in my purse for my phone and tried calling him, but it rang and went to voicemail, which Wylan hadn't bothered to set up. I buzzed again, holding the button down longer that time, and was beginning to worry when another tenant, a young sorcerer, opened the front door. He took a step back, surprised to find me there, then recovered and chuckled with embarrassment. "Hi. Guess you're going to 5B, huh?"

"That was the plan," I replied, scooping up the bag of food. "Are the buzzers not working?"

He rolled his eyes. "Temperamental. I'd tell you to ask the landlord, but as long as the building's still standing, he doesn't see the problem."

Reassured, I smiled as he held the door for me, then made the long climb upstairs. By the time I reached Wylan's floor, my still-recovering legs were burning, but anticipation carried me onward. This was even better—I'd *really* surprise him if he didn't buzz me in. Maybe we could take breakfast to the roof and enjoy the morning…

I stopped in my tracks when I saw that Wylan's door was ajar.

It was late when he got home, I told myself. *He just forgot to*

lock up. It's a crappy old building, and maybe the lock didn't catch.
No need to panic.

I knocked twice on the doorframe and called, "Wylan?
Are you up? It's me!" Pausing, I listened for movement
inside the apartment, but when only silence greeted me, I
pushed the door open wider and flipped on the light.

The den had been *tossed*. What little furniture Wylan
owned had been tipped over or thrown around the room. I
dropped the food in my shock, then ran back to Wylan's
bedroom to rouse him, only to find the bed rumpled but
empty. He'd come home last night, then, unless he'd left it
unmade Thursday morning…

As panic clawed at my stomach, I checked the
bathroom, then raced to the roof, but there was no sign of
him.

Maybe he went for a walk, I tried to reason. *Maybe he's*
redecorating. Maybe a burglar just left. Maybe that guy who let me in
was the burglar…

It was only once I returned to the apartment and
started switching on the lights that I noticed the blood. In
his bed. On the floor. On the walls.

By the time I spotted the broken antler prong by the
overturned end table, my hands were shaking, but I
managed to hold on to my phone well enough to make a
call. "Hi," I said when the call connected, "Syvin? Sorry to
bother you…"

"No trouble," she croaked. "I should be getting up.
Feeling good today?"

"I was. Uh…I'm at Wylan's place."

"Why am I not surprised? Is he all right?"

"No. He's gone."

By then, the tremor in my hands has reached my voice,
and Syvin took notice. "Annie? What's happened?"

"I don't know," I managed to tell her, "but I need
DOL here. *Now.*"

ACKNOWLEDGEMENTS

Hello again! If you've returned after *Hall of Thorns*, thank you for joining me in this new chapter. If this is your first trip to the Pactlands, however, welcome aboard! There's much more to come.

My sincere thanks go to Adam Domby, who has a ton on his plate but graciously fit me into his schedule. To the Novel Chicks, love you, ladies, and thanks for keeping me around!

And yes, here's to you, Mom and Dad.

ABOUT THE AUTHOR

When not writing fiction, Ash Fitzsimmons is an appellate attorney and an unrepentant car singer.

Find her online:
www.ashfitzsimmons.com

www.ingramcontent.com/pod-product-compliance
Lightning Source LLC
Chambersburg PA
CBHW030253200626
46816CB00002BA/628